Cumulated Fiction Index 1995-1999
compiled by
Marilyn Hicken

CDG Publishing

The Career Development Group
(of the Library Association)
acknowledge the assistance of REMPLOY
in the production of this publication
2000

M. E. Hicken
2000

CDG Publishing

A CIP record for this book is available from
The British Library

ISBN 1 901353 08 7

PREFACE

This volume contains mainly new material, since no annual volumes have been published since 1995.

It lists fiction published between 1995 and 1999, including trade paperbacks, which have not normally been listed before. As before, I have tidied up the headings to take account of current terminology; for example, HOMOSEXUALITY has now become GAY MEN. I have also cut down the number of entries under THRILLERS, since there are far more published than there have been previously. I have, instead, used the specific crime as a major heading where the thriller genre is implicit, e.g. FRAUD, KIDNAPPING.

My thanks, as always, to Holt Jackson, who supply me with a copy of their weekly CDRom, and forthcoming fiction catalogues, and to the Publication Officers of CDG, and Remploy.

Mandy Hicken   September 2000

NOTES ON THE USE OF THE INDEX

HEADINGS

The headings are categorised as follows:

1. Factual - places, people, periods of history
2. Abstract - love, hate, obsession
3. Genre - detective stories, fantasy
4. Technique - autobiographical novels, interior monologues

The headings are in alphabetical order.

PLACE AND PERIOD ENTRIES

Novels set in Great Britain are entered under the specific county or town, e.g. **Devon, Glasgow**. In all other cases, the name of the country appears first, followed by the location, e.g. **France: Paris**. Each country is indexed first by historical period, e.g.

England: 16th century; Spain: 19th century, then by location. Novels set in London are arranged in chronological order, then by location, e.g. **London: 1900-29; London: East End.**

BIOGRAPHICAL ENTRIES

Where the main character in a novel is a real person, a one line biographical description is given, followed by dates of birth and death, if known. The source for entries is Chambers' Biographical Dictionary.

CRIME FICTION

A number of categories are used for listing this type of material, as the various genres continue to expand. They are as follows:

1. Thrillers. Now only used for material which does not fall into the other categories.

2. Detective stories. Novels where the identity of the criminal is not revealed until the end of the book, or where the investigation concerns one detective.

3. Police work. Novels concerned with police procedures, where a team of police investigate more than one crime.

4. Private Eye stories. Novels concerning paid investigators, who are not connected with the police.

5. Mystery stories. Novels which fall somewhere between the detective story and the private eye story.

6. Spy stories. Novels which deal with espionage on behalf of a country.

7. Political thrillers. Novels which deal with corruption in political circles, and with terrorism and subversion.

8. Psychological thrillers. Stories in which the state of mind of criminal and victim are explored. Some are almost horror stories.

9. Suspense stories. Novels in which the tension builds up throughout the book.

10. Adventure stories. Action packed novels, usually set in foreign locations.

11. Financial thrillers. Novels set in the world of international finance, dealing with fraud and corruption.

12. Legal thrillers. Courtroom dramas.

13. Medical thrillers. Novels about hospitals, medical and genetic research.

Fictional detectives are also listed under **Detectives,etc.**, followed by the name of their creator. This is useful for tracing books where the name of the detective is known, but not that of the author.

PUBLICATION DETAILS

No dates or publishers have been listed. They can be obtained from BBIP or Book Data.

ABANDONED CHILDREN

Blumenthal, V.
   Saturday's child
Forster, M.
   Shadow baby
Murray, A.
   Orphan of Angel Street
Whitmee, J.
   Thursday's child

ABANDONED WIVES

Dunne, C.
   In the beginning

ABDUCTION

Rendell, R.
   Harm done
Thomson, R.
   The book of revelation

ABORTION

Patterson, R. N.
   No safe place
Townsend, S.
   Ghost children

ACADEMICS

Ovenden, K.
   The greatest sorrow

ACCIDENTAL DEATH

Gorman, E.
   The poker club

ACCIDENTS

DelVeccio, J. M.
   Darkness falls
Matthews, J.
   Past imperfect
Ormerod, R.
   Final toll

ACCIDENTS, AIRCRAFT

Baldacci, D.
   Total control
Crichton, M.
   Airframe
Lennon, J. R.
   The light of falling stars
Moffat, G.
   A wreath of dead moths
Peel, C. D.
   Cogan's falcons
Stewart, C.
   The kill box
Thayer, J. L.
   Terminal event
West, P.
   Terrestrials

ACCIDENTS, RAILWAY

Kingston, B.
   Gemma's journey

ACCIDENTS, ROAD

Delinsky, B.
   Coast road

ACCOUNTANTS

Taylor, D. J.
   Trespass

ACTORS

Bentley, U.
   The angel of Twickenham
Bonner, H.
   A fancy to kill for
Brandreth, G.
   Venice midnight
Brett, S.
   Dead room farce
Bron, E.
   Double take
Capriolo, P.
   The woman watching
Cookson, C.
   Riley
Dailey, J.
   Illusions
Ellis, J.
   A woman for all seasons
Ewing, B.
   The actresses
Freeman, G.
   His mistress's voice
Gill, A. A.
   Death's autograph
Grazebrook, S.
   A cameo role
   Foreign parts
Henderson, L.
   Freeze my Margarita
Hudson, H.
   Into the sunlight
Hunt, M.
   Like Venus fading
Johnson, J.
   Playing for love
Johnston, J.
   Two moons
March, H.
   The complaint of the dove
Michael, J.
   Acts of love
Nessen, R.
   Death with honors
Nye, R.
   The late Mr. Shakespeare

Paddock, T.
  Beware the dwarfs
Pearse, L.
  Charlie
Pera, P.
  Lo's diary
Potter, J.
  Greedy mouth
Prager, E.
  Roger Fishbite
Prone, T.
  Racing the moon
Reidy, S.
  The visitation
Robinson, B.
  The peculiar memories of Thomas
    Penman
Sapphire
  Push
Schaeffer, F.
  Portofino
Sebag-Montefiore, S.
  My affair with Stalin
Segrave, E.
  Ten men
Shields, D.
  Dead languages
Taylor, D.
  Pig in the middle
Teran, I.
  Dolce vita
Thomas, R.
  Moon island
Vakil, A.
  Beach boy
Van der Vyver, M.
  Childish things
Warner, A.
  The sopranos

ADOPTED CHILDREN
Arditti, M.
  Pagan and her parents
Armitage, A.
  The dark arches
Carr, I.
  Mary's child
Cleaver, C.
  The silent valley
Fawcett, P.
  The absent child
Francis, J.
  Somebody's girl
Howard, A.
  Not a bird will sing
Kay, N.
  Tina
Murphy, E.
  When day is done

Plain, B.
  Legacy of silence
Robertson, W.
  Kitty Rainbow
Sinclair, K.
  From a far country
Singer, N.
  My mother's daughter
Whitmee, J.
  Eve's daughter

ADOPTION
Holt, F.
  Some you win
Mann, J.
  The survivor's revenge
Sweetman, D.
  A tribal fever
Williams, D.
  Wishes and tears

ADULT EDUCATION CLASSES
Binchy, M.
  Evening class

ADULTERY
Ferris, P.
  Infidelity
Mead, J.
  Charlotte Street
Shearer, A.
  Box 132
Vincenzi, P.
  Almost a crime

ADVENTURE STORIES
Adair, G.
  The key of the tower
Bateman, C.
  Empire State
Canter, M.
  Down to heaven
Clancy, T. & Pieczenic, S.
  Acts of war
  Executive orders
  Games of state
Cohen, S.
  Invisible world
Cussler, C.
  Shock wave
Darnton, J.
  Neanderthal
Du Brul, J.
  Charon's landing
Forbes, C.
  Precipice
  The cauldron
Fraser, G. M.
  Flashman and the tiger

Fullerton, A.
Final dive
Gandolfi, S.
Ibiza beach
Greig, A.
The return of John MacNab
Higgins, J.
The flight of eagles
Innes, H.
Delta connection
Langley, B.
Fellrunner
The third pinnacle
Llewellyn, S.
Storm force from Navarone
The iron hotel
Thunderbolt from Navarone
MacNeill, A.
Counterplot
Double-blind
Moonblood
Miller, H.
Borrowed time
Prime target
Nichol, J.
Stinger
Nicole, C.
The trade
O'Donnell, P.
Cobra trap: stories
Peel, C. D.
Blood of your sisters
Russell, J.
Burning bright
Smethurst, W.
Sinai
Thomas, D.
Drumbeat
Whiting, C.
Hell's angels
Wood, B.
The prophetess

ADVENTURERS
Carter, R.
Barbarians

ADVERTISING
Brook, D.
Jesus and the adman
Chirnside, D.
Basket case
Vanity case
Cory, K.
The pinprick
Giancana, S.
30 seconds
Lockhart, D.
The paradise complex

Thomson, R.
Soft

AFRICA
Hudson, M.
The music in my head
Lee, M.
The lost tribe
Thomas, D.
Drumbeat

AFRICA: 19TH CENTURY
Jeal, T.
The missionary's wife

AFRICA: 1930-59
Schlee, A.
The time in Aderra

AFRICA: 1980-2000
Barnes, S.
Rogue lion safaris
Park, D.
Stone kingdoms

AFRICAN AMERICANS
McKinney-Whetstone, D.
Tumbling

AFRICANS ABROAD: BRITAIN
Gurnah, A.
Admiring silence

AGONY AUNTS
Ashworth, S.
Money talks
Bannister, J.
The primrose convention
Zigman, L.
Animal husbandry

AGORAPHOBIA
Ormerod, R.
A curtain of beads

AGRICULTURAL COLLEGES
Bere, I. de la
The understanding of Jenner
Ransfield

AIDS (DISEASE)
Glass, S.
The interpreter
Gurganus, A.
Plays well with others
Price, R.
The promise of rest

AIR CREW
Griffiths, J.
The courtyard in August

AIR PILOTS
Elgin, E.
One summer at Deer's Leap

ALAMO, BATTLE OF THE, 1836
Burke, J.
Two for Texas

ALASKA
Stein, G.
Raven stole the moon
Straley, J.
Death and the language of happiness
The curious eat themselves
The music of what happens

ALCHEMY
Chapman, R.
The secret of the world

ALCOHOLISM
Burnside, J.
The mercy boys
Denker, H.
To Marcy, with love
Thompson, H. S.
The rum diary

ALEXANDER III, KING OF SCOTLAND, 1241-86
Tranter, N.
Sword of state

ALEXANDER THE GREAT, KING OF MACEDONIA, 356-323BC
Holt, T.
Alexander at the world's end

ALGERIA: 19TH CENTURY
Moore, B.
The magician's wife

ALLEGORIES
Bradfield, S.
Animal planet

ALTERNATIVE MEDICINE
Frost, S.
The language of nightingales

ALTERNATIVE SOCIETY
Litt, T.
Beatniks

Rushkoff, D.
The Ecstasy Club
St. Aubyn, E.
On the edge

ALZHEIMER'S DISEASE
Delinsky, B.
Shades of Grace

AMATEUR THEATRICALS
Joss, M.
Fearful symmetry
Stewart, S.
Playing with stars

AMAZON, RIVER
MacNeill, A.
Moonblood

AMBITION
Bentley, U.
The angel of Twickenham
Connor, A.
Midnight's smiling
Cumper, P.
One bright child
Gray, C.
The promised land
Millhauser, S.
Martin Dressler
Mount, F.
Jem (and Sam)
Sharam, K.
Under the skin
Sheldon, S.
The best laid plans
Stuart, A.
Sin no more
Swindells, M.
Snakes and ladders
Wakefield, T.
The scarlet boy

AMERICAN CIVIL WAR, 1861-65
Cornwell, B.
The bloody ground
Coyle, H.
Until the end
Green, J.
The stars of the South
Skvorecky, J.
The bride of Texas
Smiley, J.
The all true adventures of Lidie
Newton

AMERICAN COLONIES
Ackroyd, P.
Milton in America

AMERICAN WAR OF INDEPENDENCE, 1776-83
O'Neal, R.
The Fallon blood

AMIN, IDI, UGANDAN POLITICIAN, 1925-
Foden, G.
The last king of Scotland

AMNESIA
Baker, K.
Engram
Bate, J.
The cure for love
Bonansinga, J. R.
Head case
Fiennes, R.
The sett
Garrett, A.
After you
Grimes, M.
Biting the moon
Lovesey, P.
Upon a dark night
McAlpine, G.
The persistence of memory
Morrison, C.
Frozen summer
Thubron, C.
Distance

ANATOMISTS
Andahazi, F.
The anatomist

ANGELS
Knox, E.
The vintner's luck

ANGER
Heyman, K.
The breaking

ANGLO-INDIANS
Brindley, L.
Indian summer

ANGOLA
Hurley, G.
The perfect soldier

ANIMAL RIGHTS
Coetzee, J. M.
The lives of animals

ANIMAL RIGHTS ACTIVISTS
Bradfield, S.
Animal planet
Granger, A.
A touch of mortality
Hatfield, K.
Angels alone
Hey, S.
Scare story
Palmer, F.
Red gutter

ANIMALS
Horwood, W.
The Willows at Christmas
Stranger, J.
The guardians of Staghill

ANNE BOLEYN, WIFE OF HENRY VIII, 1501-36
Maxwell, R.
The secret diary of Anne Boleyn

ANOREXIA
Grant, S.
The passion of Alice
Hanauer, C.
My sister's bones
Medoff, J.
Hungerpoint
Rosen, J.
Eve's apple

ANTARCTIC
Marshall, J. V.
White-out
Reiss. B.
Purgatory Road

ANTHROPOLOGISTS
Lancaster, G.
The Saturday girl

ANTI-COMMUNIST MOVEMENTS
Roy-Bhattacharya, J.
The Gabriel club

ANTIQUARIAN BOOKSELLERS
Buss, L.
The luxury of exile

ANTIQUE DEALERS
Ardin, W.
The Mary medallion
Cookson, C.
The lady on my left

Gash, J.
 A rag, a bone and a hank of hair
 The possessions of a lady
 The rich and the profane
Miller, J. H.
 Blythe spirit

ANTIQUES
Hamer, M.
 Dead on line
Roberts, N.
 Homeport

ANTISEMITISM
Isaacs, S.
 Red white and blue
Worboyes, S.
 Down Stepney way

ANTONY, MARK, ROMAN SOLDIER, 83-30BC
Massie, A.
 Antony

ANTS
Werber, B.
 Empire of the ants

APARTHEID
Jooste, P.
 Dance with a poor man's daughter
Niekerk, M.
 Triomf

APPALACHIAN MOUNTAINS
McCrumb, S.
 The rosewood casket

ARABIA, ANCIENT
Hariharan, G.
 When dreams travel

ARCHAEOLOGISTS
Bryers, P.
 The prayer of the bone
Ellis, K.
 An unhallowed grave
 The merchant's house
Foss, J.
 Lady in the lake
Kearsley, S.
 The shadowy horses
Kelly, S.
 The ghosts of Albi
Lewis, R.
 Angel of death
 Suddenly as a shadow
 The ghost dancers
 The shape-shifter

Siebert, S.
 Cleopatra's needle
Smethurst, W.
 Pasiphae
Wilson, G.
 The Carthaginian hoard
Wood, B.
 The prophetess

ARCHITECTS
Buckley, J.
 Xerxes
Nicholson, G.
 Female ruins

ARCHIVES
Harris, R.
 Archangel

ARCHIVISTS
Cooley, M.
 The archivist
Fotheringham, P. M.
 Death of a dusty lady

ARCTIC
Bowering, M.
 Visible worlds
Wilson, P.
 Do white whales sing at the edge of
  the world?

ARGENTINA: 1980-2000
Toibin, C.
 The story of the night

ARGYLLSHIRE
Fraser, C. M.
 Noble seed

ARISTOCRACY
Davis, M. T.
 Burning ambition
Hill, P.
 The Lion's daughter
Perez-Reverte, A.
 The fencing master
Rawlinson, P.
 The Caverel claim
Tranter, N.
 Poetic justice

ARMAGEDDON
Codrescu, A.
 Messiah

ARMS TRADE
Howard, L.
 All the Queen's men

Laurie, H.
  The gun seller
Nicole, C.
  Shadows in the sun
  The trade

ARMY LIFE: BRITISH ARMY: 18TH CENTURY
Cornwell, B.
  Sharpe's tiger

ARMY LIFE: BRITISH ARMY: 19TH CENTURY
Cornwell, B.
  Sharpe's fortress
  Sharpe's triumph

ARMY LIFE: BRITISH ARMY: 20TH CENTURY
Savage, A.
  The sword and the scalpel

ARMY LIFE: BRITISH ARMY: 1980-2000
Bullen, F.
  From pillar to post
Graham, M.
  Out of the night
Jones, A.
  Army wives
Jones, C.
  Sisters in arms
Weston, S.
  Phoenix

ARMY LIFE: BRITISH ARMY: NAPOLEONIC WAR PERIOD
Connery, T.
  Honour be damned
Mallinson, A.
  A close run thing

ARMY LIFE: US ARMY: 20TH CENTURY
Griffin, W. E. B.
  In the line of duty

AROMATHERAPY
Matthews, C.
  A whiff of scandal

ARSON
Cohen, A.
  Dream on
Craig, D.
  Torch
Homes, A. M.
  Music for torching

Pearson, R.
  Beyond recognition
Reuben, S.
  Spent matches
Rogan, B.
  Rowing in Eden
Shepherd, S.
  Embers of death
Winslow, D.
  California fire and life

ART CRITICS
Branca, A.
  Muse

ART DEALERS
Olshan, J.
  Vanitas
Schwartz, G.
  Bets and scams
Wilson. D.
  The Borgia chalice

ART FRAUD
Hill, J. S.
  Ghirlandaio's daughter

ART GALLERIES
Carr, R.
  The fine art of loving
Dewhurst, E.
  The verdict on winter

ART HISTORIANS
Frayn, M.
  Headlong
Ironside, E.
  The art of deception
Morgan, P-A.
  The Munich sabbatical
Pye, M.
  Taking lives

ART STUDENTS
Ray, K.
  Stoats and weasels

ART THEFTS
Boyd, D.
  The fiddler and the ferret
Brett, S.
  Mrs. Pargeter's point of honour
Collier, I.
  Innocent blood
Fraser, A.
  Dangerous deception
Grimes, M.
  The Stargazy

Matthews, L.
   A picture of innocence
Mayle, P.
   Chasing Cezanne
Pears, I.
   Death and restoration
Pemberton, L.
   Sleeping with ghosts
Rowlands, B.
   Copycat
Weber, D.
   The music lesson

ARTHUR, KING OF BRITAIN, FL. 6TH CENTURY
Attanasio, A. A.
   The perilous order
Cornwell, B.
   Enemy of God
   Excalibur
Hollick, H.
   Shadow of the king
Lawhead, S.
   Grail
Middleton, H.
   The Queen's captive
Whyte, J.
   The fort at river's bend
   The Saxon shore

ARTHURIAN LEGEND
Bryers, P.
   In a pig's ear
Chapman, V.
   The enchantresses
Foss, J.
   Lady in the lake
Guttridge, P.
   The once and future con
Middleton, H.
   The knight's vengeance

ARTIFICIAL INSEMINATION
Beckett, S.
   Where there's smoke

ARTISTS
Barnard, R.
   The corpse at the Haworth Tandoori
Blair, J.
   Portrait of Charlotte
Bolitho, J.
   Buried in Cornwall
Branca, A.
   Muse
Brierley, D.
   The horizontal woman
Buxton, J.
   Pity

Chevalier, T.
   Girl with a pearl earring
Daish, E.
   Avenue of poplars
Dufort, N.
   Painting out Oscar
Glaister, L.
   Sheer blue bliss
Gordon, M.
   Spending
Gurganus, A.
   Plays well with others
Hart, J.
   The stillest day
Hayes, K.
   Still life on sand
Henderson, L.
   The strawberry tattoo
Holms, J.
   Bad vibes
Howard, L.
   Now you see her
Inglis, J.
   The colour of sin
Ireland, D.
   The chosen
Joyce, M.
   Harlequin's daughter
Kilmer, N.
   Dirty linen
Mackay, S.
   The artist's widow
Ormerod, R.
   Landscape with corpse
Smart, H.
   The wild garden
Urquhart, J.
   The underpainter
Woodman, R.
   Under sail

ARTS FOUNDATIONS
Eberstadt, F.
   When the sons of heaven meet the
      daughters of Earth

ASIANS IN BRITAIN
Syal, M.
   Anita and me

ASSAYE, BATTLE OF, 1803
Cornwell, B.
   Sharpe's triumph

ASTEROIDS
Napier, B.
   Nemesis

AUSTRALIA: SYDNEY
Cleary, J.
A different turf
Dilemma
Endpeace
Five ring circus
Foster, D.
In the new country
Morrissey, D.
When the singing stops
Niles, C.
Run time
Toner, B.
All you need to know

AUSTRALIA: TASMANIA
Courtenay, B.
The potato factory
Tommo and Hawk
Flanagan, R.
The sound of one hand clapping

AUSTRIA: 19TH CENTURY
Rice, A.
Violin

AUSTRIA: 1930-59
Ibbotson, E.
A song for summer

AUSTRIA: VIENNA
Dracup, A.
Mozart's darling
Mathews, A.
Vienna blood
Roth, J.
The string of pearls

AUTHORS
Babson, M.
Miss Petunia's last case
Busia, A.
The seasons of Beento Blackbird
Byatt, A. S.
Babel tower
Caute, D.
Fatima's scarf
Cooper, D.
Guide
Dufresne, J.
Love warps the mind a little
Ellis, J.
Second time around
Fane, J.
Evening
Fraser, A.
Motive for murder
French, M.
My summer with George

Holt, H.
The fatal legacy
Hucker, H.
The real Claudia Charles
Kharitanov, M.
Lines of fate
King, J.
The Book** Prize winner
Lively, P.
Heat wave
Martini, S.
The list
Mead, J.
Sentimental journey
Mortimer, J.
Felix in the underworld
Pepper, M.
Man on a murder cycle
Ratushinskaya, I.
Fictions and lies
Rees, E.
The book of dead authors
Robertson, W.
The self-made woman
Stallwood, V.
Oxford knot
Tremain, R.
The way I found her
Van Wormer, L.
Any given moment

AUTOBIOGRAPHICAL NOVELS
Barraclough, J.
First finds
First loves
Chatterjee, A.
Across the lakes
Erofeev, V.
Moscow stations
Ginzburg, N.
The things we used to say
Hopkins, B.
Our kid
Martel, Y.
Self
Nadas, P.
A book of memories
Tennant, E.
Strangers
Theroux, P.
My other life
Vidal, G.
The season of comfort

AUTOMOBILE INDUSTRY
Baker, D.
Backroom girl
McMillan, R.
Blue collar blues

Robbins, H.
The stallion

AVIARIES
Martin, J. W.
The bird yard

AVIATION
Brown, D.
Fatal terrain
Coonts, S.
Fortunes of war
Follett, J.
Sabre
Harrison, M. J.
Signs of life
Herman, R.
Against all enemies
Humphreys, H.
Leaving Earth
Hurley, G.
Permissible limits
Lunnon-Wood, M.
Angel seven
Mendelsohn, J.
I was Amelia Earhart
Nichol, J.
Point of impact
Savarin, J. J.
McAllister's run
Stewart, C.
Shattered bone

AYRSHIRE
MacDonald, E.
Catch the moment

AZERBAIJAN
Peters, R.
The devil's garden

BABY FARMING
Mitchell, K.
A rage of innocents

BALKANS: 14TH CENTURY
Kadare, I.
The three-arched bridge

BALKANS: 1900-29
Lawrence, S.
Montenegro

BALLET
Ibbotson, E.
A company of swans

BANKING
Cohen, M. B.
The butcher's ball
Gleeson, J.
The moneymaker

BANKRUPTCY
Cavell, A.
The birthday party

BARRISTERS
Cooper, N.
Creeping ivy
Fraser, C. M.
A hallowed place
Woodford, P.
On the night

BARRY, JAMES MIRANDA, MALE IMPERSONATOR
Duncker, P.
James Miranda Barry

BASSANO, EMILIA
Baldwin, M.
Dark lady

BATH
Brown, L.
Double wedding ring
Shoo fly
Lee, C.
The killing of Cinderella
The killing of Sally Keemer
Lovesey, P.
Bloodhounds
The vault
Upon a dark night

BEARS
Kotzwinkle, W.
The bear went over the mountain
Zabor, R.
The bear comes home

BEAUFORT, MARGARET, COUNTESS OF RICHMOND, 1443-1509
Gower, I.
Destiny's child

BEAUTY
O'Neill, A.
Wayward angel
Toner, B.
All you need to know
Wilson, S.
Beauty

BEAUTY CONTESTS
Davis, V.
Queen's ransom

BEAUTY PARLOURS
Cheek, M.
Sleeping beauties

BEDFORDSHIRE
Cox, J.
Cradle of thorns

BEES
Anderson-Dargatz, G.
A recipe for bees

BEETHOVEN, LUDWIG VAN, GERMAN COMPOSER, 1770-1827
Suchet, J.
The last master; passion and anger
The last master; passion and glory
The last master; passion and pain

BEGA, SAINT
Bragg, M.
Credo

BEHAVIOUR PATTERNS
O'Connell, S.
Angel bird

BELFAST
Beattie, G.
The corner boys
Doughty, A.
A few late roses
Larkin, M.
For better, for worse
Full circle
Patterson, G.
The International
Petit, C.
The psalm killer
Wilson, R. M.
Eureka Street

BELGIUM: ANTWERP
Conrad, P.
Limousine

BELGIUM: BRUSSELS
Bailey, M.
Haycastle's cricket

BENIN
Wilson, R.
A darkening stain
Blood is dirt

BEREAVEMENT
Baker, A.
With a little luck
Cox, J.
A time for us
Duffy, B.
Last comes the egg
Forsyth, M.
Waiting for Lindsay
Howard, A.
Beyond the shining water
Jenny, Z.
The pollen room
Jones, M.
Cold in earth
Kirchhof, S.
The threefold garment
Patchett, A.
Taff
The magician's assistant
Pilcher, R.
An ocean apart
Sobin, G.
The fly-truffler
Trevor, W.
Death in summer
Trollope, J.
Next of kin
Weldon, F.
Worst fears

BETRAYAL
Plain, B.
Legacy of silence

BETS
Llewellyn, R.
The man on Platform 5

BIBLE
Wangerin, W.
The book of God

BIG GAME HUNTING
Thomas, D.
Drumbeat

BIGAMY
Barrett, M.
Intimate lies
Tayler, P.
Somewhere in between
White, G.
The beggar bride

BIOGRAPHERS
Carroll, J.
Kissing the beehive

Lennox, J.
  Some old lover's ghost
McMahon, K.
  Footsteps

BIOLOGICAL WARFARE
Adams, J.
  Hard target
Cook, R.
  Vector
De Mille, N.
  Plum Island
Deutermann, P. T.
  Zero option
Hey, S.
  Scare story
Jackson, J. H.
  Dead headers
McClure, K.
  Resurrection
Preston, R.
  The Cobra event

BIOLOGISTS
Evans, N.
  The loop

BIOTECHNOLOGY
McCarthy, W.
  Blood

BIRD WATCHING
Cleeves, A.
  High Island blues

BIRMINGHAM
Bennett, A.
  Love me tender
Cutler, J.
  Dying for millions
  Dying for power
  Dying on principle
  Dying to write
  Power on her own
Hutchinson, M.
  Abel's daughter
  For the sake of her child
Murray, A.
  Birmingham blitz
  Orphan of Angel Street
Oliver, M.
  The golden road

BISHOPS
Greeley, A. M.
  The bishop and the three kings

BLACK COUNTRY
Hutchinson, M.
  A handful of silver
Taylor, M.
  The love match

BLACK MARKET
Roberts, I.
  Walker Street

BLACKMAIL
Buchanan, D.
  Different rules
Burke, J.
  Remember me, Irene
Cohen, A.
  Dedicated angel
Dunmore, H.
  Your blue-eyed boy
George, E.
  In the presence of the enemy
Graham, C.
  A place of safety
Hammond, G.
  Sink or swim
  Twice bitten
Henderson, L.
  The black rubber dress
Kelly, S.
  Death is sweet
Linscott, G.
  Dance on blood
Mann, J.
  A private enquiry
Norman, G.
  Blue streak
Page, E.
  Hard evidence
Roome, A.
  Deceptive relations
Sharam, K.
  Under the skin
Trow, M. J.
  Maxwell's movie
Williams, D.
  Dead in the market

BLACKPOOL
Oldham, N.
  Nightmare city
  One dead witness
Prior, A.
  The old man and me again
Thornton, M.
  A stick of Blackpool rock
  Forgive our foolish ways
  Looking at the moon
  The sound of the laughter
  Wish upon a star

BLACKS

Dennis, F.
   Duppy conqueror

BLACKS: BRITAIN

Adebayo, D.
   Some kind of black
Bryan, J.
   Bernard and the cloth monkey
Carr, R.
   Brixton bwoy
Cumper, P.
   One bright child
Johnson, S.
   Gabriel's ladder
Levy, A.
   Never far from nowhere
McLeod, J.
   Stuck up a tree
Newland, C.
   The scholar

BLACKS: CANADA

Alexis, A.
   Childhood

BLACKS: UNITED STATES

Baker, C.
   Naming the new world
Beatty, P.
   The white boy shuffle
Briscoe, C.
   Big girls don't cry
Estleman, L. D.
   Stress
French, A.
   I can't wait on God
Hill, E.
   A life for a life
   Satisfied with nothin'
Jackson, B. K.
   The view from here
Morrison, T.
   Paradise
Perry, P. J.
   Stigmata
Rhodes, J. P.
   Magic city
Tyree, O.
   A do right man
   Flyy girl

BLINDNESS

Adair, G.
   A closed book
Bradley, J.
   The deep field
Lynds, G.
   Mosaic

Sillitoe, A.
   The German numbers woman
Thomson, R.
   The insult

BLOOD TRANSFUSIONS

Puckett, A.
   Chilling out

BLUE FILMS

Ison, G.
   Blue murder
Rhea, N.
   Omens of death

BOARDING KENNELS

Stranger, J.
   Perilous journey

BOARDING SCHOOLS

Bailey, J.
   Promising
Curzon, C.
   All unwary
Dunne, M.
   Blessed art thou a monk swimming
Evans, M.
   Midnight feast
Hanania, T.
   Homesick
Redmond, P.
   The wishing game
Sheepshanks, M.
   Facing the music
Tinniswood, P.
   Dolly's war

BOAT BUILDING

Monk, C.
   Water's edge

BODICE RIPPERS

Blake, J.
   Golden fancy
   Notorious angel
   Silver-tongued devil
Brandewyne, R.
   Desperado
   Glory seekers
   Passion moon rising
Deveraux, J.
   The heiress
Garwood, J.
   Ransom
   The wedding
Lindsey, J.
   A gentle feuding
   Savage thunder

Michaels, F.
   Captive innocence
   Captive secrets
   Valentina

BOHEMIANS
Teran, I.
   Dolce vita

BOMB ATTACKS
Palmer, F.
   Red gutter
   Witching hour
Pennac, D.
   The scapegoat

BONNY, ANNE, FEMALE PIRATE
MacLeod, A.
   The changeling

BOOKS
Hughes, D.
   The little book
Pamuk, O.
   The new life
Straub, P.
   The Hellfire Club

BOOKSELLERS
Block, L.
   The burglar in the rye
Cheek, M.
   Getting back Brahms
Gill, A. A.
   Starcrossed
King, R.
   Ex-libris
Macdonald, M.
   Death's autograph
   Ghost walk
   Smoke screen

BOOTLEG LIQUOR
Courtenay, B.
   The potato factory
Ripley, M.
   Bootlegged Angel

BORNEO: 19TH CENTURY
Godshalk, C. S.
   Kalimantaan

BOSNIA: SARAJEVO
Fesperman, D.
   Lie in the dark
Fullerton, J.
   The monkey house

BOSNIAN CIVIL WAR, 1995
Savarin, J. J.
   McAllister's run

BOSNIAN CONFLICT, 1992
Trench, S.
   Fran's war

BOTSWANA
Davies, C.
   Jamestown blues

BOW STREET RUNNERS
Alexander, B.
   Murder in Grub Street
   Watery grave

BOXING
Bateman, C.
   Of wee sweetie mice and men
Fraser, G. M.
   Black Ajax

BRAZIL: RIO
Fonseca, R.
   The lost manuscript

BREAST CANCER
Cook, K.
   What girls learn

BREWING INDUSTRY
Swindells, M.
   Winners and losers

BRIBERY
Keating, H. R. F.
   The bad detective

BRIDGE (GAME)
King, P.
   Your deal, Mr. Bond
Moody, S.
   Doubled in spades
   Sacrifice bid

BRIDGES
Kadare, I.
   The three-arched bridge

BRIGHTON
Marchant, I.
   In Southern waters
Paling, C.
   Deserters

BRISTOL
Randall, A.
   Kilkenny bay

Thompson, E. V.
  Lewin's Mead

BRITISH ABROAD: FRANCE
Fergusson, L.
  The chase

BRITISH ABROAD: JAPAN
Kramer, G.
  Shopping

BRITISH ABROAD: MIDDLE EAST
Micou, P.
  The leper's bell

BROADCASTING HOUSE
Paling, C.
  The silent sentry

BRONTE FAMILY
Hughes, G.
  Bronte

BRONTE, EMILY, ENGLISH NOVELIST, 1818-48
Peters, M.
  Child of earth

BROTHERS
Baker, S.
  Falling in deep
Bowering, M.
  Visible worlds
Courtenay, B.
  Tommo and Hawk
Coyle, H.
  Until the end
Dunmore, H.
  With your crooked heart
Fyfield, F.
  Staring at the light
Jones, D. W.
  Unnatural acts
McCrum, R.
  Suspicion
McGown, J.
  Plots and errors
McKay, M.
  The Lack brothers
Sweetland, M.
  Tradewind

BROTHERS AND SISTERS
Bailey, H.
  Miles and Flora
Chissick, R.
  Colourbook
Hall, G.
  Mortal remains

Lessing, D.
  Mara and Dann
Petterson, P.
  To Siberia
Purcell, D.
  Love like hate adore
Purves, L.
  Home leave
Roe, J.
  A well kept secret
Shriver, L.
  A perfectly good family
Taylor, D.
  Pig in the middle

BROWN, JOHN, AMERICAN ABOLITIONIST, 1800-59
Banks, R.
  Cloudsplitter

BULIMIA
Madden, M. E.
  Astral dance

BUSKERS
McNeill, B.
  To answer the peacock

BYRON, G. G. , 6TH BARON, ENGLISH POET, 1788-1824
Buss, L.
  The luxury of exile

BYZANTINE EMPIRE
Lawhead, S.
  Byzantium

CAESAR, JULIUS, ROMAN STATESMAN, C. 100-44BC
McCullough, C.
  Caesar
  Caesar's women

CAFES
Dennis, F.
  The last blues dance

CALL CENTRES
Thorne, M.
  Eight minutes idle

CAMBODIA: 1960-80
Hillerman, T.
  Finding Moon

CAMBRIDGE
Crombie, D.
  Dreaming of the bones

Gregory, S.
  A deadly brew
Spring, M.
  Nights in white satin
  Standing in the shadows

CAMBRIDGESHIRE
Sole, L.
  This land, this love

CANADA: 19TH CENTURY
Atwood, M.
  Alias Grace

CANADA: 1930-59
Anderson-Dargatz, G.
  The cure for death by lightning
Kavanagh, P.
  Gaff topsails

CANADA: 1960-80
Alexis, A.
  Childhood
Lundin, S.
  This river awakens

CANADA: 1980-2000
Goodwin, T.
  Blood of the forest
Harrison, S.
  The snow falcon
Ricci, N.
  Where she has gone

CANADA: BRITISH COLUMBIA
Anderson-Dargatz, G.
  A recipe for bees
  The cure for death by lightning

CANADA: MONTREAL
Farrow, J.
  City of ice

CANADA: NEWFOUNDLAND
Johnston, W.
  The colony of unrequited dreams
Kavanagh, P.
  Gaff topsails

CANADA: NOVA SCOTIA
McNeil, J.
  Hunting down home

CANADA: ONTARIO
Sakamoto, K.
  The electrical field

CANADA: QUEBEC
Reichs, K.
  Deja dead

CANADA: TORONTO
Michaels, A.
  Fugitive pieces
Wright, E.
  Death of a Sunday writer

CANADA: VANCOUVER
Gough, L.
  Heartbreaker
  Memory lane

CANALETTO, ITALIAN PAINTER, 1697-1768
Laurence, J.
  Canaletto and the case of the privy
    garden
  Canaletto and the case of
    Westminster Bridge

CANALS
Bannister, J.
  The hireling's tale
Fforde, K.
  Life skills
Spridgeon, G.
  The return of the Green Boaters

CANCER
Curtis, N.
  The last place you look
Frost, S.
  The language of nightingales
McClure, K.
  Pandora's helix

CANNIBALISM
Haloche, L.
  Pleasures of the flesh

CANOEING
Bell, P.
  A multitude of sins

CANONISATION
Redmon, A.
  The head of Dionysos

CANTERBURY
Anthony, M. D.
  Midnight come
Oldfield, P.
  Pieces of silver

CAPITALISM
Banks, I.
The business

CAR INDUSTRY
Torrington, J.
The devil's carousel

CAR THEFTS
Price, R.
Freedomland

CARDIFF
Craig, D.
The tattooed detective
Torch
McKenzie, H.
The way things were
Williams, D.
A terminal case
Dead in the market
Williams, J.
Five pubs, two bars and a nightclub

CARERS
Brett, B.
Mother

CARMICHAEL, SIR JOHN OF LANARKSHIRE, FL. 16THC
Tranter, N.
A rage of regents

CARS
Hammond, G.
Fine tune
Myers, A.
Murder in the motor stable

CARTOGRAPHERS
Cowan, J.
A mapmaker's dream

CARTOONISTS
Lennon, J. R.
The funnies

CARVER, RAYMOND, AMERICAN POET, 1939-88
Maxwell, M.
That other lifetime

CASANOVA, GIACOMO, ITALIAN ADVENTURER, 1725-98
Miller, A.
Casanova

CASTAWAYS
Chorlton, W.
Latitude zero

CATHARS
Tanner, J.
The shores of midnight

CATHEDRAL CITIES
Feeny, C.
A matter of time
Palliser, M.
The unburied
Palmer, F.
Murder live
Simons, P.
Angels and men

CATHEDRALS
Edwards, R. D.
Murder in a cathedral
Greenwood, D. M.
A grave disturbance
Holt, H.
Death of a Dean
Pewsey, E.
Unholy harmonies

CATHOLIC CHURCH
Alexander, D.
The fifth gospel
Folsom, A.
Day of confession
Kavanagh, P.
Gaff topsails
Luard, E.
Marguerite
Miller, W. M.
Saint Leibowitz and the wild horse woman
Spencer, L.
Then came heaven

CATHOLICS AND PROTESTANTS
Doughty, A.
Stranger in the place

CATS
Alexander, C.
Mrs. Chippy's last expedition
Babson, M.
Miss Petunia's last case
Braun, L. J.
The cat who knew Shakespeare
The cat who played post office
The cat who said cheese
The cat who sang for the birds
The cat who saw stars
The cat who tailed a thief

King, G.
  The golden cat
  The wild road

CATTLE RANCHES
Dailey, J.
  Notorious
McCarthy, C.
  Cities of the plain
Roberts, N.
  Montana sky
Turner, N.
  These is my words
Williamson, P. G.
  Heart of the West

CATTLE STATIONS
Morrissey, D.
  Heart of the dreaming

CELTS
Sampson, F.
  A casket of earth

CEMETERIES
Reynolds, S.
  A gracious plenty

CENTRAL AMERICA: 1930-59
Merrick, J.
  Horse latitudes

CENTRAL AMERICA: 1980-2000
Chai, A. J.
  Eating fire and drinking water
Didion, J.
  The last thing he wanted
Maw, J.
  Nothing but trouble

CHANGE OF IDENTITY
Marchmont, G.
  Wild grapes
Pye, M.
  Taking lives

CHANNEL ISLANDS: GUERNSEY
Bachmann, D.
  An elusive freedom
  Winds of change
Binding, T.
  Island madness
Dewhurst, E.
  Alias the enemy

CHANNEL ISLANDS: JERSEY
Blair, E. N.
  Half hidden

Falconer, E.
  A barefoot wedding

CHARACTER STUDIES: MEN
Barrow, A.
  The man in the moon
Binding, T.
  A perfect execution
Blackaby, M.
  Look what they've done to the blues
Blumenthal, V.
  Kempton's journey
Boyd, W.
  Armadillo
Brookner, A.
  Altered states
Brown, J. G.
  The wrecked, blessed body of
    Shelton Lafleur
Buarque, C.
  Benjamin
Busia, A.
  The seasons of Beento Blackbird
Doyle, R.
  A star called Henry
Dunne, C.
  A name for himself
Erdrich, L.
  Tales of burning love
Fane, J.
  Money matters
Gale, P.
  Tree surgery for beginners
Guterson, D.
  East of the mountains
Hamilton, J.
  The short history of a prince
Harrison, S.
  Heaven's on hold
Hart, C.
  The harvest
Humphreys, E.
  The gift of a daughter
Ireland, K.
  The man who never lived
Jacobi, S.
  A short series of discrete problems
Kennedy, D.
  The big picture
Klima, I.
  The ultimate intimacy
Kristof, A.
  Yesterday
Lingard, A.
  The fiddler's leg
McIlvanney, W.
  The kiln
McMurtry, L.
  Duane's depressed

Michaels, A.
Fugitive pieces
Middleton, S.
Necessary ends
Morley, J. D.
Destiny
Mourby, A.
The four of us
We think the world of him
Norman, H.
The museum guard
Parks, T.
Destiny
Parsons, T.
Man and boy
Perlman, E.
Three dollars
Richler, M.
Barney's version
Roth, H.
Requiem for Harlem
Roth, J.
Rebellion
Russo, R.
Straight man
Salmon, E.
Titus
Seaward, B.
The avalanche
Shearer, C.
The wonder book of the air
Shields, C.
Larry's party
Simpson, M.
A regular guy
Stadler, M.
Allan Stein
Thomas, S.
Absent fathers
Tyler, A.
A patchwork planet
Updike, J.
Bech at bay
Wall, A.
Bless the thief
Williams, N.
Forty something
Wiseman, T.
Genius Jack
Wolfe, T.
A man in full
Woodford, P.
On the night
Yehoshua, A. B.
Open heart

CHARACTER STUDIES: WOMEN
Adamoli, V.
Sons, lovers, etc.

Adamson, Z.
Touch the sky
Anderson-Dargatz, G.
A recipe for bees
Appignanesi, L.
A good woman
Atwood, M.
Alias Grace
Benison, T.
The arrogance of women
Benzie, A.
The angle of incidence
Berg, E.
Range of motion
Bradford, B. T.
A sudden change of heart
Her own rules
Power of a woman
Brady, J.
The emigre
Brookfield, A.
The godmother
Brookner, A.
Falling slowly
Undue influence
Visitors
Burton, B.
Not just a soldier's war
Cobbold, M.
The purveyor of enchantment
Courtenay, B.
Jessica
Creer, G.
Cradle to grave
Crewe, C.
Falling away
Dailey, J.
Notorious
Davidson, C. T.
The priest fainted
Doyle, R.
The woman who walked into doors
Duffy, S.
Eating cake
Dunn, S.
Commencing our descent
Edwards, P.
The search for Kate Duval
Forster, M.
The memory box
Friedman, R.
Vintage
Geary, T.
Shouting at the ship men
Glaister, L.
The private parts of women
Goodwin, K.
Sleeping with random beasts

Gould, J.
  Till the end of time
Grant, L.
  The cast iron shore
Haff, B. H.
  Shame
Hall, B.
  The Saskiad
Hill, S.
  The service of clouds
Hinxman, M.
  Losing touch
Hutchinson, M.
  For the sake of her child
Irving, J.
  A widow for one year
James, S.
  Two loves
Kasischke, L.
  Suspicious river
Lambert, A.
  Golden lads and girls
Lingard, A.
  Figure in a landscape
Lively, P.
  Spiderweb
Lyons, G.
  Lucy Leighton's journey
  Perdita's passion
  Poppy Penhaligon's progress
MacLaverty, B
  Grace notes
Maitland, S.
  Brittle joys
Marsh, J.
  Iris
Marsh, W.
  Amy Wingate's journal
Michaels, F.
  Celebration
Nahai, G. B.
  Moonlight on the avenue of faith
Neil, B.
  A history of silence
Norman, H.
  Susanna
Nugent, F.
  Drawing from life
O'Neill, A.
  Wayward angel
Perriam, W.
  Coupling
  Second skin
Plain, B.
  Secrecy
Raife, A. .
  The larach
Rhodes, E.
  Portrait of Chloe

Roe, J.
  A new leaf
  The topiary garden
Rowntree, K.
  An innocent diversion
Spencer, L.
  That Camden summer
Steinberg, A. N.
  First hands
Stevens, A.
  Finding Maggie
Sully, S.
  The daisy chain
Sussman, S.
  Young wives' tales
Swick, M. A.
  Evening news
Swindells, M.
  Snakes and ladders
Tayler, P.
  Cutting the sweetness
Taylor, E. R.
  Tomorrow
Traynor, J.
  Sister Josephine
Weldon, F.
  Worst fears
Windsor, V.
  Saint and warrior
Wynne-Jones, G.
  Ordinary miracles
Young, L.
  Baby love

CHEFS
Myers, A.
  Murder in the motor stable
  Murder with Majesty

CHEMICAL WARFARE
Harlow, B.
  Circle William
Sebastian, T.
  Ultra

CHESHIRE
James, E.
  A sense of belonging
Marston, A. E.
  The hawks of Delamere
Reimann, A.
  Wise child
Spencer, S.
  The Salton killings
  Those golden days
Stranger, J.
  Perilous journey

CHESS

Glavinic, T.
Carl Haffner's love of the draw

CHILD ABDUCTION

Cleeves, A.
The baby-snatcher
Harmetz, A.
Off the face of the earth
Parker, T. J.
Where serpents lie

CHILD ABUSE

Adams, J.
Cast the first stone
Atkins, A.
A fine and private place
Benzie, A.
The angle of incidence
Davidson, T.
Scar culture
Fox, , Z. A.
Cradle and all
Harte, L.
Losing it
Jonker, J.
Sadie was a lady
Leroy, M.
Trust
Masters, P.
Catch the fallen sparrow
Nykanen, M.
Hush
Steel, D.
The long road home
Wingfield, R. D.
Winter Frost

CHILD BRIDES

Rabinyan, D.
Persian brides

CHILD PORNOGRAPHY

Gadney, R.
The Achilles heel

CHILD SEXUAL ABUSE

Johnson, R. A.
A kind of hush
Oldham, N.
One dead witness
Prager, E.
Roger Fishbite
Robinson, P.
Wednesday's child
Sapphire
Push

CHILDBIRTH

Kidman, F.
Ricochet baby

CHILDHOOD

Alexis, A.
Childhood
Atkins, A.
On our own
Baker, N.
The everlasting story of Nory
Barraclough, J.
First finds
Berne, S.
A crime in the neighbourhood
Bingham, K.
Mummy's legs
Burt, G.
The dandelion clock
Cobbold, M.
Frozen music
Darling, J.
Crocodile soup
Davies, C.
Jamestown blues
Deane, S.
Reading in the dark
Devoto, P. C.
My last days as Roy Rogers
Dillon, D.
Itchycooblue
Fenkl, H. I.
Memories of my ghost brother
Fraser, S.
Specs war
Gavron, J.
Moon
Grimes, M.
Hotel Paradise
Grossman, D.
The zigzag kid
Halliwell, A.
The cuckoo's parting cry
Hanania, T.
Homesick
Hedges, P.
An ocean in Iowa
Hornby, N.
About a boy
Iskander, F.
The old house under the cypress tree
Jooste, P.
Dance with a poor man's daughter
Levy, D.
Billy and girl
Matthew, C.
A nightingale sang in Fernhurst Road
McEwan, T.
Arithmetic

Papandreou, N.
  Father dancing
Perera, S.
  Haven't stopped dancing yet
Petterson, P.
  To Siberia
Purves, L.
  Regatta
Richards, J.
  The innocence of roast chicken
Roy, A.
  The god of small things
Ryan, M.
  The song of the tide
Sadiq, Z.
  38 Bahadurabad
Saxton, J.
  Someone special
Syal, M.
  Anita and me
Toksvig, S.
  Whistling for the elephants
Vinci, S.
  A game we play

CHILDRENS' HOMES
Taylor, A. G.
  In guilty night

CHILE: 19TH CENTURY
Allende, I.
  Daughter of fortune

CHILE: 1930-59
Agosin, M.
  A cross and a star

CHILE: 1980-2000
Dorfman, A.
  The nanny and the iceberg

CHIMPANZEES
Self, W.
  Great apes

CHINA: 19TH CENTURY
Carter, R.
  Barbarians

CHINA: 20TH CENTURY
Wood, B.
  Perfect harmony

CHINA: 1900-29
Whiting, C.
  The Japanese princess

CHINA: 1930-59
Chang, M.
  A choice of evils
Chiu, M. L.
  Gone forever
West, P.
  The tent of orange mist

CHINA: 1980-2000
See, L.
  The flower net
  The interior
Ying, H.
  Summer of betrayal

CHINESE ABROAD: BRITAIN
Roberts, I.
  Limehouse lady

CHINESE MEDICINE
Wood, B.
  Perfect harmony

CHOCOLATE
Harris, J.
  Chocolat

CHOIRS
Warner, A.
  The sopranos

CHRISTMAS
Gaarder, J.
  The Christmas mystery
Moore, C.
  Santa and Pete

CHURCH OF ENGLAND
Taylor, A.
  The four last things

CHURCH POLITICS
Greenwood, D. M.
  Mortal spoils

CHURCHES
Taylor, A. G.
  The mortal sickness

CIRCUSES
Chalfoun, M.
  Roustabout

CITY LIFE
Bandele-Thomas, B.
  The street

CIVIL RIGHTS MOVEMENT
Brand, D.
In another place, not here
Rivers, C.
Camelot

CIVIL SERVANTS
Perry, A.
Traitor's Gate

CIVIL WAR, ENGLISH, 1642-51
Cannam, H.
A clouded sky
Carter, N.
Harvest of swords
King's men crow
Stand by the colours
Storming party
Hines, J.
The puritan's wife
Sweetman, D.
A tribal fever
Tomson, J. M.
Devil on my shoulder

CLAIRVOYANCE
Evans, M.
Inheritors
Graziunas, D.
Thinning the predators
Greeley, A. M.
Irish mist
Haines, C.
Touched
Passman, D.
The visionary
Smethurst, W.
Woken's eye

CLAY INDUSTRY
Gower, I.
Sweet Rosie
Summers, R.
Primmy's daughter
White rivers

CLEANERS
Dewar, I.
Giving up on ordinary
Truss, L.
Going loco
Watson, S.
The perfect treasure

CLEOPATRA, QUEEN OF EGYPT, 69-30BC
George, M.
The memoirs of Cleopatra

CLERGY
Anthony, M. D.
Midnight come
Braun, T.
Free spirits
Charles, K.
Unruly passions
Edwards, R. D.
Murder in a cathedral
Greenwood, D. M.
A grave disturbance
Heavenly vices
Mortal spoils
Gregson, J. M.
A turbulent priest
Perry, A.
Brunswick Gardens
Rhodes, P.
The trespassers
Rose, L.
Heaven's door
Kingdom come
Secombe, F.
Pastures new
Taylor, A.
The judgement of strangers
Templeton, A.
Past praying for
Wilbourne, D.
A vicar's diary
Williams, D.
A terminal case

CLITORIS
Andahazi, F.
The anatomist

CLOCKMAKING
Moring, M.
In Babylon

CLONING
Craven, W.
Fountain society
Steel, D.
The Klone and I

CLYDESIDE
Craig, M.
The river flows on
Henderson, M.
The holy city
Hood, E.
Time and again

COACH TOURS
Wallington, M.
Happy birthday, Mr. Shakespeare

COAL MINING
Smith, M. C.
Rose
Trotter, J. M.
Chasing the dream

COLD WAR
Bennett, F.
Making enemies

COLLAPSE OF CIVILISATION
Gee, M.
The ice people

COLLECTORS
Wilson, D.
Cumberland's cradle

COLLEGES
Cutler, J.
Dying for power
Dying on principle
Kean, R.
The pledge
Kelly, N.
Old wounds

COLOMBIA
Lewis, S.
Taking chances

COMA
Coupland, D.
Girl friend in a coma
Delinsky, B.
Coast road

COMEDIANS
Barrow, A.
The man in the moon
Capurro, S.
Fowl play

COMEDY FESTIVALS
Guttridge, P.
No laughing matter

COMMUNISM
Roth, P.
I married a communist

COMMUNITY CENTRES
Wilson, P.
Noah, Noah

COMMUTERS
Matthews, C.
Let's meet on Platform 8

COMPETITIONS
Manby, C.
Deep heat

COMPOSERS
McEwan, I.
Amsterdam

COMPUTER GAMES
Locke, T.
One false move
Pugh, D.
Foolproof
Tasker, P.
Samurai boogie

COMPUTER PROGRAMMERS
Lyons, D.
Dog days

COMPUTER VIRUSES
Besher, A.
Mir

COMPUTERS
Bronson, P.
The first $20million is always the hardest
Clancy, T.
Ruthless. com
Franklet, D.
Bad memory
Harry, E. L.
Society of the mind
Knox, B.
Death bytes
Larsen, M.
Uncertainty
Mathews, A.
Vienna blood
McLaren, J.
Press send
Murphy, M.
Goodnight, my angel
Watson, I.
Hard questions

CONFERENCES
Palmer, F.
Hot Toddy

CONFESSIONS
Belsky, R.
Playing dead
Roberts, M.
Fair exchange

CONFIDENCE TRICKSTERS
Cannell, S. J.
  King con
Howard, E. J.
  Falling
Kessel, J.
  Corrupting Dr. Nice
Rowntree, K.
  Mr. Brightly's evening off
Yorke, M.
  False pretences

CONGO: 1960-80
Bennett, R.
  The catastrophist
Kingsolver, B.
  The poisonwood Bible

CONSCIENTIOUS OBJECTORS
Murphy, T.
  Christ in khaki

CONSERVATION
Charbonneau, L.
  The magnificent Siberian
Fielding, K.
  Untrodden ways
Siddons, A. R.
  Low country

CONSERVATIONISTS
Bailey, M.
  Haycastle's cricket
Barr, N.
  Endangered species
Cleeves, A.
  The crow trap
Elegant, R. S.
  The big brown bears
Merriman, C.
  State of desire

CONSPIRACIES
Backhouse, F.
  By other means
Baker, K.
  Inheritance
Blake, S.
  The butcher bird
Carroll, J.
  Kissing the beehive
Edwards, M.
  Eve of destruction
Estleman, L. D.
  The witchfinder
Folsom, A.
  Day of confession
Fraser, S.
  Montague's whore

Freeling, N.
  A dwarf kingdom
Garrison, P.
  Fire and ice
Goodwin, T.
  Seeds of destruction
Higgins, G. V.
  A change of gravity
Kellerman, F.
  Serpent's tooth
Kennealy, J.
  The forger
La Plante, L.
  Cold heart
Lockhart, D.
  The paradise complex
Ludlum, R.
  The Matarese countdown
Macaulay, T.
  Brutal truth
Martini, S.
  Critical mass
Mezrich, B.
  Threshold
Norman, H.
  The pact
Roberts, B.
  The victory snapshot
Sutherland, G.
  East of the city
Thomson, J.
  Burden of innocence
Urban, M. L.
  The illegal
Wilson. D.
  The Borgia chalice

CONSTRUCTION INDUSTRY
Davis, V.
  Getting away with it
Ooi, Y-M.
  The flame tree

CONTEMPORARY CULTURE
Gallagher, H.
  Teeth

CONVENTS
Leon, D.
  The death of faith

COOKS
Laurence, J.
  Appetite for death
Smith, D.
  The circus
Temple, L. J.
  Bread on arrival

CORN MILLS
Dickinson, M.
  The miller's daughter

CORNWALL
Aitken, R.
  Cornish harvest
  Deep waters
Barker, A. L.
  The Haunt
Benson, P.
  The shape of clouds
Bingham, C.
  A grand affair
Bolitho, J.
  Buried in Cornwall
  Exposure of evil
  Framed in Cornwall
  Snapped in Cornwall
  Victims of violence
Burley, W. J.
  Wycliffe and the redhead
Chapman, J.
  The soldier's girl
Clayton, M.
  Dead men's bones
  Death is the inheritance
  The prodigal's return
  The word is death
Cook, G.
  Porthellis
  Roscarrock
Everett, P.
  The voyages of Alfred Wallis
Goddard, R.
  Beyond recall
Grimes, M.
  The Lamorna Wink
Hawksley, E.
  Crossing the Tamar
Hedgecoe, J.
  Breakfast with Dolly
Henley, J.
  Family ties
  Somebody's lover
Hill, E. A.
  The driftwood fire
Hines, J.
  The lost daughter
Jackson, J.
  The iron road
Mann, J.
  A private enquiry
Matthews, J. W.
  A silver flood
  A vein of richness
Montague, J.
  Child of the mist

Roe, J.
  A new leaf
Ross, M.
  Like a diamond
  The Carringtons of Helston
  Tomorrow's tide
Saville, D.
  Capability's Eden
Shepherd, S.
  Twilight curtain
Sinclair, E.
  Her father's house
Summers, R.
  Primmy's daughter
  September morning
  White rivers
Thompson, E. V.
  Moontide
Titchmarsh, A.
  The last lighthouse keeper
Todd, C.
  Wings of fire
Tremayne, K.
  Adam Loveday
Wesley, M.
  Part of the furniture
White, G.
  Veil of darkness

CORPORATIONS
Banks, I.
  The business
Flusfeder, D. L.
  Like plastic
Garber, J. R.
  Vertical run
Heffernan, W.
  The dinosaur club
Heiney, P.
  Domino's effect
Lynn, M.
  Insecurity
Stanley, G.
  Nagasaki six

CORRESPONDENCE, NOVELS IN THE FORM OF
Conlon, E.
  A glassful of letters
Gaarder, J.
  Vita brevis
Latham, E.
  Silences of the heart
Maraire, N.
  Zenzele

CORRUPTION
Allbeury, T.
  Shadow of a doubt

Ryan, M.
  The song of the tide
Sinclair, E.
  The path through the woods
Swinson, A.
  The cousin's tale
Willett, M.
  Second time around

COWBOYS
Vanderhaeghe, G.
  The Englishman's boy

CREATIVE WRITING
Cutler, J.
  Dying to write

CRETE
Baker, D.
  Some day I'll find you

CRIBB, TOM, CHAMPION BOXER
Fraser, G. M.
  Black Ajax

CRIME
Ballard, J. G.
  Cocaine nights
Cameron, J.
  It was an accident
Cole, M.
  The runaway
Grey, P.
  Cutter's Wharf
Mortimer, J.
  Felix in the underworld
Noll, I.
  Head count

CRIMEAN WAR, 1853-56
Bainbridge, B.
  Master Georgie
Douglas, G.
  Soldiers in the mist
  The devil's own
  The valley of death
Dymoke, J.
  The making of Molly March
Harrod-Eagles, C.
  The winter journey

CRIMES OF PASSION
Cole, M.
  Two women

CRIMINAL JUSTICE SYSTEM
Anonymous
  A time for justice

CRIMINALS
Arnott, J.
  The long firm
Atwood, M.
  Alias Grace
Boyle, J.
  Hero of the underworld
Dillon, P.
  Truth
Little, E.
  Another day in paradise
Martin, D.
  In the hat
May, S.
  The nudist colony
McMurtry, L. & Ossana, D.
  Pretty Boy Floyd
Williams, G.
  Diamond geezers

CROSSWORD PUZZLES
Saunders, J.
  Thicker than water

CRUISES
Hall, J. W.
  Buzz cut
Straley, J.
  The angels will not care
Warren, T.
  Full steam ahead
Winterson, J.
  Gut symmetries
Woodman, R.
  Act of terror

CRUSADES
Hillier, D.
  Fire and shadow
McCaughrean, G.
  Lovesong
Rivele, S. J.
  A booke of days

CUBA: 19TH CENTURY
Conde, M.
  Windward heights

CUBA: HAVANA
King, F.
  Ash on an old man's sleeve
Palmer, F.
  Hoodwinked
Smith, M. C.
  Havana Bay

CUBANS ABROAD: US
Parker, B.
  Suspicion of deceit

CUCHULAINN, IRISH MYTHOLOGICAL HERO
Eickhoff, R. L.
The feast

CULTS
Burgh, A.
The cult
Caveney, P.
1999
King, L. R.
A monstrous regiment of women

CUMBRIA
Bragg, M.
The soldier's return

CURSES
Battison, B.
The witch's familiar
Cook, J.
Kill the witch
Erskine, B.
House of echoes
Gordon, F.
Thorn
O'Neill, A.
A family cursed
Veevers, M.
Bloodlines

CUSTER, GEORGE ARMSTRONG, AMERICAN SOLDIER, 1839-76
Blake, M.
Marching to Valhalla
Chiaventone, F. J.
A road we do not know

CUSTOMS AND EXCISE
Gadney, R.
The Achilles heel

CYBERNETICS
Harry, E. L.
Society of the mind

CYCLING
North, F.
Cat
Waddington, J.
Bad to the bone

CZECHOSLOVAKIA: PRAGUE
Klima, I.
The ultimate intimacy
Skeggs, D.
The phoenix of Prague

Sterling, B.
Holy fire

DALI, SALVADOR, SPANISH ARTIST, 1904-89
Dronfield, J.
Resurrecting Salvador

DANCERS
Ibbotson, E.
A company of swans
Parker, J.
The stars shine bright
Pearse, L.
Ellie
Steel, D.
Granny Dan

DARTMOOR
North, S.
The lie of the land
Thompson, E. V.
Cast no shadows
Willett, M.
Starting over

DARWIN, CHARLES, ENGLISH NATURALIST, 1809-92
McDonald, R.
Mr. Darwin's shooter

DATING AGENCIES
Fyfield, F.
Blind date
Todd, C.
Staying cool

DAVID, MASTER OF KENNEDY, SCOTTISH NOBLEMAN, FL. 16TH CENTURY
Tranter, N.
A flame for the fire

DAY TRIPS
Brune, H.
Day trippers

DEAF PEOPLE
Pemberton, V.
The silent war
Seth, V.
An equal music

DEAN, JAMES, FILM ACTOR, 1931-55
Toperoff, S.
Jimmy Dean prepares

DEATH

Crace, J.
Being dead
Gaarder, J.
Through a glass darkly
Kirchhof, S.
The threefold garment

DEATH THREATS

Gano, J.
Arias of blood

DEBT COLLECTORS

Hightower, L.
The debt collector

DEBUTANTES

Melville, A.
Debutante

DECADENCE

Gambotto, A.
The pure weight of the heart

DECEIT

Gadol, P.
The long rain

DENTISTS

Armstrong, V.
Dead in the water

DEPARTMENT STORES

Burns, P.
Goodbye, Piccadilly: Packards at war
Packards
Hill, P.
Murder in store
Pennac, D.
The scapegoat

DERBYSHIRE

George, E.
In pursuit of the proper sinner
McDermid, V.
A place of execution

DESIGNERS

Baker, D.
Backroom girl

DETECTIVE STORIES

Adams, J.
Cast the first stone
Final frame
Aird, C.
After effects
Stiff news

Airth, R.
River of darkness
Alexander, B.
Murder in Grub Street
Ardin, W.
The Mary medallion
Armstrong, D.
Thought for the day
Bannister, J.
The hireling's tale
Barnard, R.
No place of safety
The corpse at the Haworth Tandoori
Battison, B.
Jeopardy's child
Mirror image
The witch's familiar
Truths not told
Bell, P.
A multitude of sins
Benison, C. C.
Death at Buckingham Palace
Bolitho, J.
An absence of angels
Exposure of evil
Finger of fate
Framed in Cornwall
Sequence of shame
Snapped in Cornwall
Victims of violence
Bonner, H.
A fancy to kill for
Bowen, G.
A killing spring
Bowker, D.
The butcher of Glastonbury
Brett, S.
Dead room farce
Brookmyre, C.
Quite ugly one morning
Burke, J.
Dear Irene
Burke, J.
Remember me, Irene
Burley, W. J.
Wycliffe and the redhead
Butler, G.
Coffin's game
Coffin's ghost
Carson, P.
Cold steel
Casley, D. J.
Death under par
Charles, P.
Fountain of sorrow
Last boat to Camden Town
Clayton, M.
Dead men's bones
Death is the inheritance

Woods, J. G.
  A murder of no consequence
  The General's dog

DETECTIVES, ETC.

Archer, Owen
  Robb, C.
Barnaby, Chief Inspector
  Graham, C.
Brannigan, Kate
  McDermid, V.
Bray, Nell
  Linscott, G.
Bulman, George
  Royce, K.
Campbell, Letty
  Fritchley, A.
Coffin, John
  Butler, G.
Colorado, Kat
  Kijewski, K.
Croft, Mike, Det. Insp.
  Adams, J.
Cunningham, John
  Hammond, G.
Dallas, Eve
  Robb, J. D.
Delchard, Ralph
  Marston, E.
Devlin, Sean
  Higgins, J.
Didier, Auguste
  Myers, A.
Faro, Inspector
  Knight, A.
Fizz & Buchanan
  Holms, J.
Fyfe, David, Det. Chief Inspector
  Paul, W.
Garrity, Callaghan
  Trocheck, K. H.
Gently, George, Det. Supt.
  Hunter, A.
Ghote, Inspector
  Keating, H. R. F.
Grant, Celia
  Sherwood, J.
Ho, Holly-Jean
  Lin-Chandler, I.
Hope, Matthew
  McBain, E.
Howard, Jeri
  Dawson, J.
Kincaid, Duncan, Det. Ch. Insp.
  Crombie, D.
Lynley, Thomas, Det. Ch. Insp
  George, E.
Malone, Scobie
  Cleary, J.

Mayo, Det. Inspector Gil
  Eccles, M.
McNally, Archie
  Sanders, L.
Millhone, Kinsey
  Grafton, S.
Mitchell, Meredith
  Granger, A.
Mitchell, Mitch
  Kershaw, V.
Peters, Toby
  Kaminsky, S. M.
Peterson, Det. Sgt Wes
  Ellis, K.
Piercy, Joanna, Det. Insp
  Masters, P.
Pitt, Thomas
  Perry, A.
Pluke, Montague, Det. Insp.
  Rhea, N.
Qwilleran, Jim
  Braun, L. J.
Rawlings, John
  Lake, D.
Reilly, Regan
  Clark, C. H.
Robicheaux, Dave
  Burke, J. L.
Roger the Chapman
  Sedley, K.
Rook, Jim
  Masterton, G.
Roper, Ian, Det. Insp.
  Bolitho, J.
Ryan, Father Blackie
  Greeley, A. M.
Scudder, Matt
  Block, L.
Simpson, Tim
  Malcolm, J.
Sister Fidelma
  Tremayne, P.
Skinner, Bob, ACC
  Jardine, Q.
Slider, Bill, Det. Ch. Insp.
  Harrod-Eagles, C.
Sloan, C. D. Ch. Insp
  Aird, C.
Spenser
  Parker, R. B.
Swann, Cassie
  Moody, S.
Tansey, Det. Supt.
  Penn, J.
Thanet, Luke, Det. Insp.
  Simpson, D.
Trevelyan, Rose
  Bolitho, J.

Varady, Fran
 Granger, A.
Zen, Aurelio
 Dibdin, M.

DEVELOPING COUNTRIES
Park, D.
 Stone kingdoms

DEVON
Bonner, H.
 For death comes softly
Ellis, K.
 An unhallowed grave
 The Armada boy
 The merchant's house
Goring, A.
 The mulberry field
Jecks, M.
 Moorland hanging
 The abbot's gibbet
Kingsnorth, J.
 Landscapes
Marston, A. E.
 The wildcats of Exeter
Staples, M. J.
 Bright day, dark night
Willett, M.
 Hattie's mill
 Holding on
 Second time around
 The dipper

DIAMONDS
O'Brien, G.
 Cleaning up

DIARIES, NOVELS IN THE FORM OF
Alexander, C.
 Mrs. Chippy's last expedition
Fielding, H.
 Bridget Jones's diary
George, S.
 The journal of Mrs. Pepys
Jones, M.
 Cold in earth
Marsh, W.
 Amy Wingate's journal
Matthew, C.
 A nightingale sang in Fernhurst Road
Morley, D.
 Sing a lonely song
Orton, J.
 Between us girls
Turner, N.
 These is my words
Weir, A.
 Does my bum look big in this?

DIAZ, RODRIGO (EL CID), SPANISH NOBLEMAN, 1043-99
Michaels, F.
 Tender warrior

DINNER PARTIES
Davis, A.
 The dinner

DINOSAURS
Bear, G.
 Dinosaur summer

DIPLOMATS
Schlee, A.
 The time in Aderra

DISABLED PEOPLE
Brown, J. G.
 The wrecked, blessed body of
  Shelton Lafleur
Kingston, B.
 Gemma's journey
Lingard, A.
 The fiddler's leg
Reynolds, S.
 A gracious plenty
Rosenberg, P. M.
 Daniel's dream

DISASTERS
Callison, B.
 Ferry down
Ouellette, P.
 The third pandemic

DISFIGUREMENT
Traynor, J.
 Divine

DISSENTERS, RELIGIOUS
Perez Galdos, B.
 Dona Perfecta

DIVORCE
Cheek, M.
 Three men on a plane
Davis, M. T.
 Gallachers
Delinsky, B.
 A woman's place
Grazebrook, S.
 Page two
Johnson, D.
 Le divorce
Kaye, G.
 Late in the day

Rhodes, E.
  Spring music
Roberts, N.
  Finding the dream
Thorne, N.
  A family affair

DIXON, JEREMIAH, BRITISH SURVEYOR, 1733-79
Pynchon, T.
  Mason and Dixon

DOCTORS
Aird, C.
  After effects
Charles, P.
  Last boat to Camden Town
Collins, W.
  The marriage of souls
Connor, A.
  Midnight's smiling
Cook, J.
  Blood on the Borders
Fielding, K.
  A secret place
  Ravensdale spring
  Untrodden ways
Gash, J.
  Prey dancing
Hilliard, G.
  Golden rain
Jacobson, A.
  False accusations
MacDonald, E.
  Kirkowen's daughter
Naish, N.
  A time to learn
Rhodes, P.
  Whispers
Segal, E.
  Only love
Stephens, K.
  Sign of the moon
Withall, M.
  Fields of heather
  The poppy orchard
Yehoshua, A. B.
  Open heart

DOG BREEDING
Hammond, G.
  Dogsbody
  Twice bitten
Veevers, M.
  Bloodlines

DOG FIGHTING
Howell, L.
  The director's cut

DOGS
Auster, P.
  Timbuktu
Berger, J.
  King
Burgh, A.
  Breeders
Hammond, G.
  A shocking affair
Stranger, J.
  Perilous journey

DOMESTIC VIOLENCE
Dawson, J.
  Trick of the light
Doyle, R.
  The woman who walked into doors
Evans, P.
  The carousel keeps turning
Gom, L.
  Freeze frame
Harvey, J.
  Still water
Jonker, J.
  Walking my baby back home
McGown, J.
  Picture of innocence
Neel, J.
  A timely death
Quindlen, A.
  Black and blue
Rendell, R.
  Harm done
Sharp, L.
  Crows over a wheatfield
Waite, E.
  Kingston Kate

DORSET
Thorne, N.
  Past love
Todd, C.
  Search the dark

DOUBLE AGENTS
Banville, J.
  The untouchable

DOWNSIZING
Perlman, E.
  Three dollars

DRAG ARTISTS
Rodi, R.
  Drag queen

DREAMS
Grimsley, J.
  My drowning

Rosenberg, P. M.
  Daniel's dream
Smith, M. M.
  One of us

DREYFUS, ALFRED, FRENCH SOLDIER, 1859-1935
Rubens, B.
  I, Dreyfus

DRIVING LESSONS
McBain, E.
  Driving lessons
Norwich, W,
  Learning to drive

DROPOUTS
Calisher, H.
  In the slammer with Carol Smith
Stone, O.
  A child's night dream

DROUGHT
Carrington, R.
  A thirst for rain
Marlow, M.
  Dry
Moloney, S.
  A dry spell

DROWNING
Grimes, M.
  Hotel Paradise

DRUG ADDICTS
Calisher, H.
  In the slammer with Carol Smith
Davies, L.
  Candy
Hendricks, V.
  Iguana love
Kays, K.
  Wasted
Keyes, M.
  Rachel's holiday
Marchant, I.
  In Southern waters
McDowell, N.
  Four in the morning
Miller, E.
  Like being killed
Shepherd, S.
  Embers of death
Stewart, S.
  Sharking
Welsh. I.
  Ecstasy
Yablonsky, L.
  The story of junk

DRUG MANUFACTURE
Johansen, I.
  Long after midnight
Keating, H. R. F.
  Asking questions
Palmer, F.
  Dark forest
Stewart, E.
  The solution

DRUG RESEARCH
Gibb, N.
  Blood red sky
Hill, R.
  The wood beyond

DRUG TRAFFIC
Andrews, C.
  Deep as the marrow
Battison, B.
  Truths not told
Blincoe, N.
  The dope priest
Brune, H.
  Your house is mine
Carcaterra, L.
  Apaches
Caveney, P.
  1999
Chisnell, M.
  The delivery
Clayton, M.
  Dead men's bones
Collins, L.
  Tomorrow belongs to us
Conway, S.
  Damaged
Danks, D.
  Torso
Dold, G.
  Schedule two
Eccles, M.
  Killing me softly
Falconer, C.
  Triad
Farris, J.
  Solar eclipse
Ferrigno, R.
  Heartbreaker
Gill, B.
  Death of a busker king
Gilstrap, J.
  At all costs
Gulvin, J.
  Close quarters
  Sorted
Harvey, J.
  Last rites

Hensher, P.
  Pleasured
James, B.
  Eton crop
  Lovely mover
  Panicking Ralph
  Top banana
Jones, J.
  After Melissa
Leather, S.
  The solitary man
Masters, A.
  The good and faithful servant
  The speed queen
McEldowney, E.
  The sad case of Harpo Higgins
Medland, M.
  Point of honour
Miller, J. R.
  The last family
Morell, J.
  The targeting of Robert Alvar
Pawson, S.
  Last reminder
  The Judas sheep
Plate, P.
  Police and thieves
Rayner, R.
  Murder book
Robinson, P.
  Dead right
Ross, J.
  Murder! murder! burning bright
Siler. J.
  Easy money
Sillitoe, A.
  The German numbers woman
Stewart, E.
  The solution
Strong, T.
  White viper
Strongman, P.
  Cocaine
Titchmarsh, A.
  The last lighthouse keeper
Waites, M.
  Mary's prayer
Whitnell, B.
  Deep waters
Wilson, A.
  Truth or dare
Yallop, D.
  Unholy alliance

DRUGS
Cooper, D.
  Guide
Morton, C. W.
  Rage sleep

Rushkoff, D.
  The Ecstasy Club

DRUIDS
Harris, E.
  The twilight child

DUNBAR, PATRICK, EARL OF
Tranter, N.
  Envoy extraordinary

DUNDEE
Burnside, J.
  The mercy boys

DURHAM
Fawcett, P.
  Village wives
Gill, E.
  The road to Berry Edge
Horne, U.
  A time to heal
Jenkins, R.
  The Duke's agent
Robertson, W.
  A thirsting land
  Children of the storm
Trotter, J. M.
  Never stand alone

EARHART, AMELIA, AVIATOR, 1898-1937
Mendelsohn, J.
  I was Amelia Earhart

EARTHQUAKES
Alletzhauser, A.
  Quake

EAST AFRICA: 18TH CENTURY
Smith, W.
  Monsoon

EAST ANGLIA
Blacker, T.
  Revenance
Lynton, P.
  Innocence
Marshall, S.
  A late lark singing
  Strip the willow
Sebald, W. G.
  The rings of Saturn
Taylor, D. J.
  Trespass
Wilson, T.
  The poppy path
  The strawberry sky

EAST GERMANY: 1980-2000
Brussig, T.
Heroes like us

EAST INDIA COMPANY
McNeill, E.
Dusty letters

EAST INDIES
Chorlton, W.
Latitude zero

ECCENTRICS
Brink, A.
Devil's valley
Desai, K.
Hullabaloo in the guava orchard
Ellmann, L.
Man or mango?
Gowdy, B.
Mister Sandman
Haylock, J.
Body of contention
Jackson, M.
The underground man
Legge, G.
Near neighbours
Lock, S.
Nothing but the truth
Magrs, P.
Does it show?
Marsh, W.
The quick and the dead
Miller, A.
Ingenious pain
Sealy, A.
The Everest Hotel

EDINBURGH
Dewar, I.
Women talking dirty
Douglas, A.
As the years go by
Catherine's land
Frame, R.
The lantern bearers
Holms, J.
Bad vibes
Thin ice
Jardine, Q.
Gallery whispers
Murmuring the judges
Skinner's ghosts
Skinner's mission
Skinner's ordeal
Johnston, P.
Body politic
The bone yard

Knight, A.
Murder by appointment
The Coffin Lane murders
Lindsay, F.
A kind of dying
Idle hands
McNeill, E.
Money troubles
Rankin, I.
The hanging garden

EDWIN, SAINT, KING OF NORTHUMBRIA, C585-633
Sampson, F.
The flight of the sparrow

EGYPT
Smethurst, W.
Sinai

EGYPT, ANCIENT
Doherty, P. C.
The Horus killings
The mask of Ra
George, M.
The memoirs of Cleopatra
Holland, T.
The sleeper in the sands
Jacq, C.
Ramses: under the Western Acacia
Ramses; the lady of Abu Simbel
The battle of Kadesh
The black Pharaoh
The son of the light
The temple of a million years

EGYPT: 18TH CENTURY
Rufin, J. C.
The Abyssinian

EGYPT: 19TH CENTURY
Howard, R.
Bonaparte's invaders
Jakeman, J.
The Egyptian coffin

EGYPT: 1900-29
Pearce, M.
Death of an effendi
The fig tree murder
The last cut

EGYPT: 1980-2000
Soueif, A.
The map of love

EL SALVADOR
Benitez, S.
Bitter grounds

ELDERLY
Anderson, B.
Proud garments
Frewen, F.
The tortoise shell

ELECTIONS
Grippando, J.
The abduction

ELECTRIC POWER
Belfer, L.
City of light

ELECTRONICS
Page, M.
Night secrets

ELEPHANTS
Gowdy, B.
The white bone

ELIJAH, BIBLICAL PROPHET
Coelho, P.
The fifth mountain

**ELIOT, THOMAS STEARNS, POET
AND DRAMATIST, 1888-1965**
Cooley, M.
The archivist

ELIZABETH I, QUEEN, 1533-1603
Finney, P.
Unicorn's blood
Maxwell, R.
The Queen's bastard

EMERALDS
Boucheron, R.
Victoria's emeralds

EMPIRE STATE BUILDING
Bateman, C.
Empire State

EMPLOYERS
Hijuelos, O.
Empress of the splendid season

ENCLOSED COMMUNITIES
Swinfen, A.
The anniversary
Treuer, D.
Little

ENDANGERED SPECIES
Montero, M.
You, darkness

O'Brien, D.
Brendan Prairie

ENGAGEMENTS
Finnamore, S.
Old maid

ENGLAND, NORTH EAST
Carr, I.
Chrissie's children
Gill, E.
Under a cloud-soft sky
Robertson, W.
Kitty Rainbow

ENGLAND, PREHISTORIC
Cornwell, B.
Stonehenge

ENGLAND: 1ST CENTURY
Rowe, R.
The Germanicus mosaic
Wishart, D.
The horse coin

ENGLAND: 6TH CENTURY
Bradley, M. Z.
Lady of Avalon
Cornwell, B.
Enemy of God
Excalibur
Lawhead, S.
Grail
Miles, R.
Guenevere: the Queen of the summer
country
Whyte, J.
The Saxon shore
The sorcerer

ENGLAND: 7TH CENTURY
Bragg, M.
Credo
Sampson, F.
A casket of earth

ENGLAND: 8TH CENTURY
Cusack, W.
The edge of vengeance

ENGLAND: 11TH CENTURY
Baltuck, N.
Kingdom come
Marston, A. E.
The hawks of Delamere
The lions of the north
The serpents of Harbledown
The stallions of Woodstock
The wildcats of Exeter

Marston, E.
    The foxes of Warwick
Pernell, S.
    The gift and the promise
Rathbone, J.
    The last English king

ENGLAND: 12TH CENTURY
Chadwick, E.
    The love knot
Clare, A.
    Fortune like the moon
Highsmith, D.
    Master of the keys
Hill, P.
    Countess Isabel
    Curtmantle
    The supplanter
Hillier, D.
    Fire and shadow
Morson, I.
    A psalm for Falconer
    Falconer and the face of God
    Falconer and the great beast
Penman, S. K.
    Cruel as the grave
    The Queen's man

ENGLAND: 13TH CENTURY
Chadwick, E.
    The marsh king's daughter
Gellis, R.
    A mortal bane
Hill, P.
    The Lion's daughter

ENGLAND: 14TH CENTURY
Alexander, V.
    The love knot
Baer, A.
    Medieval women
Doherty, P. C.
    A tournament of murders
    The demon archer
    The devil's domain
    The devil's hunt
    The field of blood
Hall, D.
    Kemp; the road to Crecy
Harding, P.
    The assassin's riddle
Jecks, M.
    Belladonna at Belstone
    Moorland hanging
    Squire Throwleigh's heir
    The abbot's gibbet
    The Crediton killings
    The leper's return

Robb, C.
    A spy for the redeemer
    The king's bishop
    The riddle of St. Leonard's

ENGLAND: 15TH CENTURY
Adams, R.
    The outlandish knight
Doherty, P. C.
    The rose demon
Gower, I.
    Destiny's child
Gregory, S.
    A bone of contention
    A deadly brew
    A wicked deed
    An unholy alliance
Sedley, K.
    The brothers of Glastonbury
    The Saint John's fern
    The weaver's inheritance
    The wicked winter

ENGLAND: 16TH CENTURY
Baker, K.
    In the garden of Eden
Baldwin, M.
    Dark lady
Buckley, F.
    The doublet affair
    The Robsart mystery
Chisholm, P. F.
    A plague of angels
    A surfeit of guns
Clynes, M.
    The relic murders
Cook, J.
    Blood on the Borders
    Death of a lady's maid
    Kill the witch
    Murder at the Rose
Finney, P.
    Unicorn's blood
Maxwell, R.
    The Queen's bastard
    The secret diary of Anne Boleyn
Pownall, D.
    The catalogue of men
Radley, S.
    New blood from old bones
Tannahill, R.
    Fatal majesty

ENGLAND: 17TH CENTURY
Armitage, A.
    The seamstress
Chapman, R.
    The secret of the world

Davies, S.
  Impassioned clay
Elgin, E.
  Scapegoat for a Stuart
George, S.
  The journal of Mrs. Pepys
Gregory, P.
  Earthly joys
  Virgin earth
Hines, J.
  The lost daughter
  The puritan's wife
Holland, T.
  Deliver us from evil
Lynton, P.
  Innocence
Mount, F.
  Jem (and Sam)
Nye, R.
  The late Mr. Shakespeare
Palliser, M.
  Matthew's prize
Pears, I.
  An instance of the fingerpost
Potter, C.
  The witch
  The witch's son

ENGLAND: 18TH CENTURY
Alexander, B.
  Watery grave
Bell, J.
  Silk town
Griffin, N.
  The requiem shark
Kinsolving, W.
  Mister Christian
Koen, K.
  Now face to face
Lake, D.
  Death on the Romney Marsh
Limb, S.
  Enlightenment
March, H.
  The complaint of the dove
  The devil's highway
Miller, A.
  Ingenious pain
Mountain, F.
  Isabella
Norman, D.
  Blood royal
  Shores of darkness
Smith, W.
  Monsoon
Summers, R.
  A safe haven
Taverner, J.
  Rebellion

ENGLAND: 19TH CENTURY
Barron, S.
  Jane and the genius of the place
  Jane and the man of the cloth
  Jane and the unpleasantness at
    Scargrave Manor
  Jane and the wandering eye
Bedford, W.
  The freedom tree
Billington, R.
  Perfect happiness
Blair, J.
  The other side of the river
  The seaweed gatherers
Broomfield, J.
  A song in the street
Carey, P.
  Jack Maggs
Chesney, M.
  A marriage of convenience
Cookson, C.
  The branded man
  The desert crop
  The upstart
Courtenay, B.
  The potato factory
Cox, J.
  Cradle of thorns
  Tomorrow the world
Davies, J. W.
  To the ends of the earth
Dymoke, J.
  The making of Molly March
Etchells, O.
  The Jericho trumpet
Everett, P.
  The voyages of Alfred Wallis
Fawcett, Q.
  Embassy Row
Fraser, G. M.
  Black Ajax
Gill, E.
  Under a cloud-soft sky
Goring, A.
  No enemy but winter
  The mulberry field
Graham, M.
  A bitter legacy
Harrod-Eagles, C.
  The hidden shore
  The mirage
  The outcast
  The winter journey
Hawksley, E.
  Crossing the Tamar
Heaven, C.
  The love child
Howard, A.
  Promises lost

Tomorrow's memories
Hughes, G.
  Bronte
Hutchinson, M.
  A love forbidden
  A promise given
  Abel's daughter
Jackson, J.
  The iron road
Jackson, M.
  The underground man
Jacobs, A.
  Hallam Square
  Jessie
Jakeman, J.
  Fool's gold
  The Egyptian coffin
Jeffrey, E.
  Far above rubies
  Hannah Fox
Jenkins, R.
  The Duke's agent
Matthews, J. W.
  A silver flood
  A vein of richness
Minton, M.
  Fortune's daughter
Monk, C.
  Water's edge
Montague, J.
  Child of the mist
Myers, A.
  Murder with Majesty
Naish, N.
  A time to learn
Newberry, S.
  A charm of finches
O'Brian, P.
  The yellow admiral
Paige, F.
  So long at the fair
Palliser, M.
  The unburied
Perry, A.
  Ashworth Hall
  The twisted root
Peters, M.
  Child of earth
Robertson, W.
  Kitty Rainbow
Rogow, R.
  The problem of the missing hoyden
Russell, N.
  The dried-up man
Smith, M. C.
  Rose
Sole, L.
  This land, this love

Stirling, J.
  The workhouse girl
Tennant, E.
  Elinor and Marianne
  Emma in love
Terry, C.
  My beautiful mistress
Thompson, E. V.
  Cast no shadows
  Lewin's Mead
  Moontide
  Somewhere a bird is singing
Thorne, N.
  Return to Wuthering Heights
Tremayne, K.
  Adam Loveday
Trow, M. J.
  Lestrade and the devil's own
Truss, L.
  Tennyson's gift
Waters, S.
  Tipping the velvet
Wiggin, H.
  Trouble on the wind
Willsher, A.
  So shall you reap
  The fruitful vine
Wood, V.
  Children of the tide
  The Romany girl

ENGLAND: 20TH CENTURY
Frost, S.
  Redeem the time
Graham, M.
  A bitter legacy
Lambert, A.
  Golden lads and girls
Lennox, J.
  Some old lover's ghost

ENGLAND: 1900-29
Airth, R.
  River of darkness
Aitken, R.
  Cornish harvest
Andrews, L.
  Liverpool songbird
  Where the Mersey flows
Andrews, L. M.
  Angels of mercy
Baker, A.
  A Liverpool lullaby
  A Mersey duet
  Mersey maids
  The price of love
Barker, P.
  Another world

Bennett, A.
  Love me tender
Brindley, L.
  Indian summer
  Lizzie
Bryant, J.
  Waiting for the tide
Carr, A.
  The last summer
Carr, I.
  Love child
  Mary's child
Clark, C. C.
  The workroom girls
Connor, A.
  The moon is my witness
Dickinson, M.
  Chaff upon the wind
  The miller's daughter
Drummond, E.
  Act of valour
Eadith, J.
  A very loud voice
Flynn, K.
  Rainbow's end
Forrester, H.
  Mourning doves
Fraser, S.
  The imperialists
Gill, E.
  Snow angels
Hartnett, D. W.
  Brother to dragons
Howard, A.
  When morning comes
Hudson, H.
  Winter roses
Hutchinson, M.
  A handful of silver
  Bitter seed
  For the sake of her child
  No place of angels
Hylton, S.
  Footsteps in the rain
Jacobs, A.
  Our Lizzie
Jeffrey, E.
  Dowland's Mill
Kay, N.
  Tina
King, L. R.
  A letter of Mary
Lightfoot, F.
  Lakeland Lily
  Manchester pride
Linscott, G.
  Dead man's music
Maskell, V.
  Shopkeepers

McAlpine, G.
  The persistence of memory
Mitchell, J.
  Dancing for joy
Monk, C.
  Different lives
  On the wings of the storm
Murphy, E.
  Comfort me with apples
  When day is done
Murray, A.
  Orphan of Angel Street
Myers, A.
  Murder in the motor stable
Newberry, S.
  A charm of finches
  The painted sky
Oldfield, P.
  Lady of the night
Page, L.
  At the toss of a sixpence
  Just by chance
Parker, J.
  The stars shine bright
Pemberton, M.
  Yorkshire Rose
Reed, C. W.
  To reason why
Robertson, W.
  Children of the storm
Ross, M.
  Like a diamond
  The Carringtons of Helston
  Tomorrow's tide
Saunders, J.
  A different kind of love
Spencer, S.
  Those golden days
Stuart, A.
  Loyalty defiled
Summers, R.
  White rivers
Tate, J.
  No one promised me tomorrow
  Riches of the heart
Taylor, M.
  The love match
Thomas, L.
  Other times
Thornton, M.
  A stick of Blackpool rock
Todd, C.
  A test of wills
Wilson, T.
  The poppy path

ENGLAND: 1930-59
Andrews, L. M.
  From this day forth

Murphy, E.
Honour thy father
Murray, A.
Birmingham blitz
Oldfield, P.
Pieces of silver
Oliver, M.
The golden road
Page, L.
Any old iron
Palmer, E.
The dark side of the sun
Pearse, L.
Ellie
Pemberton, M.
Magnolia Square
Prior, A.
The old man and me again
Raymond, D.
The sea family
Reimann, A.
Wise child
Riviere, W.
Echoes of war
Roberts, I.
Walker Street
Robertson, D.
Wait for the day
Robertson, W.
A thirsting land
Sallis, S.
Touched by angels
Saxton, J.
Still waters
Sinclair, E.
Her father's house
Sole, L.
Spring will come
Staples, M. J.
Bright day, dark night
Summers, R.
September morning
Tate, J.
For the love of a soldier
Taylor, A.
The lover of the grave
Taylor, A. G.
The mortal sickness
Thornton, M.
Forgive our foolish ways
Looking at the moon
Trotter, J. M.
Chasing the dream
Vincenzi, P.
Windfall
Vites, C.
Class of '39
Waite, E.
Kingston Kate

Wesley, M.
Part of the furniture
Whitmee, J.
Eve's daughter
Wilson, T.
The strawberry sky
Withall, M.
The poppy orchard

ENGLAND: 1960-80
Andrews, L.
The sinister side
Armitage, A.
The dark arches
Byatt, A. S.
Babel tower
Cookson, C.
The bonny dawn
The lady on my left
The solace of sin
Currie, E.
She's leaving home
Evans, P.
A smile for all seasons
Ferrari, L.
The girl from Norfolk with the flying
table
Graham, L.
The ten o'clock horses
Gray, C.
The promised land
Haslam, J.
Rosy Smith
Lawton, J.
A little white death
Lee, M.
Annie
MacAndrew, A.
Party pieces
Pearse, L.
Charlie
Stephens, K.
Return to Stonemoor
Syal, M.
Anita and me
Taylor, T.
Kicking around
Warren, T.
Full steam ahead

ENGLAND: 1980-2000
King, J.
England away
MacAndrew, A.
Party pieces
Trotter, J. M.
Never stand alone

ENGLISH ABROAD: SRI LANKA
Roberts, K.
The flower boy

ENTERTAINMENT INDUSTRY
Smith, R.
I must confess

ENTREPRENEURS
Millhauser, S.
Martin Dressler
Simpson, M.
A regular guy

EROTIC NOVELS
Jaivin, L.
Eat me
Latow, R.
Embrace me
Her one obsession
Only in the night
Secret souls
The pleasure seekers
The sweet caress
Thomas, R.
Customs of the country

ESCAPED CONVICTS
Deaver, J.
A maiden's grave
Gorman, E.
The silver scream
Hurwitz, G. A.
The tower

ESCAPED PRISONERS
Leather, S.
The solitary man

ESCAPES
Dawson, J.
Magpie
Duffy, B.
Last comes the egg
Kinsolving, W.
Mister Christian
Lansdale, J. R.
Freezer burn
Renton, A.
Winter butterfly
Waller, R. J.
Puerto Vallarta squeeze

ESSEX
George, E.
Deception on his mind
Jeffrey, E.
Dowland's Mill

Lord, E.
The Bowmaker girls
Newberry, S.
Tilly's family

ESTATE AGENTS
Tayler, P.
Moving on

ETHICS
McEwan, I.
Amsterdam

ETHNIC CLEANSING
Easterman, D.
The final judgement

EUROPE, EASTERN
Conway, S.
Damaged
Hoffman, A.
Two for the devil
Mann, J.
The survivor's revenge

EUROPE: 15TH CENTURY
Dunnett, D.
Caprice and Rondo

EUROPE: 16TH CENTURY
Carter, N.
King of coins
Knave of swords
Doherty, P. C.
The soul slayer

EUROPE: 17TH CENTURY
King, R.
Ex-libris
Mahjoub, J.
The carrier

EUROPE: 18TH CENTURY
Pavic, M.
Last love in Constantinople

EUROPE: 19TH CENTURY
Perry, A.
Weighed in the balance

EUROPE: 20TH CENTURY
Williams, R.
Lunch with Elizabeth David

EUROPE: 21ST CENTURY
Hillier, D.
Homeland

EUROPE: 1930-59
Bennett, F.
  Making enemies
Clarasc, M.
  Wandering Angus
Farhi, M.
  Children of the rainbow
Fast, H.
  The bridge builder's story
Stafford, E.
  Whirlwind

EUTHANASIA
Aird, C.
  Stiff news
Graham, M.
  Practicing wearing purple

EVANGELISM
Rose, L.
  Heaven's door
Yallop, D.
  Unholy alliance

EVIL
Baker, T.
  The boy who kicked pigs
Boast, P.
  Deus
Collier, I.
  Spring tide
Follett, K.
  The third twin
Greeley, A. M.
  Blackie at sea
Hewson, D.
  Epiphany
Hightower, L.
  No good deed
Hutson, S.
  Purity
Kellerman, J.
  Survival of the fittest
Kennedy, S.
  Charlotte's friends
Moody, S.
  Sacrifice bid
Morrison, T.
  Paradise
Murphy, M.
  Goodnight, my angel
Newman, R.
  Manners
Pepper, M.
  The short cut
Rice, A.
  Servant of the bones
Seymour, M.
  The telling

Turnbull, P.
  Embracing skeletons

EXCHANGE PROGRAMMES
North, F.
  Polly

EX-CONVICTS
Bunker, E.
  Dog eat dog
Cameron, J.
  Brown bread in Wengen
Gough, L.
  Memory lane
Kerr, P.
  A five year plan
Mosley, W.
  Always outnumbered, always
    outgunned
Power, M. S.
  Dealing with Kranze
Scholefield, A.
  Bad timing

EXORCISM
Doherty, P. C.
  The haunting
Rickman, P.
  Midwinter of the spirit

EXPATRIATES
Haylock, J.
  Body of contention
Tan, H. H.
  Foreign bodies

EXPERIMENTAL NOVELS
Brooke-Rose, C.
  Next
Ryman, G.
  253; the print remix

EXPLORERS
Alexander, C.
  Mrs. Chippy's last expedition
Barrett, A.
  The voyage of the Narwhal

EX-SERVICEMEN
Bragg, M.
  The soldier's return
Butler, R. O.
  The dark green sea
Evans, E.
  Carter Clay
Gologorsky, E.
  The things we do to make it home
Masters, A.
  The men

Quinnell, A. J.
  Message from hell
Todd, C.
  A test of wills
Vites, C.
  Passing shadows

EXTORTION
Battison, B.
  Poetic justice

EXTRA-MARITAL RELATIONSHIPS
Plain, B.
  Promises

EX-WIVES
Lutz, J.
  The ex

FACIAL RECONSTRUCTION
Johansen, E.
  The face of deception

FACISM
Marlow, M.
  Hell's children

FACTORIES
Heiney, P.
  Golden apples

FAIRGROUNDS
Jones, C.
  Stealing the show

FAIRS
Evans, P.
  The carousel keeps turning

FAIRY TALES
Donoghue, E.
  Kissing the witch

FAITH
Simons, P.
  Losing faith
St. John M.
  A pure clear light

FALCONRY
Saville, D.
  The hawk dancer

FALCONS
Harrison, S.
  The snow falcon

FALKLAND ISLANDS
Kent-Payne, V.
  Longdon

FALKLANDS WAR, 1982
Barnacle, H.
  Day one
Nichol, J.
  Exclusion zone
Trotter, J. M.
  For love and glory

FAMILY CHRONICLES
Andrews, V.
  Heart song
  Hidden jewel
  Melody
  Olivia
  Tarnished gold
  Unfinished symphony
Barker, C.
  Galilee
Blair, E.
  Flower of Scotland
  Goodnight, sweet prince
Carr, A.
  The last summer
Collier, C.
  A house full of women
  Past remembering
Craig, M.
  The river flows on
Daish, E.
  Emma's Christmas rose
  Emma's family
  Emma's journey
Davey, A. R.
  Winter in Paradise Square
Davis, M. T.
  A kind of immortality
Delaney, F.
  Desire and pursuit
Dickinson, M.
  Reap the harvest
Dorris, M.
  Cloud chambers
Drummond, E.
  Act of valour
Dunnett, D.
  Caprice and Rondo
Elgin, E.
  Windflower wedding
Elis, I. F.
  Return to Lleifior
Ellis, J.
  Far to go
Evans, M.
  Inheritors

Fast, H.
  An independent woman
Fraser, C. M.
  Noble seed
Gordon, K.
  The peacock fan
Gower, I.
  Dream catcher
  Firebird
  Sweet Rosie
Graham, M.
  A bitter legacy
Harrod-Eagles, C.
  The hidden shore
  The mirage
  The outcast
  The winter journey
Hines, J.
  The lost daughter
Hogan, L.
  Solar storms
Ikeda, S. D.
  What the scarecrow said
Jacobs, A.
  Hallam Square
  Spinners Lake
James, E.
  The house above the sea
Jong, E.
  Of blessed memory
Kagan, E.
  Blue heaven
Kelly, S.
  A complicated woman
  A sense of duty
Lee, M.
  Dancing in the dark
Ling, P.
  Crown wars
Marchmont, G.
  A roving eye
McMahon, K.
  Footsteps
Michaels, F.
  Vegas rich
  Vegas sunrise
Moring, M.
  In Babylon
Murari, T.
  Steps from paradise
Nicole, C.
  The red gods
  The scarlet generation
O'Neill, A.
  A family cursed
O'Neill, J.
  Turn of the tide
Pemberton, L.
  Sleeping with ghosts

Puzo, M.
  The last Don
Ratushinskaya, I.
  The Odessans
Raymond, D.
  The sea family
Reeman, D.
  Dust on the sea
Robertson, W.
  A thirsting land
Roth, P.
  American pastoral
Savage, A.
  The sword and the scalpel
Shearer, C.
  The wonder book of the air
Skelton, A. S.
  Family story
Smith, W.
  Monsoon
Spencer, S.
  South of the river
Staples, M. J.
  Churchill's people
  Fire over London
  The Camberwell raid
  The family at war
Summers, R.
  Primmy's daughter
  September morning
  White rivers
Thorne, N.
  Past love
Updike, J.
  In the beauty of the lilies
Vites, C.
  Passing shadows
Watson, L.
  Justice
Welch, R.
  Groundwork
Willett, M.
  Holding on
  Starting over
Willsher, A.
  So shall you reap
  The fruitful vine
  The sower went forth
Withall, M.
  Where the wild thyme grows

FAMILY HISTORY
Dally, E.
  Remembered dreams

FAMILY LIFE
Alliott, C.
  Dangerous games
  The real thing

The dinner lady
Yeomans, S.
  Miss Bugle saw God in the cabbages
Zuravleff, M. K.
  The frequency of souls

FAMINE
Graham, B.
  The whitest flower

FANTASY
Anthony, P.
  Earth
  Yon ill wind
Arden, T.
  Sultan of moon and stars
  The harlequin's dance
  The King and Queen of swords
Asaro, C.
  The radiant seas
Ash, S.
  Songspinners
  The lost child
Asher, M.
  The eye of Ra
Asimov, I.
  Magic
Attanasio, A. A.
  Octoberland
  The dark shore
  The shadow eater
Banks, I.
  A song of stone
Barnes, J.
  Earth made of glass
Beagle, P. S.
  The innkeeper's song
Belle, P.
  Blood imperial
Bending
  Bending the landscape; ed. by N.
    Griffith
Bibby, J.
  Ronan's rescue
Bradley, R. J.
  Lady in Gil
  Lady Pain
  Scion's lady
Brooks, T.
  Angel fire east
  First King of Shannara
  Knight of the word
  Running with the demon
  Star Wars: the phantom menace
Brust, S.
  Dragon
Bunch, C.
  The demon king
  The seer king

The warrior king
Chadbourn, M.
  World's end
Cherryh. C. J.
  Cloud's rider
Chetwynd-Hayes, R.
  World of the impossible
Claremont, C.
  Shadow dawn
Coe, D. B.
  The outlanders
Cole, A.
  The gods awaken
  When the gods slept
  Wolves of the gods
Constantine, S.
  Sea dragon heir
Cool, T.
  Secret realms
Cooper, L.
  Our lady of the snow
  Sacrament of the night
  The king's demom
Coran, M.
  Darkfell
Cross, R. A.
  The white guardian
De Lint, C.
  Someplace to be flying
  Trader
Denning, T.
  Pages of pain
Dietz, W. C.
  Soldier for the Empire
Donaldson, S.
  Reave the just (short stories)
  The gap into ruin
Doyle, D.
  The stars asunder
Drake, D.
  Servant of the dragon
Duane, D.
  On Her Majesty's wizardly service
  The book of night with moon
Eddings, D.
  Polgara the sorceress
Elliott, K.
  King's dragon
  Prince of dogs
  The burning stone
Ellis, A. T.
  Fairy Tale
Ellison, H.
  Edgeworks; 4
England, B.
  No man's land
Erikson, S.
  Gardens of the moon

Farland, D.
  Brotherhood of the wolf
  The sum of all men
Feist, R. E.
  Krondor; the assassins
  Krondor; the betrayal
  Rage of a demon king
Flint, J.
  Habitus
Flying
  The flying sorcerers; ed. by P.
    Haining
Foster, A. D.
  Greenthieves
  Mid-Flinx
  Slipt
  The dig
  The howling stones
Furey, M.
  Dhiammarra
  Harp of winds
  The heart of Myrial
  The sword of flame
Gaiman, N.
  Stardust
Gemmell, D. A.
  Dark moon
  Echoes of the great song
  Midnight falcon
  The complete chronicles of the
    Jerusalem Man
  The legend of Deathwalker
  Winter warriors
Goodkind, T.
  Blood of the fold
  Soul of the fire
  Temple of the winds
Gordon, F.
  Changeling
Green, N.
  Dark star
Greenwood, E. & Grubb, J.
  Cormyr
  Elminster in Myth Drannor
Hamilton, P. F.
  The naked god
  The neutronium alchemist
  The reality dysfunction
Harlan, T.
  The shadow of Ararat
Harman, A.
  The scrying game
Harrison, H. & Holm, J.
  King and emperor
  Stars and Stripes forever
Hawksley, H.
  Dragonstrike
Hobb, R.
  Assassin's quest

Royal assassin
Ship of magic
The mad ship
Holdstock, R.
  Gates of ivory
Home, S.
  Come before Christ and murder love
Horwood, W.
  Seekers at the Wulfrock
Houghton, G.
  The apprentice
Hubbard, R. L.
  Typewriter in the sky
Jacoby, K.
  Exile's return
  Voice of the demon
Johnson, O.
  The forging of the shadows
Jones, D. W.
  A sudden wild magic
  The dark lord of Derkholm
Jones, J. V.
  A cavern of black ice
  Master and fool
  The barbed coil
Jordan, R.
  A crown of swords
  The path of daggers
  The path of daggers
Kay, G. G.
  Sailing to Sarantium
Kearney, P.
  The heretic kings
  The iron wars
Kerr, K. & Kreighbaum, M.
  Palace
  The black raven
  The red wyvern
Kilworth, G.
  A midsummer's nightmare
  Land-of-mists
  The princely flower
  The roof of voyaging
King, G.
  The wild road
King, S.
  Wizard and glass
La Plante, R.
  Tegne; soul warrior
Lackey, M.
  Owlflight
  Owlsight
  Storm breaking
  The silver gryphon
Lawhead, S.
  The iron lance
Lee, T.
  When the lights go out

Leith, V.
  The company of glass
Leroux, L.
  One hand clapping
Lessing, D.
  Mara and Dann
Lisle, H.
  Diplomacy of wolves
Lustbader, E.
  Dragons on the sea of night
Lynn, E. A.
  Dragon's winter
Mann, P.
  The burning forest
Marco, J.
  The jackal of Nar
Martin, G. R. R.
  A clash of kings
  A game of thrones
May, J.
  Magnificat
  Sky trillium
McAuley, P. J.
  Child of the river
McCaffrey, A
  A diversity of dragons
  Dinosaur planet
  Freedom's challenge
  Freedom's choice
  Nimisha's ship
  Red star rising
  Survivors
  The MasterHarper of Pern
  The tower and the hive
McCaffrey, A. & Ball, M.
  Acorna
McKay, M.
  The Lack brothers
Meyers, R. S.
  Murder in Malruan
Meynard, Y.
  The book of knights
Mieville, C.
  King Rat
Miller, R.
  Myst
  Myst: the book of Ti'ana
Modesitt, L. E.
  Fall of angels
  The death of chaos
Moorcock, M.
  The war amongst the angels
Navarro, Y.
  Music of the spears
Naylor, G.
  Backwards
Nicholls, S.
  Bodyguard of lightning

Nichols, A.
  The pathless way
Noon, J.
  Automated Alice
Nylund, E. S.
  Pawn's dream
Parker, K. J.
  Colours in the street
Perry, A.
  Tathea
Pinto, R.
  The chosen
Powers, T.
  Earthquake weather
Rawn, M.
  The golden key
  The Mageborn traitor
  The ruins of Ambrai
Redfield, J.
  The tenth insight
Reichert, M. Z.
  Beyond Ragnarok
  Prince of demons
  Spirit fox
  The children of wrath
Reimann, K.
  A tremor in the bitter earth
Rice, A.
  Exit to Eden
Roberts, J. M.
  Murder in Tarsis
Rusch, K. K.
  Rival
Russell, K.
  Mike and Gaby's space gospel
Ryan, F.
  The sundered world
Saberhagen, F.
  Shiva in steel
Salvatore, R. A.
  Passage to dawn
  The spine of the world
Sandman
  The Sandman book of dreams
Shusterman, N.
  Thief of souls
Siegel, J.
  Prospero's children
Silverberg, R.
  Lord Prestimion
Smith, M. M.
  Spares
Stackpole, M. A.
  I, Jedi
Stirling, S. M.
  The domination
  The reformer
Tarr, J.
  White mare's daughter

Taylor, R.
  Arash-Felloren
  Caddoran
  The return of the sword
Tepper, S. S.
  The family tree
Turtledove, H.
  A world of difference
  How few remain
  Worldwar: upsetting the balance
Vance, J.
  Night lamp
Vinge, V.
  A deepness in the sky
Ware, P.
  Beyond freedom
  Flight of the mariner
Watson, I.
  Oracle
Weber, D.
  The apocalypse troll
  The War God's own
Weis, M. & Perrin, D.
  Hung out
  Robot blues
  The doom brigade
  The soul forge
Wells, A.
  Exile's challenge
Williams, M.
  Allamanda
  Arcady
Williams, T.
  City of golden shadow
  Mountain of black glass
Williamson, P. G.
  Orbus's world
  The orb and the spectre
  The soul of the orb
Wingrove, D.
  The marriage of the living dark
Wolfe, G.
  Exodus from the long sun
Wurts, J.
  Fugitive prince
  Grand conspiracy
Wylie, J.
  Across the flame

FAR EAST: 1930-59
Jenkins, R.
  Leila

FAR EAST: 1980-2000
Cohen, S.
  Invisible world

FARMING
Anderson-Dargatz, G.
  The cure for death by lightning
Dickinson, M.
  Reap the harvest
Graham, B.
  The whitest flower
Heiney, P.
  Domino's effect
MacDonald, E.
  Catch the moment
Masters, P.
  Scaring crows
Newberry, S.
  A charm of finches
North, S.
  The lie of the land
Ramsay, E.
  Harvest of courage
Summers, E.
  Caleb's kingdom
Tope, R.
  A dirty death
Trollope, J.
  Next of kin
Wheeler, R. S.
  The buffalo commons

FASHION TRADE
Armstrong, L.
  Front row
Butler, G.
  Butterfly
Clark, C. C.
  The workroom girls
Holden, W.
  Simply divine
James, J.
  The wedding suit
Krantz, J.
  Spring collection
Minton, M.
  Fortune's daughter
Worboyes, S.
  Red sequins

FATHERS AND CHILDREN
Gillespie, J.
  Brothers to be
Makepeace, M.
  The would-begetter
Perez, L. M.
  Geographies of home

FATHERS AND DAUGHTERS
Bail, M.
  Eucalyptus
Boyt, S.
  The characters of love

Burns, C.
  Dust raising
Crombie, D.
  Kissed a sad goodbye
Flanagan, R.
  The sound of one hand clapping
Glaister, L.
  Easy peasy
Hutchinson, M.
  A handful of silver
Jacobs, A.
  Like no other
Jacques, J.
  A lazy eye
Kay, R.
  Return journey
Kearney, R.
  Walking at sea level
Kennedy, A. L.
  Everything you need
Lancaster, G.
  Dayton and daughter
Loraine, P.
  Ugly money
Love, A.
  Mallingford
MacDonald, E.
  Kirkowen's daughter
Nevin, J.
  Past recall
Nicholson, G.
  Female ruins
Pingeot, M.
  First novel
Pipkin, B.
  Unwelcome love
Roberts, M.
  Impossible saints
Robertson, D.
  Illusion
Simpson, M.
  A regular guy
Walker, A.
  By the light of my father's smile
Worboys, A.
  Relative strangers

FATHERS AND SONS
Adams, J.
  Final frame
Boyd, D.
  The fiddler and the ferret
De Laszlo, M.
  Dancing on her own
Dews, B.
  Three sons of three fathers
Fernyhough. C.
  The auctioneer

Inglis, J.
  The colour of sin
Jaffe, M. G.
  Dance real slow
Joyce, G.
  Indigo
Matthiessen, P.
  Lost man's river
Myerson, J.
  Your father
Prior, A.
  The old man and me again
Rathbone, J.
  Blame Hitler
Yasar Kemal
  Salman the solitary

FAWKES, GUY, ENGLISH CONSPIRATOR, 1570-1606
Elgin, E.
  Scapegoat for a Stuart

FEELINGS
Hill, S.
  The service of clouds

FEMINISM
Bowker, D.
  The secret sexist
Paretsky, S.
  Ghost country

FEMINISTS
Lambkin, D.
  The hanging tree

FENCES
Mills, M.
  The restraint of beasts

FENCING
Perez-Reverte, A.
  The fencing master

FENS
Chadwick, E.
  The marsh king's daughter
Grimes, M.
  The case has altered
Lennox, J.
  Some old lover's ghost

FERTILITY CLINICS
Case, J.
  The genesis code

FERTILITY SYMBOLS
Gardam, J.
  The green man

Tasker, P.
  Buddha kiss
West, M.
  Vanishing point

FINANCIERS
Kessler, D.
  The other victim

FIRE SERVICE
Grey, P.
  Good Hope Station

FISH FARMING
Barker, R.
  The hook

FISHES
Winton, T.
  Blueback

FISHING
Hammond, G.
  Sink or swim

FISHING INDUSTRY
Bedford, W.
  The freedom tree
Davidson, D.
  The girl with the creel
Dickinson, M.
  The fisher lass
Huth, A.
  The wives of the fishermen
Matthews, J. W.
  A silver flood
Short, A.
  The herring summer
Watkins, P.
  The story of my disappearance

FLASHBACK STORIES
Barraclough, J.
  Another summer
Brown, A.
  Audrey Hepburn's neck
Cox, J.
  Miss you forever
Crombie, D.
  Kissed a sad goodbye
Daly, I.
  Unholy ghosts
Darling, J.
  Crocodile soup
DelVeccio, J. M.
  Darkness falls
French, N.
  The memory game

Freud, E.
  Gaglow
Hewson, D.
  Epiphany
Hill, R.
  On Beulah Height
  The wood beyond
Hines, B.
  Elvis over England
Hook, P.
  The soldier in the wheatfield
Ironside, E.
  The accomplice
James, B.
  The last enemy
Mason, R.
  The drowning people
McKenna, J.
  The last fine summer
Mead, J.
  Sentimental journey
Minot, S.
  Evening
Ryan, M.
  The promise
Seymour, M.
  The telling
Thynne, J.
  The shell house
Tremain, R.
  The way I found her
Van der Vyver, M.
  Childish things
Wendorf, P.
  The toll house

FLATS
Manby, C.
  Flatmates
Mead, J.
  Charlotte Street
Smith, C.
  Kensington Court
Thomas, L.
  Kensington Heights

FLOODS
Gano, J.
  Inspector Proby's weekend

FOLKLORE, CHINESE
Garner, A.
  Strandloper
Tan, A.
  The hundred secret senses

FOLKLORE, IRISH
Eickhoff, R. L.
  The feast

FOOD
Lanchester, J.
The debt to pleasure

FOOD POISONING
Cook, R.
Toxin

FOOTBALL
Bower, M.
Football seasons
Brady, K.
United!
Gallivan, J.
Oi, ref!
King, J.
The football factory
Palmer, F.
Final score
Stein, M.
Red card
White lines
Trotter, J. M.
Chasing the dream

FOOTBALL HOOLIGANISM
Brimson, D.
Hooligan
The crew
Samson, K.
Awaydays

FORENSIC PSYCHOLOGISTS
Ablow, K. R.
Projection
Sultan, F.
Help line
Over the line

FORENSIC SCIENCE
Cornwell, P.
Black notice
Cause of death
Point of origin
Unnatural exposure
Deaver, J.
The bone collector
Johansen, I.
The killing game
McCrery, N.
The spider's web
Reichs, K.
Death du jour
Deja dead

FOREST OF DEAN
Gregson, J. M.
Accident by design

FOREST RANGERS
McGarrity, M.
Mexican hat

FORESTS
Powers, C. T.
In the memory of the forest

FORGERY
Jardine, Q.
A coffin for two
Kennealy, J.
The forger
Knox, B.
The counterfeit killers
Nabb, M.
The monster of Florence
Worboys, A.
Relative strangers

FORTUNE TELLERS
North, S.
Seeing is deceiving

FOSSILS
Lambkin, D.
The hanging tree

FOSTER CHILDREN
Fitch, J.
White oleander

FRANCE: 1ST CENTURY
Harris, E.
The sacrifice stone

FRANCE: 12TH CENTURY
Chadwick, E.
The champion
McCaughrean, G.
Lovesong
McNeill, E.
A garden of briars

FRANCE: 18TH CENTURY
Gulland, S.
Tales of passion, tales of woe
Howard, R.
Bonaparte's sons

FRANCE: 19TH CENTURY
Cordell, A.
Send her victorious
Gavin, C.
One candle burning
Kalpakian, L.
Cosette
Knox, E.
The vintner's luck

Moore, B.
    The magician's wife
Reed, J.
    Dorian
Roberts, M.
    Fair exchange
Zencey, E.
    Panama

FRANCE: 1900-29
Magnan, P.
    The murdered house

FRANCE: 1930-59
Makine, A.
    The crime of Olga Arbyeline

FRANCE: 1960-80
Rouaud, J.
    The world more or less

FRANCE: 1980-2000
Fleming, A.
    This means mischief

FRANCE: ALBI
Kelly, S.
    The ghosts of Albi

FRANCE: AVIGNON
Janes, J. R.
    Madrigal

FRANCE: BORDEAUX
Friedman, R.
    Vintage

FRANCE: BURGUNDY
Hebden, J.
    Pel the patriarch

FRANCE: LANGUEDOC
Tanner, J.
    The shores of midnight

FRANCE: NORMANDY
Forrester, H.
    Madame Barbara

FRANCE: PARIS
Bober, R.
    What news of the war?
Bourdouxhe, M.
    Marie
Grayson, R.
    And death the prize
    Death in the skies
Griffiths, J.
    The courtyard in August

Janes, J. R.
    Gypsy
Johnson, D.
    Le divorce
Makine, A.
    Le testament Francais
Pennac, D.
    The fairy gunmother
    The scapegoat
Stadler, M.
    Allan Stein
Tremain, R.
    The way I found her
Zencey, E.
    Panama

FRANCE: PERIGORD
Fergusson, L.
    The chase

FRANCE: PROVENCE
Bogner, N.
    To die in Provence
English, L.
    Children of light
Harris, E.
    The sacrifice stone
Hutchison, W.
    Before the fact
Luard, E.
    Marguerite
Magnan, P.
    The murdered house
Matthews, J.
    Past imperfect
Mayle, P.
    Anything considered
Ryan, L.
    A taste of freedom
Sobin, G.
    The fly-truffler

FRANCE: PYRENEES
Chaplin, P.
    Happy hour
Hebden, J.
    Pel is provoked

FRANCE: RENNES
McNeill, B.
    To answer the peacock

FRAUD
Ardin, W.
    The Mary medallion
Armstrong, D.
    Thought for the day
Billheimer, J.
    The contrary blues

Blake, P.
  Waiting for the sea to be blue
Branton, M.
  The love parade
Brett, S.
  Mrs. Pargeter's plot
Cleary, J.
  Five ring circus
Cleeves, A.
  High Island blues
Cutler, J.
  Staying power
Evans, L.
  JFK is missing
Haley, J.
  When beggars die
  Written in water
Hammond, G.
  Dogsbody
Harrison, R.
  Murder by design
Higgins, G. V.
  A change of gravity
Jardine, Q.
  A coffin for two
Lewis, R.
  Suddenly as a shadow
  The ghost dancers
Luard, N.
  Silverback
Mann, J.
  A private enquiry
Neel, J.
  A timely death
Ormerod, R.
  The seven razors of Ockam
Rawlinson, P.
  The Caverel claim
Roberts, B.
  The victory snapshot
Rowntree, K.
  Mr. Brightly's evening off
Swindells, M.
  Sunstroke
Wilson, R.
  Blood is dirt

FRENCH AND INDIAN WAR, 1754-60
Coyle, H.
  Savage wilderness

FRENCH REVOLUTION, 1789-99
Baldwin, M.
  The first Mrs. Wordsworth
Piercy, M.
  City of darkness, city of light

FRIENDSHIP
Ames, J.
  The extra man
Anderson, B.
  House guest
Andrews, L.
  The ties that bind
Andrews, V.
  Orphans
Arditti, M.
  Pagan and her parents
Ashworth, S.
  Just good friends
Bacon, M.
  Friends and relations
  The ewe lamb
Bagshawe, L.
  Tall poppies
  Venus envy
Banks, L. R.
  Fair exchange
Barraclough, J.
  No time like the present
Bennett, A.
  A little learning
Berg, E.
  Range of motion
Binchy, M.
  Evening class
Blume, J.
  Summer sisters
Bond, F. A.
  Changing step
  Old acquaintances
Boucheron, R.
  Friends and neighbours
Brampton, S.
  Concerning Lily
Brookfield, A.
  Marriage games
  Single lives
Bullen, F.
  From pillar to post
Canin, E.
  For kings and planets
Capriolo, P.
  The woman watching
Carey, H.
  Some sunny day
Cartmell, S.
  Papal whispers
Chambers, C.
  Learning to swim
Chidgey, C.
  In a fishbone church
Clayton, V.
  Out of love
Cobbold, M.
  Frozen music

Ovenden, K.
  The greatest sorrow
Parkin, S.
  Take me home
Pearse, L.
  Ellie
Pemberton, L.
  Dancing with shadows
Pizzey, E.
  The wicked world of women
Pullinger, K.
  The last time I saw Jane
Ramster, J.
  Ladies' man
Reed, C. W.
  Mirror images
Richards, B.
  Don't step on the lines
Richards, J.
  Touching the lighthouse
Riviere, W.
  Echoes of war
Roberts, I.
  London's pride
Robertson, D.
  Wait for the day
Roe, J.
  Eating grapes downwards
Ross, L.
  All the blood is red
Rowlands, B.
  A hive of bees
Ryan, M.
  Glenallen
Sallis, S.
  Come rain or shine
  Touched by angels
Saxton, J.
  You are my sunshine
Simons, P.
  Angels and men
Smart, H.
  The wild garden
Smith, A.
  What about me?
Smith, C.
  Double exposure
Stephens, K.
  Sign of the moon
Stevens, A.
  November tree
Stranger, J.
  The guardians of Staghill
Stuart, A.
  Sin no more
Sutton, H.
  Bank Holiday Monday
Swift, G.
  Last orders

Thomas, L.
  Kensington Heights
Thorne, N.
  Class reunion
Weir, A.
  Onwards and upwards
Wells, L.
  My turn now
Wells, R.
  Divine secrets of the ya-ya sisterhood
Whitmee, J.
  The lost daughters
Willett, M.
  The dipper
Wilson, A. N.
  A watch in the night
Wilson, P.
  Days of good hope
Wilson, T.
  The strawberry sky
Wynne-Jones, G.
  Wise follies
Yeomans, S.
  Miss Bugle saw God in the cabbages

FUNDAMENTALIST GROUPS
Cutler, J.
  Dying for power
Diehl, W.
  Reign in hell

FUND-RAISING
Ormerod, R.
  The seven razors of Ockam

FUTURE, STORIES OF THE
Ackroyd, P.
  The Plato papers
Barnes, J.
  England, England
Cross, N.
  Christendom
Currie, E.
  The Ambassador
Ferriss, L.
  The misconceiver
Gee, M.
  The ice people
Halperin, J. L.
  The truth machine
Johnston, P.
  Body politic
  The bone yard
  Water of death
Kerr, P.
  The second angel
Kirk, P.
  The keepers

Mosse, K.
  Crucifix Lane
Preston, P.
  Bess
Rathbone, J.
  Trajectories
Robb, J. D.
  Ceremony in death
  Glory in death
  Naked in death
  Rapture in death
  Vengeance in death
Russell, M. D.
  The sparrow
Updike, J.
  Toward the end of time

GALOIS, EVARISTE, FRENCH MATHEMATICIAN, 1811-32
Petsinis, T.
  The French mathematician

GAMBLING
Martin, L. J.
  Sounding drum
Noon, J.
  Nymphomation

GANGSTERS
Burgess, M.
  Bloodtide
Conway, S.
  Damaged
Selby, H.
  The willow tree
Spencer, S.
  The paradise job
Zahavi, H.
  Donna and the fatman

GARDENERS
Barrie, A.
  The linden tree
Gregory, P.
  Earthly joys
  Virgin earth
Harbouri, P.
  Our lady of the serpents
Titchmarsh, A.
  Mr. MacGregor

GARDENS
Bloom, A.
  Mistress of Melthorpe
Fforde, K.
  Wild designs
Saville, D.
  Capability's Eden

Sherwood, J.
  Shady borders
Wiggin, H.
  In the heart of the garden

GAWILGHUN, SIEGE OF, 1803
Cornwell, B.
  Sharpe's fortress

GAY COMMUNITIES
Cleary, J.
  A different turf

GAY MEN
Aitken, G.
  Vanity fierce
Arditti, M.
  Pagan and her parents
Blincoe, N.
  Manchester slingback
Bradshaw, P.
  Lucky baby Jesus
Buxton, J.
  Pity
Capurro, S.
  Fowl play
Frame, R.
  The lantern bearers
Grimsley, J.
  Dream boy
Holleran, A.
  The beauty of men
Hollinghurst, A.
  The spell
Kharitanov, M.
  Under house arrest
Leavitt, D.
  The page turner
LeVay, S.
  Albrick's gold
Picano, F.
  The book of lies
Ramster, J.
  Ladies' man
Ronan, F.
  Lovely
Thomas, R.
  Customs of the country
Van Sant, G.
  Pink
White, E.
  The farewell symphony
Whyte, C.
  The gay decameron
Wilcox, J.
  Plain and normal
Woodrell, D.
  Tomato red

GEISHAS
Golden, A.
  Memoirs of a geisha

GENEALOGISTS
Edwards, P.
  The search for Kate Duval

GENETIC ENGINEERING
Barnard, C.
  The donor
Case, J.
  The genesis code
Currie, E.
  The Ambassador
Harrison, M. J.
  Signs of life
Huggins, J. B.
  Cain
LeVay, S.
  Albrick's gold
MacDonald, E.
  The infiltrator
McDermid, V.
  Blue genes
Smith, H.
  Alison Wonderland

GENETIC RESEARCH
Cordy, M.
  The miracle strain
Follett, K.
  The third twin
McCabe, J.
  Paper

GENETICISTS
Mawer, S.
  Mendel's dwarf

GENOCIDE
Lustbader, E.
  Pale Saint

GEOLOGISTS
Bradley, J.
  The deep field
Reiss. B.
  Purgatory Road

GERMANY: 17TH CENTURY
Wallace, C.
  The Pied Piper's poison

GERMANY: 19TH CENTURY
Buckley, J.
  Xerxes

GERMANY: 1900-29
Freud, E.
  Gaglow

GERMANY: 1930-59
Greeley, A. M.
  A midwinter's tale
Palmer, W.
  The pardon of Saint Anne
Ransmayr, C.
  The dog king
Schlink, B.
  The reader

GERMANY: 1980-2000
Krausser, H.
  The great Bagarozy
Wilson, J.
  Turmfalke: case 3788

GERMANY: BERLIN
Hensher, P.
  Pleasured
Shea, M.
  The Berlin Embassy

GERMANY: HAMELIN
Wallace, C.
  The Pied Piper's poison

GERMANY: MUNICH
Morgan, P-A.
  The Munich sabbatical

GIANTS
Davis, M. T.
  The Clydesiders
Mantel, H.
  The giant, O'Brien
McCracken, E.
  The giant's house

GIFTED CHILDREN
Jacques, J.
  A lazy eye
Nonhebel, C.
  Eldred Jones, Lulubelle and the most
  high

GLASGOW
Benzie, A.
  The angle of incidence
Craig, M.
  When the lights come on again
Davis, M. T.
  A kind of immortality
  The Clydesiders
Henderson, M.
  Bloody Mary

Jardine, Q.
  Wearing purple
Knox, B.
  The Lazarus widow
Livoni, G.
  Candyfloss martyrs
McGregor, H. R.
  Schrodinger's baby
Paige, F.
  The lonely shore
Scott, M.
  Night mares
Stirling, J.
  Prized possessions
  The piper's tune
Turnbull, P.
  The man with no face

GLASTONBURY
Bowker, D.
  The butcher of Glastonbury

GLITZ
Bagshawe, L.
  The movie
Barrett, M.
  Dangerous obsession
  Elle
Barry, M.
  Dark desire
Beauman, S.
  Danger zones
  Sextet
Blair, L.
  Fascination
Booth, P.
  Temptation
Brown, S.
  Exclusive
Carr, R.
  The fine art of loving
Collins, J.
  Dangerous kiss
  Thrill!
Cooper, J.
  Appassionata
  Score
Corbett, V. and others
  Best of enemies
Edmonds, L.
  Playing with fire
Gould, J.
  Second love
Kaiser, J.
  Last night in Rio
Krentz, J. A.
  Absolutely positive
Lewis, S.
  Chasing dreams

Last resort
Wildfire
McNaught, J.
  Remember when
Michaels, F.
  Vegas heat
Pacter, T.
  To love, honour and betray
Pulitzer, R.
  The Palm Beach story
Robbins, H.
  Tycoon
Roberts, N.
  Daring to dream
Spindler, E.
  Forbidden fruit
Stephenson, J.
  Pandora's diamond
Taylor, J.
  Anything for love
Vincenzi, P.
  The dilemma

GLOBAL WARMING
Johnston, P.
  Water of death
Lessing, D.
  Mara and Dann

GLOUCESTERSHIRE
Gregson, J. M.
  Girl gone missing
Limb, S.
  Enlightenment

GOD
Cosse, L.
  A corner of the veil

GODFATHERS AND GODSONS
Marsh, W.
  Facing the music

GOLD
Langley, B.
  The third pinnacle

GOLD MINING
Hebbard, F.
  Branigan
Shaw, P.
  The glittering fields
Straley, J.
  The curious eat themselves
Wheeler, R. S.
  Flint's truth

GOLF

Hamer, M.
  Dead on line
Murphy, M.
  The kingdom of Shivas Irons
Pakenham, K.
  A green too far
Porter, G.
  Open conspiracy
Shackelford, G.
  The good doctor returns

GOLF TOURNAMENTS

Hunt, R.
  The man trap

GOOD AND EVIL

Brandreth, G.
  Who is Nick Saint?
Brooks, T.
  Running with the demon
Gately, I.
  The assessor
Harris, E.
  The twilight child
Levin, I.
  Son of Rosemary
Maurensig, P.
  The Luneburg variation

GOSSIP

Woods, S.
  Dirt

GOTHIC ROMANCES

Adams, J.
  Bird
Adler, E.
  No regrets
Allen, C. V.
  Claudia's shadow
Argers, H.
  The gilded lily
Armitage, A.
  Annabella
  Cambermere
  Jason's dominion
Barlow, L.
  Intimate betrayal
Brandewyne, R.
  Presumed guilty
Coffman, V.
  A splash of rubies
  Emerald flame
  The vampyre of Moura
  The wine dark opal
  Tiger's eye
Coulter, C.
  Moonspun magic

Edgar, P.
  The secret within
Ellis, J.
  The Geneva rendezvous
  The Italian affair
  Villa Fontaine
  When the summer people have gone
Favier, P.
  A price too high
Forsyth, F.
  The Phantom of Manhattan
Goring, A.
  Return to Moondance
Graham, H.
  Liar's moon
Gray, C.
  Masquerade
Harris, J.
  The evil seed
Hawksley, E.
  Tempting fortune
Hessayon, J. P.
  The Helmingham rose
Hodge, J. A.
  Bride of dreams
Hooper, K.
  Amanda
Horne, U.
  The jewel streets
Hoskyns, T.
  Peculiar things
Hylton, S.
  The sunflower girl
Jackson, J.
  A place of birds
James, M.
  The final reckoning
Joyce, M.
  The house by the shore
Lamb, C.
  Deep and silent waters
  Walking in darkness
Lowell, E.
  Forget me not
McCabe, H.
  Raven's mill
Mills, C.
  Love and lies
Moline, K.
  Belladonna
Oliver, M.
  Veiled destiny
Page, L.
  Isabella
Parker, U-M.
  Taking control
Patterson, R. N.
  Silent witness

Pearse, L.
  Camellia
Quincey, E.
  Forgotten sins
  Her mother's sins
Sole, L.
  Flame child
Spindler, E.
  Fortune
Steel, D.
  Malice
Stewart, S.
  Floodtide
  Mood indigo
Stockenberg, A.
  Beyond midnight
Stratton, P.
  The devil's bride
Townsend, L.
  Chasing Rachel
Whitmee, J.
  Belladonna
Whitney, P. A.
  Amethyst's dreams
Williams, M.
  Flowering thorn
Wood, B.
  Curse this house
  Yesterday's child
Wood, V.
  Emily
Worboys, A.
  Hotel girl
  Seasons of the senses
  You can't sing without me

GOURMETS
Lanchester, J.
  The debt to pleasure

GOVERNESSES
Harrod-Eagles, C.
  Dangerous love

GRAFFITI
Harbouri, P.
  Graffiti

GRAIL, HOLY
Ashley, M. editor
  Chronicles of the Holy Grail

GRANDFATHERS AND GRANDDAUGHTERS
Heller, Z.
  Everything you know
Morley, D.
  Sing a lonely song

GRANDFATHERS AND GRANDSONS
Hood, D.
  The chess men

GRANDMOTHERS AND GRANDDAUGHTERS
Brink, A.
  Imaginings of sand
Campbell, B. M.
  Singing in the comeback choir
Dally, E.
  Remembered dreams
Glanfield, J.
  Portraits in an album
Hart, E.
  The order of the star
McMahon, K.
  Footsteps

GREAT EXHIBITION, 1851
Minton, M.
  The breathless summer

GREECE, ANCIENT
Apostolou, A.
  A murder in Thebes
Holt, T.
  Alexander at the world's end
McCullough, C.
  The song of Troy
Merlis, M.
  Pyrrhus
Pressfield, S.
  Gates of fire
Wolf, C.
  Medea

GREECE: 1980-2000
Bawden, N.
  A nice change
Harbouri, P.
  Our lady of the serpents
Hylton, S.
  Separate lives
Papandreou, N.
  Father dancing
Woodhouse, S.
  Other lives

GREECE: 20TH CENTURY
Davidson, C. T.
  The priest fainted

GREECE: ATHENS
Harbouri, P.
  Graffiti

GREECE: CORFU
Daish, E.
Summer romance

GREECE: SALONIKA
Redmon, A.
The head of Dionysos

GREEK ISLANDS
Townsend, L.
Night of the storm

GREENLAND
Goodwin, T.
Seeds of destruction

GRIEF
Blumenthal, V.
Chasing eagles
Carroll, J.
The marriage of sticks
Crowell, J.
Necessary madness
Delaney, F.
The amethysts
Doughty, A.
Summer of the hawthorn
Esstman, B.
Mare's milk
Hamilton, J.
After Flora
The good Catholic
Irving, J.
A widow for one year
James, E.
Act of faith
Jones, M.
Cold in earth
McDermott, A.
Charming Billy
Mooney, B.
Intimate letters
Paige, F.
The swimming pool
Scofield, S.
Plain seeing
Shreve, A.
The pilot's wife
Tem, M.
Black river
Trapido, B.
The travelling horn player
Vickers, E.
The way of gentleness
Weber, K.
The music lesson
Yoshimoto, B.
Amrita

GUADELOUPE
Conde, M.
Windward heights

GUENEVERE, QUEEN
Miles, R.
Guenevere: the Queen of the summer
country

GUERRILLA WARFARE
Hurley, G.
The perfect soldier

GUILT
Barker, R.
The hook
Blanchard, S.
The paraffin child
Burgh, A.
The cult
Denker, H.
To Marcy, with love
Hamilton, J.
The good Catholic
Hart, J.
The stillest day
Park, D.
Stone kingdoms
Sutherland, G.
East of the city
Taylor, A.
The judgement of strangers

GUITARS
Nicholson, G.
Flesh guitar

GULF WAR SYNDROME
Nichol, J.
Vanishing point

GULF WAR, 1991
Blinn, J.
The aardvark is ready for war
Farley, C. J.
My favourite war
Sigaud, D.
Somewhere in a desert

GUN CLUBS
Hunt, D.
Trick shot

GUNPOWDER PLOT, 1603
Elgin, E.
Scapegoat for a Stuart

GUN-RUNNING
Nicole, C.
Guns in the desert

GUNS
Chisholm, P. F.
A surfeit of guns
Hammond, G.
Follow that gun
Walker, M. W.
All the dead lie down

GURUS
Kellerman, F.
Jupiter's bones

GUYANA
D'Aguiar, F.
Dear future
Kempadoo, O.
Buxton spice
Morrissey, D.
When the singing stops

GYMNASIIUMS
Henderson, L.
Too many blondes

GYPSIES
Farhi, M.
Children of the rainbow
Rowlands, B.
The cherry pickers
Wendorf, P.
One of us is lying
The toll house
Wood, V.
The Romany girl

HAIRDRESSERS
Edwards, D.
Better love next time

HALF-CASTES
Traynor, J.
Divine

HALF-SISTERS
Roberts, N.
Born in shame

HARASSMENT
Spring, M.
Nights in white satin

HARBOUR MASTERS
Woodman, R.
Captain of the Caryatid

HAREMS
Chamberlin, A.
The reign of favoured women

HAROLD II, KING, 1022-66
Rathbone, J.
The last English king

HATE
Adams, J.
Cast the first stone
Anthony, E.
The legacy
Hawksley, H.
Absolute measures
Hutchinson, M.
No place of angels

HAULAGE COMPANIES
Jones, C.
Running the risk

HAWAII
Flora, K.
Death in paradise
Kissick, G.
Winter in Volcano

HAWKS
Winn, M.
Redtails in love

HEADTEACHERS
Belfer, L.
City of light
McMahon, K.
Confinement

HEALING
Eidson, T.
Hannah's gift
Evans, M.
Inheritors
Howatch, S.
A question of integrity
Lancaster, G.
The precious gift

HEALTH FARMS
Laurence, J.
Diet for death

HEALTH INSPECTORS
Puckett, A.
Chilling out
Shadows behind a screen

HEART TRANSPLANTS
Buchanan, E.
Pulse
Connelly, M.
Blood work
Royle, N.
The matter of the heart

HEIRLOOMS
Frost, S.
Redeem the time

HENRY I, KING, 1068-1135
Hill, P.
The supplanter

HENRY II, KING, 1133-89
Hill, P.
Curtmantle

HERMAPHRODITES
Flanagan, M.
Adele

HERMITS
Desai, K.
Hullabaloo in the guava orchard

HEROES
Oates, J. C.
Broke heart blues

HIGHWAYMEN
March, H.
The devil's highway
Norman, D.
Blood royal

HIJACKING
Griffiths, J.
The courtyard in August
Tonkin, P.
Hell gate

HIMALAYAS
Kerr, P.
Esau
Podrug, J.
Frost of heaven
Sealy, A.
The Everest Hotel

HIRED KILLERS
Block, L.
Hit man
Cameron, J.
It was an accident
Deaver, J.
The devil's teardrop

Garber, J. R.
In a perfect state
Huberman, C.
Eminent domain
Lindsey, D. L.
Requiem for a glass heart
Masters, A.
I want him dead
Quinton, A.
This mortal coil

HISTORIANS
Fry, S.
Making history

HISTORICAL ROMANCE
Aiken, J.
Lady Catherine's necklace
Balogh, M.
A chance encounter
An honest deception
Barker, A.
His Lordship's gardener
Barraclough, J.
Loving and learning
Chesney, M.
His Lordship's pleasure
Miss Davenport's Christmas
Silken bonds
The chocolate debutante
The dreadful debutante
The glitter and the gold
Clitheroe, S.
Secret of Ware
Collier, G. K.
The golden web
Coulter, C.
Calypso magic
Daish, E.
The vineyard inheritance
Duffy, E.
Proud heart, fair lady
Dymoke, J.
Cassie's captain
Erle, J.
Scandal's daughter
Favier, P.
A masquerade too far
A temptation too great
Fenson, J.
Roscoe, Emily and all the little
bastards
Gillespie, J.
The reluctant baronet
Hatcher, R. L.
Kiss me, Katie
Hawksley, E.
The cabochon emerald
The Hartfield inheritance

Kaye, G.
Mistress of Calverley
Lightfoot, F. M.
A woman beyond price
Lindsey, J.
Man of my dreams
Minton, M.
Sea of love
The strident whisper
Morgan, K.
The vagabond judge
Quick, A.
Mischief
With this ring
Stratton, P.
The unromantic lady
Street, M.
See a fine lady
The confession of Fitzwilliam Darcy
Walsh, S.
The Cornwell bride
Wiggs, S.
Briar Rose

HIT AND RUN ACCIDENTS
Moody, S.
Dummy hand
Schwartz, J. R.
Reservation Road

HIV (DISEASE)
Rhodes, P.
Whispers

HOLIDAY REPS
Butts, C.
Is Harry on the boat?

HOLIDAY VILLAGES
Ballard, J. G.
Cocaine nights

HOLIDAYS
Barfoot, J.
Some things about flying
Barraclough, J.
Another summer
Bawden, N.
A nice change
Connolly, J.
Summer things
Daish, E.
Summer romance
Grant-Adamson, L.
Undertow
Melville, A.
The longest silence
Oakley, A.
A proper holiday

Schaeffer, F.
Portofino
Smith, C.
Double exposure
Sutton, H.
Bank Holiday Monday
Waller, L.
Eden
Whitnell, B.
The fragrant harbour

HOLOCAUST
Delaney, F.
The amethysts
Farhi, M.
Children of the rainbow
Skibell, J.
A blessing on the moon

HOLOCAUST SURVIVORS
Dershowitz, A. M.
Just revenge
Krich, R. M.
Blood money

HOME EXCHANGES
Binchy, M.
Tara Road

HOMELESS
Barnard, R.
No place of safety
Berger, J.
King
Brooke-Rose, C.
Next
Walker, M. W.
All the dead lie down

HONG KONG
Burdett, J.
The last six million seconds
Davis, J. G.
The year of dangerous loving
Falconer, C.
Triad
Luk, H.
China bride
Theroux, P.
Kowloon Tong
Tonkin, P.
The action
West, C.
Death of a red mandarin
Whitnell, B.
The fragrant harbour
Wilson, G.
Bezique

HOROLOGY

Wilkins, C.
The horizontal instrument

HORROR STORIES

Ablow, K. R.
Denial
Alten, S.
Meg
The trench
Andrews, C.
Legacies
Andrews, V.
Hidden jewel
Atkins, P.
Big thunder
Wishmaster
Bachman, R.
The regulators
Barker, C.
Sacrament
Brenchley, C.
Light errant
Shelter
Brite, P. Z.
Exquisite corpse
Campbell, R.
The house on Nazareth Hill
Cave, H. B.
Isle of the whisperers
Caveney, P.
Bad to the bone
Chadbourn, M.
Scissorman
The Eternal
Clark, S.
Darker
Judas tree
King Blood
Vampyrrhic
Cleaver, C.
The wishing tree
Dark
Dark of the night; edited by S. Jones
Dark terrors 2
Donnelly, J.
Incubus
Twitchy eyes
Douglas, J.
Hard shoulder
Zoo event
Dronfield, J.
The locust farm
Farris, J.
Dragonfly
Fowler, C.
Personal demons
Gordon, F.
The burning altar

Gray, M.
Furnace
Hall, K.
Dark debts
Harris, S.
Straker's Island
The devil on May Street
Herbert, J.
'48
Others
Holland, T.
Deliver us from evil
Hunter, G.
Law of the wild
James, P.
Alchemist
The truth
Jetmundsen, N.
The soulbane stratagem
Jones, J. V.
Where the children cry
King, S.
Bag of bones
Desperation
The girl who loved Tom Gordon
Klavan, A.
The uncanny
Koontz, D. R.
Fear nothing
Seize the night
Sole survivor
Ticktock
Laws, S.
Chasm
Somewhere south of midnight
Laymon, R.
After midnight
Among the missing
Bite
Body rides
Come out tonight
Fiends
The midnight tour
Little, B.
Guests
Houses
The store
Lumley, B.
E-Branch: invaders
Necroscope; the lost years 2
The house of doors; second visit
Lynch, P.
Carriers
Masterton, G.
Faces of fear
The chosen child
The house that Jack built
Tooth and claw

Masterton, J.
  The terror
Morris, M.
  Genesis
  Longbarrow
  Mr. Bad Face
Rickman, P.
  The wine of angels
Rose, D.
  Pest maiden
Rovin, J.
  Vespers
Russell, J.
  Blood
  Celestial dogs
Saul, J.
  The Blackstone chronicles
  The presence
Slade, M.
  Shrink
  Zombie
Stine, R. L.
  Superstitious
Trewinnard, P
  The pastor
Veevers, M.
  Bloodlines
White, G.
  Unhallowed grave

HORSE BREEDING
McCormac, R.
  Playing dead

HORSE RACING
Baker, D.
  Ride for a fall
Bingham, C.
  The nightingale sings
Francis, D.
  10lb penalty
  To the hilt
Francome, J.
  False start
  High flyer
  Safe bet
  Tip off
Jones, C.
  Going the distance
Pitman, R.
  Blood ties
  The third degree
Power, M. S.
  Nathan Crosby's fan mail

HORSES
Dimmick, B.
  In the presence of horses

Jones, C.
  Running the risk
Merrick, J.
  Horse latitudes
Robinson, S-A.
  Riding out

HOSPITALS
Burgh, A.
  On call
Carson, P.
  Scalpel
Cooper, N.
  Fruiting bodies
Cuthbert, M.
  The silent cradle
Daish, E.
  Ryan's quadrangle
Evans, E.
  Carter Clay
Feinstein, L.
  Likely to die
Gordon, R.
  The last of Sir Lancelot
Rayner, C.
  Fourth attempt
Robinson, L. R.
  Intensive care

HOSTAGES
Anscombe, R.
  Shank
Deaver, J.
  A maiden's grave
Gorman, E.
  Runner in the dark
Peters, R.
  The devil's garden
Rendell, R.
  Road rage
Walker, M. W.
  Under the beetle's cellar

HOTEL BOATS
Fforde, K.
  Life skills

HOTELIERS
Ustinov, P.
  Monsieur Rene

HOTELS
Adamson, P.
  Facing out to sea
Barker, A. L.
  The Haunt
Bawden, N.
  A nice change

Bingham, C.
  A grand affair
Downes, F.
  The long snake tattoo
Doyle, R.
  Alva
Fraser, A.
  Dangerous deception
Haylock, J.
  Body of contention
Holms, J.
  Bad vibes
Hylton, S.
  Easter at the Lakes
Maskell, V.
  Worlds apart
Patterson, G.
  The International
Raife, A.
  Belonging
  Grianan
Sealy, A.
  The Everest Hotel

HOUSE PARTIES
Perrick, P.
  Evermore

HOUSEKEEPERS
Santiago, E.
  America's dream

HOUSES
Barraclough, J.
  The Villa Violetta
Boyle, J.
  The spirit of the family
Brindley, L.
  Indian summer
Cookson, C.
  The solace of sin
Erskine, B.
  House of echoes
Glanfield, J.
  Portraits in an album
Goddard, R.
  Set in stone
Graham, M.
  A bitter legacy
Hayes, K.
  Cloud music
James, E.
  A sense of belonging
Love, A.
  Mallingford
Makepeace, M.
  Out of step
Marsh, W.
  The quick and the dead

Marysmith, J.
  The philosopher's house
Montero, G.
  The Villa Marini
Raife, A.
  Drumveyn
Stephens, K.
  Felstead
Stewart, M.
  Rose Cottage
Sutton, H.
  The househunter
Thayer, N.
  Belonging
Thynne, J.
  The shell house
Wendorf, P.
  One of us is lying
Willett, M.
  Hattie's mill

HOUSES, CONSERVATION OF
Clayton, V.
  Dance with me
Johnson, P.
  Under construction

HOUSING ESTATES
Richards, B.
  Throwing the house out of the
    window

HULL
Wood, V.
  Children of the tide

HUMOROUS NOVELS
Aitken, G.
  Fifty ways of saying fabulous
Alliott, C.
  Rosie Meadows regrets
Anderson, D.
  Futon fever
Baddiel, D.
  Time for bed
Bailey, J.
  An angel in waiting
Barker, N.
  Wide open
Beatty, P.
  The white boy shuffle
Bellamy, G.
  The mystery of men
  The power of women
Blackaby, M.
  Look what they've done to the blues
Blake, C.
  It's my party

O'Connell, T.
Sex, lies and litigation
Pearson, C.
Look no hands
Pennac, D.
Write to kill
Peters, L.
Premature infatuation
Reading between the lies
Plass, A.
The sacred diary of Adrian Plass
Pratchett, T.
Carpe jugulum
Feet of clay
Hogfather
Jingo
The fifth elephant
The last continent
Rankin, R.
A dog called Demolition
Apocalypso
Nostradamus ate my hamster
Sex and drugs and sausage rolls
Snuff fiction
Sprout mask replica
The Brentford chainstore massacre
The dance of the voodoo handbag
Revell, N.
House of the spirit levels
Robinson, B.
The peculiar memories of Thomas
Penman
Scott, C. K.
Low alcohol
Selby, M.
All that glisters
Gargoyles and port
That awkward age
Shames, L.
Welcome to Paradise
Sharpe, T.
The midden
Spence, A.
Way to go
Stowe, R.
One good thing
Summers, J.
Frogs and lovers
Syal, M.
Life isn't all ha ha hee hee
Sykes, E.
Smelling of roses
Theroux, M.
A stranger in the Earth
Toksvig, S.
Whistling for the elephants
Toner, B.
An organised woman

Toner, M.
Seeing the light
Townsend, S.
Adrian Mole, the cappucino years
Truss, L.
Going loco
Tennyson's gift
Walshe, P.
The latecomer
Welsh. I.
Filth
Woolf, I.
The trials of Tiffany Trott
Wroe, G.
Slaphead
Wynne-Jones, G.
Wise follies

HUNDRED YEARS WAR
Hall, D.
Kemp: passage at arms
Kemp; the road to Crecy

HUNGARY: 1930-59
Nadas, P.
The end of a family story

HUNGARY: 1960-80
Roy-Bhattacharya, J.
The Gabriel club

HUNGARY: 1980-2000
Swinfen, A.
The travellers

HUNGARY: BUDAPEST
Roy-Bhattacharya, J.
The Gabriel club

HUNGER
Rosen, J.
Eve's apple

HUNTING
Sullivan, M. T.
The purification ceremony

HURRICANES
Buchanan, E.
Act of betrayal

HYPNOTHERAPY
Craig, K.
Some safe place

HYPNOTISM
Carey, P.
Jack Maggs

Margolis, S.
  The hypnotist

ICE SKATING
Thomson, M. F.
  Dreams of gold

ICEBERGS
Follett, J.
  Second Atlantis
Tonkin, P.
  Meltdown

IDLENESS
Marchant, I.
  In Southern waters

ILLEGAL IMMIGRANTS
Collins, M.
  Emerald underground
Creswell, S.
  A sort of homecoming
George, E.
  Deception on his mind
Hall, P.
  Dead on arrival
Scholefield, A.
  The drowning mark

ILLEGITIMATE CHILDREN
Kay, N.
  Gift of love
Mills, J.
  The hearing
Mortimer, J.
  Felix in the underworld

ILLNESS
Bohjalian, C.
  The law of similars
Brady, J.
  Death comes for Peter Pan
Denker, H.
  A place for Kathy Cameron
Woodford, P.
  Jane's story

IMMIGRANTS
Ardizzone, T.
  In the garden of Papa Santuzzu
Baker, K.
  Dreamland
Fuentes, C.
  The crystal frontier
Graves, H.
  Beyond the purple hills
Jakes, J.
  America dreams

Messud, C.
  The last life

IMPERSONATORS
Kavanagh, S.
  Wired to the moon
Kluge, P. F.
  Biggest Elvis

IMPOSTORS
Corby, V.
  Something stupid
Doyle, R.
  Executive action
Duncker, P.
  James Miranda Barry
Grimes, M.
  The Stargazy
Morson, I.
  A psalm for Falconer

IMPOTENCE
Lefcourt, P.
  The woody

INCEST
Fraser, C. M. & Galloway, F. I.
  The poppy field
Harvey, J.
  Last rites
Pennington, L.
  The stalking of Eve
Sapphire
  Push
Stuart, A.
  The war zone
Tepper, N.
  The happy hunting grounds

INDECENT EXPOSURE
Spring, M.
  Standing in the shadows

INDIA: 18TH CENTURY
Cornwell, B.
  Sharpe's tiger

INDIA: 19TH CENTURY
Cornwell, B.
  Sharpe's fortress
Gordon, K.
  The peacock fan
Hussein, A.
  The weary generations
McNeill, E.
  Dusty letters
Sinclair, K.
  From a far country

INDIA: 20TH CENTURY
Hussein, A.
The weary generations
Murari, T.
Steps from paradise

INDIA: 1900-29
Brindley, L.
Indian summer
Hylton, S.
Footsteps in the rain

INDIA: 1930-59
Baldwin, S. S.
What the body remembers
Kapur, M.
Difficult daughters

INDIA: 1960-80
Mistry, R.
A fine balance
Roy, A.
The god of small things

INDIA: 1980-2000
Desai, A.
Fasting, feasting
Desai, K.
Hullabaloo in the guava orchard
Godden, R.
Cromartie v. the god Shiva
Jha, R. K.
The blue bedspread
Sharma, Y.
The buffalo thief
Vakil, A.
Beach boy
Whitaker, P.
Eclipse of the sun

INDIA: AHALLABAD
Mukerjee, R.
Toad in my garden

INDIA: BOMBAY
Forbes, L.
Bombay ice
James, C.
The silver castle
Keating, H. R. F.
Asking questions

INDIA: CALCUTTA
Chatterjee, A.
Across the lakes
Chaudhuri, A.
Freedom song
Divakaruni, C. J.
Sister of my heart

Gupta, S.
A sin of colour
Keating, H. R. F.
Bribery, corruption also

INDIA: PUNJAB
Baldwin, S. S.
What the body remembers

INDIANS ABROAD: UNITED STATES
Divakaruni, C. J.
The mistress of spices

INDO-CHINA: 1930-59
Murphy, Y.
The sea of trees

INDONESIA
Gray, C.
The torrent

INDUSTRIAL ESPIONAGE
Pipkin, B.
Silent agony
Watson, I.
Hard questions

INFERTILITY
Asher, J.
The longing
Elton, B.
Inconceivable
Krich, R. M.
Fertile ground

INFIDELITY
Jackson, S.
Living other lives
Mooney, B.
Intimate letters
St. John M.
A pure clear light

INHERITANCE
Anthony, E.
The legacy
Baker, K.
Inheritance
Barrett, M.
Breach of promise
Barrie, A.
The linden tree
Bentley, U.
The sloping experience
Bolitho, J.
Framed in Cornwall
Clayton, M.
Death is the inheritance

Delaney, F.
  Pearl
Edwards, M.
  The devil in disguise
Fraser, C.
  Beyond forgiveness
Fraser, C. M.
  An inheritance
Goddard, R.
  Beyond recall
Graham, M.
  Practicing wearing purple
Hammond, G.
  Dogsbody
Hawksley, E.
  Crossing the Tamar
Hill, P.
  Countess Isabel
Hood, E.
  Rowan Cottage
Knight, S.
  Out of the blue
McGown, J.
  Picture of innocence
  Plots and errors
Mullins, E.
  The devil's work
O'Connell, C.
  Flight of the stone angel
Page, E.
  Intent to kill
Rawlinson, P.
  The Caverel claim
Roberts, N.
  Montana sky
Seymour, A.
  The sins of the mother
Shorten, E.
  Katie Colman crosses the water
Shriver, L.
  A perfectly good family
Smith, M.
  Legacy
Sweetland, M.
  Tradewind
Thayer, N.
  Belonging
Vincenzi, P.
  Windfall
Wendorf, P.
  One of us is lying
Whitehead, B.
  Secrets of the dead
Willett, M.
  Second time around
Woodhouse, S.
  Other lives

INNER CITIES
Selby, H.
  The willow tree

INNS
Howard, A.
  Tomorrow's memories
Norman, D.
  Blood royal

INSANITY
Boylan, C.
  Beloved stranger
Glaister, L.
  The private parts of women
Hall, M.
  The art of breaking glass
Hinxman, M.
  Losing touch
Lovesey, P.
  Death duties
Mootoo, S.
  Cereus blooms at night
Reynolds, A.
  Insanity
Self, W.
  Great apes

INSURANCE
Silver, J.
  Assumption of risk
Sutherland, G.
  East of the city

INSURANCE INVESTIGATORS
Johnson, B.
  Bad moon rising
Reuben, S.
  Spent matches
Stanley, G.
  Nagasaki six
Winslow, D.
  California fire and life

INTELLECTUALS
Daley, D.
  The strange letter Z

INTELLIGENCE SERVICES
Barnacle, H.
  Day one

INTERIOR DESIGNERS
Babson, M.
  The multiple cat
Baker, D.
  A man possessed
Grant, R. E.
  By design

Ray, K.
  A fine restoration
Stewart, S.
  Kissing shadows

INTERIOR MONOLOGUES
Cirino, M.
  Name the baby
Gray, S.
  Breaking hearts
Landis, J. D.
  Lying in bed

INTERNET
Cannell, S. J.
  Final victim
Green, J.
  Jemima J.

INVESTMENT BROKERS
Pugh, D.
  Body blow

IRAN: 1900-29
Rabinyan, D.
  Persian brides

IRAN: 1960-80
Buchan, J.
  A good place to die

IRELAND, ANCIENT
Doughty, A.
  Summer of the hawthorn
Mantel, H.
  The giant, O'Brien

IRELAND: 7TH CENTURY
Tremayne, P.
  The monk who vanished
  The spider's web
  The subtle serpent
  Valley of the shadow

IRELAND: 11TH CENTURY
Llywelyn, M.
  Pride of lions

IRELAND: 18TH CENTURY
Warnock, G.
  The silk weaver

IRELAND: 19TH CENTURY
Gebler, C.
  How to murder a man
Graham, B.
  The whitest flower
O'Neill, A.
  A family cursed

IRELAND: 20TH CENTURY
Collier, C.
  A house full of women
Delaney, F.
  Desire and pursuit
Doyle, R.
  A star called Henry
Welch, R.
  Groundwork

IRELAND: 1900-29
Hardy, C.
  The last days of innocence
Macklan, A.
  The house by the sea
O'Neill, A.
  A family cursed
  Wayward angel
O'Neill, A.
  Where shadows walk

IRELAND: 1930-59
Cleaver, C.
  The wishing tree
Flynn, K.
  Rose of Tralee
Leitch, M.
  The smoke king
Lyons, G.
  The perfect family
Ryan, M.
  Glenallen
Taylor, A.
  The woman of the house

IRELAND: 1960-80
Dunne, M.
  Blessed art thou a monk swimming
Mackenna, J.
  The last fine summer
O'Neill, J.
  Leaving home

IRELAND: 1980-2000
Binchy, M.
  Tara Road
Bingham, C.
  The nightingale sings
Cleaver, C.
  The silent valley
Conlon, E.
  A glassful of letters
Cremins, R.
  A sort of homecoming
Doughty, A.
  Stranger in the place
Doyle, R.
  Alva

Gill, B.
  Death of a busker king
Hamilton, H.
  Sad bastard
Horne, U.
  The boy in the moon
Kavanagh, S.
  Wired to the moon
Kelly, C.
  She's the one
O'Brien, E.
  Down by the river
  Wild December
O'Neill, J.
  Turn of the tide
Ryan, L.
  A taste of freedom
Ryan, M.
  The song of the tide
Thompson, K.
  Thin air

IRELAND: CLARE
Conway, J.
  Cereal love
Gill, B.
  The death of an Irish sea wolf
Roberts, N.
  Born in shame

IRELAND: CONNEMARA
Daly, I.
  Unholy ghosts
McCormac, R.
  Playing dead

IRELAND: CORK
Hayes, K.
  Cloud music
Ryan, J.
  Dismantling Mr. Doyle

IRELAND: DUBLIN
Boylan, C.
  Room for a single lady
Carson, P.
  Cold steel
Conlon, E.
  A glassful of letters
Hughes, S.
  The detainees
Johnston, J.
  Two moons
Lyons, G.
  The other cheek
McEldowney, E.
  The sad case of Harpo Higgins
O'Connor, J.
  The salesman

Parsons, J.
  Mary, Mary
Ryan, M.
  The seduction of Mrs. Caine
Sheridan, P.
  44

IRELAND: MAYO
Heiney, P.
  Golden apples

IRELAND: MONAGHAN
Gebler, C.
  How to murder a man

IRELAND: WATERFORD
Lusby, J.
  Flashback

IRISH ABROAD: BRITAIN
Casey, P.
  The water star
Healy, D.
  Sudden times
McDonald, J. F.
  Tribe

IRISH POLITICAL DISTURBANCES, 1968-
Anthony, P.
  The fragile peace
Beattie, G.
  The corner boys

IRISH POLITICAL UNREST
Fraser, S.
  Montague's whore

IRISH REBELLION, 1916-21
Hardy, C.
  The last days of innocence
Llywelyn, M.
  1916

IRISH REPUBLICAN ARMY
Bradby, T.
  Shadow dancer
Gulvin, J.
  Close quarters
O'Rourke, F. M.
  The poison tree

ISLAM
Caute, D.
  Fatima's scarf

ISLANDS
Garland, A.
  The beach

Tonkin, P.
  Tiger Island
Waller, L.
  Eden

ISLE OF MAN
Dyson, S.
  Fairfield Rose

ISLE OF WIGHT
Barnes, J.
  England, England
Daish, E.
  Emma's Christmas rose
Truss, L.
  Tennyson's gift

ISOLATED COMMUNITIES
Baker, W.
  The raven bride
Barnard, R.
  The corpse at the Haworth Tandoori
Bowering, M.
  Visible worlds
Garland, A.
  The beach
Huneven, M.
  Round rock
McNeil, J.
  Hunting down home
Moffat, G.
  Running dogs
Morrow, B.
  Giovanni's gift

ISOLATION
Benson, P.
  The shape of clouds

ISRAEL, ANCIENT
Boast, P.
  Sion
Whitehouse, M.
  The book of Deborah

ISRAEL: 1945-
Williams, B.
  Crusaders

ISRAEL: 1980-2000
Abecassis, E.
  The Qumran mystery
Grossman, D.
  The zigzag kid
Land, J.
  Pillars of Solomon

ISRAEL: JERUSALEM
Stone, R.
  Damascus Gate

ITALIANS ABROAD: CANADA
Ricci, N.
  Where she has gone

ITALY: 13TH CENTURY
Heritage, J.
  Set fire to Sicily

ITALY: 15TH CENTURY
Eyre, E.
  Dirge for a doge
Proud, L.
  A tabernacle for the sun
Wilson, D.
  The swarm of heaven

ITALY: 16TH CENTURY
Andahazi, F.
  The anatomist
Cowan, J.
  A mapmaker's dream

ITALY: 18TH CENTURY
Moor M. de
  The virtuoso
Williams, J. M.
  Scherzo

ITALY: 19TH CENTURY
Ross, K.
  The devil in music
St. Aubin de Teran, L.
  The palace

ITALY: 1930-59
Barraclough, J.
  The Villa Violetta

ITALY: 1980-2000
Brizzi, E.
  Jack Frusciante has left the band
Curzon, C.
  Guilty knowledge
Hellenga, R.
  The fall of a sparrow
Odone, C.
  The shrine
Pewsey, E.
  Volcanic airs
Prantera, A.
  Letter to Lorenzo
Roberts, N.
  Homeport

ITALY: FLORENCE

Nabb, M.
  The monster of Florence
Proud, L.
  A tabernacle for the sun
Ryan, M.
  The promise

ITALY: MILAN

Williams, T.
  Big Italy

ITALY: NAPLES

Buss, L.
  The luxury of exile
Dibdin, M.
  Cosi fan tutte

ITALY: PIEDMONT

Aspler, T.
  The beast of Barbaresco
Dibdin, M.
  A long finish

ITALY: PORTOFINO

Schaeffer, F.
  Portofino

ITALY: ROME

Pears, I.
  Death and restoration
Turnbull, P.
  The justice game

ITALY: SICILY

Seymour, G.
  Killing ground

ITALY: SIENA

Crane, T.
  Siena summer

ITALY: TUSCANY

Hill, J. S.
  Ghirlandaio's daughter
Humphreys, E.
  The gift of a daughter

ITALY: UMBRIA

Unsworth, B.
  After Hannibal

ITALY: VENICE

Eyre, E.
  Dirge for a doge
Girardi, R.
  Vaporetto 13
Hayes, K.
  A patch of green water

Heritage, J.
  Set fire to Sicily
Leon, D.
  A noble radiance
  Acqua alta
  Fatal remedies
  The death of faith
Stewart, S.
  Kissing shadows
Williams, J. M.
  Scherzo

JACKSON, ANDREW, AMERICAN PRESIDENT, 1767-1845

Stone, I.
  The President's lady

JACOBITE REBELLION, 1715

Taverner, J.
  Rebellion

JACOBITES

Norman, D.
  Blood royal

JAMES, IV, KING OF SCOTLAND, 1473-1513

Tranter, N.
  A flame for the fire

JAPAN: 17TH CENTURY

Rowlands, L. J.
  Bundori
  The concubine's tattoo
  The way of the traitor

JAPAN: 19TH CENTURY

Grey, A.
  Tokyo Bay

JAPAN: 1930-59

Golden, A.
  Memoirs of a geisha
Hollands, J.
  The exposed

JAPAN: 1980-2000

Alletzhauser, A.
  Quake
Hill, T.
  Skin
Murakami, H.
  The wind-up bird chronicle
Oe, K.
  A quiet life
Stanley, G.
  Nagasaki six

Tasker, P.
   Samurai boogie

JAPAN: TOKYO
Brown, A.
   Audrey Hepburn's neck
Kramer, G.
   Shopping
Tasker, P.
   Buddha kiss

JAPANESE ABROAD: UNITED STATES
Ikeda, S. D.
   What the scarecrow said

JAZZ MUSICIANS
Compton, D. G.
   Back of town blues
Granelli, R.
   Out of nowhere
Kay, J.
   Trumpet
Munoz Molina, A.
   Winter in Lisbon
Straub, P.
   Pork Pie Hat
Zabor, R.
   The bear comes home

JEALOUSY
Berry, E.
   The scourging of poor little Maggie
Crane, T.
   The raven hovers
Lambkin, D.
   The hanging tree
Loraine, P.
   Ugly money
Newberry, S.
   The painted sky
Shreve, A.
   The weight of water
Taylor, A.
   The judgement of strangers
Williamson, N.
   Ming's kingdom
Yasar Kemal
   Salman the solitary

JESUITS
Russell, M. D.
   The sparrow

JESUS CHRIST
Abecassis, E.
   The Qumran mystery
Byrne, M.
   Heaven looked upwards

Mailer, N.
   The Gospel according to the Son
Whitehouse, M.
   The book of Deborah

JEWELLERY TRADE
Oliver, M.
   The golden road
Roper, M.
   Cutting the rocks

JEWELS
Fonseca, R.
   The lost manuscript
Roth, J.
   The string of pearls

JEWS
Horn, S.
   Four mothers
Rabinyan, D.
   Persian brides

JEWS: BRITAIN
Freeman, G.
   His mistress's voice
Rayner, J.
   Day of atonement
Waterstone, T.
   A passage of lives

JEWS: CHILE
Agosin, M.
   A cross and a star

JEWS: EUROPE
Shalom Alekhem
   The song of songs

JEWS: NEW ZEALAND
Gee, M.
   Live bodies

JEWS: PERSECUTION
Clegg, A.
   Where birds don't sing
Cregan, C.
   Valkyrie
Fast, H.
   The bridge builder's story
Hoffman, A.
   Two for the devil
Pemberton, L.
   Sleeping with ghosts
Skibell, J.
   A blessing on the moon

JEWS: UNITED STATES
Jong, E.
  Of blessed memory
Mamet, D.
  The old religion
Rabinovitch, D.
  Flora's suitcase
Singer, I. B.
  Shadows on the Hudson

JOAN OF ARC, SAINT, C. 1412-31
Marcantel, P.
  An army of angels

JOANNE OF ACRE, DAUGHTER OF EDWARD I
Alexander, V.
  The love knot

JOCKEYS
Baker, D.
  Ride for a fall

JOSEPHINE, EMPRESS, WIFE OF NAPOLEON, 1763-1814
Gulland, S.
  Tales of passion, tales of woe

JOURNALISTS
Armstrong, L.
  Front row
Bannister, J.
  Critical angle
Bedford, M.
  Exit, orange and red
Blake, S.
  The butcher bird
Bradshaw, P.
  Lucky baby Jesus
Brink, A.
  Devil's valley
Brookmyre, C.
  Country of the blind
Buchanan, E.
  Suitable for framing
Burke, J.
  Dear Irene
Burke, J.
  Hours
  Liar
  Remember me, Irene
Burns, J.
  Nark
  Snap
Coleridge, N.
  With friends like these
Craft, M.
  Body language

Delinsky, B.
  Lake news
Farley, C. J.
  My favourite war
Frost, S.
  Redeem the time
Hall, P.
  Dead on arrival
  Perils of the night
Hammond, G.
  Dogsbody
Harrison, C.
  Manhattan nocturne
Hayter, S.
  Nice girls finish last
Heald, T.
  Stop press
Hey, S.
  Scare story
  Sudden unprovided death
Hill, P.
  The small black knife
Holden, W.
  Simply divine
Ignatius, D.
  A firing offence
Kelly, C.
  She's the one
Lee-Potter, E.
  Hard copy
Mann, J.
  Hanging fire
Mathews, A.
  Vienna blood
Matthews, L.
  A picture of innocence
McDermid, V.
  A place of execution
McEwan, I.
  Amsterdam
Preston, J.
  Ink
Purcell, D.
  Sky
Richards, B.
  The silver river
Roome, A.
  Bad Monday
  Deceptive relations
Sharam, K.
  Rough exposure
Shepherd, S.
  Twilight curtain
Shreve, A.
  The weight of water
Sinclair, J.
  Dangerous games
Singh. A.
  Give 'em hell, Hari

Stock, F.
  A foreign country
Stuart, A.
  Barefoot angel
Theroux, M.
  A stranger in the Earth
Thompson, H. S.
  The rum diary
Waites, M.
  Mary's prayer
Walker, M. W.
  Under the beetle's cellar
Walters, M.
  The echo
Wheeler, R. S.
  Flint's truth

JOURNEYS

Auster, P.
  Spring will come
  Timbuktu
Blevins, W.
  The rock child
Clement, C.
  Theo's odyssey
Conroy, P.
  Beach music
Frazier, C.
  Cold mountain
Gemmell, N.
  Cleave
Hines, B.
  Elvis over England
Ireland, D.
  The chosen
Kearney, R.
  Walking at sea level
Lawhead, S.
  Byzantium
Lessing, D.
  Mara and Dann
Lyons, G.
  Lucy Leighton's journey
Murray, L.
  Fredy neptune
North, F.
  Chloe
Pamuk, O.
  The new life
Raphael, F.
  Coast to coast
Weller, A.
  Land of the golden clouds
Wilson, P.
  Do white whales sing at the edge of
    the world?

JUDEA, ANCIENT

Crace, J.
  Quarantine

JUDGES

Anonymous
  A time for justice
Gustafsson, L.
  The tale of a dog
Mills, J.
  The hearing

JUDICIAL SYSTEM

Cornwell, J.
  Fear and favour

JURORS

Ashford, J.
  A web of circumstances
Friedman, P.
  Grand jury
Van Wormer, L.
  Jury duty

JUSTICE

Dillon, P.
  Truth

KELSEY, NANCY, AMERICAN PIONEER

Holland, C.
  An ordinary woman

KENNETH II, KING OF SCOTLAND

Tranter, N.
  High kings and Vikings

KENT

Andrews, L.
  The sinister side
Mackay, S.
  The orchard on fire

KENYA

Lambkin, D.
  The hanging tree

KENYA: 1930-59

Gavron, J.
  Moon

KENYA: 1980-2000

Blake, P.
  Heat of the moment

KENYA: NAIROBI
Casley, D. J.
Death under par
Marciano, F.
Rules of the wild

KIDNAPPING
Andrews, C.
Deep as the marrow
Asher, H.
The predators
Backhouse, F.
Within the walls
Baker, J.
Walking with ghosts
Blumenthal, V.
Saturday's child
Carcaterra, L.
Apaches
Carson, P.
Scalpel
Child, L.
Die trying
Coburn, A.
Birthright
Cooper, N.
Creeping ivy
Curzon, C.
All unwary
Davis, V.
Queen's ransom
Deaver, J.
The bone collector
Easterman, D.
The final judgement
Eccles, M.
Killing me softly
Freeling, N.
One more river
Garrison, P.
Fire and ice
George, E.
In the presence of the enemy
Granger, A.
Keeping bad company
Gray, C.
The torrent
Grippando, J.
The abduction
Holms, J.
Thin ice
James, D.
The fortune teller
Karr, J.
Catch me if you can
Leib, F. A.
The house of pain
Leon, D.
A noble radiance

Listfield, E.
The last good night
Luk, H.
China bride
Maitland, B.
The Chalon heads
Martin, J. W.
The bird yard
Moggach, D.
Seesaw
Morgenroth, K.
Kill me first
Morrissy, M.
Mother of Pearl
Rogow, R.
The problem of the missing hoyden
Sandford, J.
Mind prey
Scholefield, A.
Bad timing
Simons, P.
Eleven hours
Smith, M. A.
New America
Straub, P.
The Hellfire Club
Washburn, S.
Into thin air
Whiting, C.
The Japanese princess

KING, MARTIN LUTHER, CIVIL RIGHTS LEADER, 1929-68
Johnson, C.
Dreamer

KINGSTON UPON THAMES
Waite, E.
Kingston Kate

KNIGHTS AT ARMS
Chadwick, E.
The champion

KNIGHTS TEMPLAR
Boast, P.
Deus
Hillier, D.
Fire and shadow

KOREA
Limon, M.
Jade lady burning
Stout, M.
One thousand chestnut trees

LAKE DISTRICT
Howell, L.
The director's cut

Lightfoot, F.
Lakeland Lily
Larkrigg Fell
The bobbin girls
Moffat, G.
The lost girls
Mountain, F.
Isabella

LANCASHIRE
Connor, A.
Midnight's smiling
The moon is my witness
Cox, J.
A time for us
The devil you know
Tomorrow the world
Dyson, S.
One golden summer
Eadith, J.
A very loud voice
Etchells, O.
The Jericho trumpet
Gregson, J. M.
Missing, presumed dead
To kill a wife
Hamilton, R.
Paradise Lane
Howard, A.
Tomorrow's memories
Hylton, S.
Footsteps in the rain
Jacobs, A.
Hallam Square
Our Lizzie
Spinners Lake
Lancaster, G.
The Saturday girl
Morson, I.
A psalm for Falconer
Vites, C.
Class of '39

LANDLORDS
Gebler, C.
How to murder a man
Pugh, D.
Body blow

LANDOWNERS
Blair, E.
An apple from Eden
Fraser, C. M.
Ullin Macbeth
Torres, A. T.
Dona Ines versus oblivion

LANDSCAPE GARDENERS
Saville, D.
Capability's Eden

LAW OF LAURISTON, JOHN, SCOTTISH FINANCIER, 1671-1729
Gleeson, J.
The moneymaker

LAWYERS
Dooling, R.
Brainstorm
Fraser, C.
An immoral code
Fyfield, F.
Staring at the light
Gadol, P.
The long rain
Harrington, E.
Daddy darling
James, P. D.
A certain justice
Krich, R. M.
Speak no evil
Meek, M. R. D.
A house to die for
O'Connell, T.
Sex, lies and litigation
Ooi, Y-M.
The flame tree
Parker, B.
Suspicion of deceit
Ramsay, E.
The quality of mercy
Roberts, B.
Robbery with malice
Siddons, A. R.
Fault lines
Stockley, G.
Blind judgment
Turnbull, P.
The justice game

LEBANESE CIVIL WAR
Daoud, H.
The house of Mathilde

LEBANON
Hanania, T.
Unreal city

LEBANON: BEIRUT
Daoud, H.
The house of Mathilde
Gibeily, C. A.
Blueprint for a prophet
Gibran, K.
Broken wings

Hanania, T.
Homesick

LECTURERS
Cutler, J.
Dying to score
MacLeod, C.
Exit the milkman
Reah, D.
Only darkness

LEGAL PHOTOGRAPHERS
Hall, J. W.
Body language

LEGAL THRILLERS
Adler, E.
All or nothing
Amato, A.
Lady Gold
Armstrong, C.
Silencer
Arnold, C.
Due process
Imperfect justice
Wrongful death
Baldacci, D.
The simple truth
Bettle, J.
Natural causes
Bohjalian, C.
Midwives
Burke, J.
Cimarron rose
Carrington, R.
Dead fish
Darden, C.
The trials of Nikki Hill
Davies, J.
On appeal
Undisclosed material
Davis, J. G.
The year of dangerous loving
Davis, R.
Abuse of process
Hung jury
The oath
Deverell, W.
Street legal; the betrayal
Dias, D.
Above the law
Error of judgement
Rule of law
Finder, J.
High crimes
Frieder, P.
Signature murder
Friedman, P.
Grand jury

No higher law
Grisham, J.
The partner
The runaway jury
The street lawyer
Gruenfeld, L.
The expert
The halls of justice
Hall, G.
A cement of blood
Higgins, G. V.
Sandra Nichols found dead
Hillstrom, R.
Letter of intent
Iles, G.
The quiet game
Jacobs, J.
Motion to dismiss
Kessler, D.
A fool for a client
Reckless justice
Klempner, J. T.
Felony murder
Korelitz, J. H.
A jury of her peers
Lescroart, J. T.
Nothing but the truth
MacDougal, B.
Breach of trust
Margolin, P. M.
The burning man
Meltzer, B.
Dead even
The tenth justice
O'Shaughnessy, P.
Invasion of privacy
Parker, B.
Criminal justice
Patterson, R. N.
Dark lady
Silent witness
The final judgment
Rosenberg, N.
Abuse of power
Ruffa, D. W.
The defense
Salaman, N.
A state of shock
Scottoline, L.
Mistaken identity
Rough justice
Running from the law
Stewart, E.
Jury double
Turow, S.
Personal injuries
Wesson, M.
A suggestion of death
Render up the body

Wilhelm, K.
The best defence
Willett, S.
The deal
Williams, N.
Without prejudice

LEGENDS, AFRICAN
Thompson, E. V.
Mud huts and missionaries

LEICESTER
Palmer, F.
Black gold

LEICESTER, ROBERT DUDLEY, EARL OF, ENGLISH COURTIER, 1533-1588
Maxwell, R.
The Queen's bastard

LEICESTERSHIRE
Hodges, J.
The girl with brains in her feet
Page, L.
Any old iron
At the toss of a sixpence
Just by chance
Willsher, A.
So shall you reap
The fruitful vine
The sower went forth

LESBIANS
Bennett, S.
A question of love
Brand, D.
In another place, not here
Clarke, C.
The wolf ticket
Dorcey, M.
Biography of desire
Fritchley, A.
Chicken feed
Chicken out
Gunthorp, D.
Georgiana's closet
Herring, P. J.
A moment's indiscretion

LETTERS
Buss, L.
The luxury of exile

LIARS
McGregor, H. R.
Schrodinger's baby

LIBERIA: 1980-2000
Cobb, J.
Seafighter

LIBRARIANS
McCracken, E.
The giant's house

LIE DETECTORS
Cooper, N.
Sour grapes

LIGHTHOUSE KEEPERS
Fraser, C. M.
Kinvara

LIGHTHOUSE TENDERS
Woodman, R.
Captain of the Caryatid

LIGHTHOUSES
Titchmarsh, A.
The last lighthouse keeper

LINCOLNSHIRE
Dickinson, M.
Chaff upon the wind
Reap the harvest
The fisher lass
The miller's daughter
Mackie, M.
Spring fever
Smethurst, W.
Woken's eye

LINDBERGH FAMILY
Coburn, A.
Birthright

LINDISFARNE
Cusack, W.
The edge of vengeance

LIONS
Barnes, S.
Rogue lion safaris

LITERARY AGENTS
Upcher, C.
Falling for Mr. Wrong
Van Wormer, L.
Any given moment

LITERARY CIRCLES
Waugh, H.
The chaplet of pearls

LITERARY RESEARCH
Wall, A.
  The lightning cage

LITTLE BIGHORN, BATTLE OF, 1876
Chiaventone, F. J.
  A road we do not know
Skimin, R.
  The river and the horsemen

LIVERPOOL
Andrews, L.
  Liverpool songbird
  The ties that bind
  Where the Mersey flows
Andrews, L. M.
  From this day forth
  Liverpool lamplight
  When tomorrow dawns
Baker, A.
  A Liverpool lullaby
  A Mersey duet
  Mersey maids
  The price of love
  With a little luck
Compton, D. G.
  Back of town blues
Currie, E.
  She's leaving home
Downes, F.
  The long snake tattoo
Edwards, M.
  Eve of destruction
  First cut is the deepest
  The devil in disguise
Ellis, R.
  Ears of the city
  Mean streets
Flynn, K.
  Liverpool Taffy
  No silver spoon
  Rainbow's end
  Rose of Tralee
Forrester, H.
  Madame Barbara
  Mourning doves
Francis, J.
  Another man's child
  Kitty and her boys
  Somebody's girl
Hamilton, R.
  The Bells of Scotland Road
  The corner house
Holt, F.
  Some you win
Howard, A.
  Beyond the shining water

Promises lost
Jonker, J.
  Sadie was a lady
  Sweet Rosie O'Grady
  The pride of Polly Perkins
  Try a little tenderness
  Walking my baby back home
Lee, M.
  Annie
  Dancing in the dark
  Put out the fires
  Through the storm
Murphy, E.
  Comfort me with apples
  Honour thy father
  When day is done
Newman, J.
  Life class
Smith, A.
  What about me?

LOCAL COUNCILLORS
Flynn, R.
  A public body

LODGERS
Boylan, C.
  Room for a single lady
Clayton, V.
  Past mischief

LOGGING
Goodwin, T.
  Blood of the forest

LONDON
Boast, P.
  Deus
Rutherford, E.
  London

LONDON UNDERGROUND
Hill, T.
  Underground

LONDON: 17TH CENTURY
Marston, E.
  The King's evil

LONDON: 18TH CENTURY
Alexander, B.
  Murder in Grub Street
Lake, D.
  Death at the Devil's Tavern
  Death in the Peerless Pool
Laurence, J.
  Canaletto and the case of
    Westminster Bridge

LONDON: 19TH CENTURY

Buxton, J.
  Pity
Fraser, S.
  Montague's whore
Freeman, G.
  His mistress's voice
Hardy, C.
  Far from home
Harrison, R.
  Draught of death
  Facets of murder
  Murder by design
Hudson, H.
  Into the sunlight
King, A.
  A handful of sovereigns
  Bow belles
Minton, M.
  The breathless summer
O'Neill, G.
  The lights of London
Perry, A.
  Bedford Square
  Brunswick Gardens
  Pentecost Alley
  The silent cry
  Traitor's Gate
  Whited sepulchres
Roberts, B.
  Sherlock Holmes and the harvest of
    death
  Sherlock Holmes and the royal flush
Staples, M. J.
  The ghost of Whitechapel
Thomson, E.
  A time before Oliver
Waters, S.
  Affinity

LONDON: 1900-29

Bowling, H.
  The whispering years
Burns, P.
  Packards
Carr, I.
  Lovers meeting
Chapman, E.
  Damaged fruit
Davey, A. R.
  Winter in Paradise Square
King, A.
  Frankie's manor
Lord, E.
  A better life
  The turning tides
Newberry, S.
  Tilly's family

Nicolson, C.
  The golden city
Oldfield, J.
  After hours
Pemberton, V.
  My sister Sarah
Roberts, I.
  Limehouse lady
Spencer, S.
  South of the river
Stuart, A.
  Sin no more
Waite, E.
  Nippy
Warner, E.
  A sparrow from the smoke
Williams, D.
  Ellie of Elmleigh Square
  Katie's kitchen

LONDON: 1930-59

Bowling, H.
  As time goes by
  Down Milldyke way
  One more for Saddler Street
  The Chinese lantern
  The glory and the shame
  When the pedlar called
Burns, P.
  Goodbye, Piccadilly: Packards at war
Carey, H.
  Some sunny day
Carr, A.
  The last summer
Casey, P.
  The water star
Cole, H.
  Julia's war
Evans, P.
  Yesterday's friends
Grey, P.
  Cutter's Wharf
  Good Hope Station
Kelly, T.
  The cut
Oldfield, J.
  All fall down
O'Neill, G.
  Cissie Flowers
  Dream on
Pemberton, M.
  Coronation summer
Pemberton, V.
  Nellie's war
  The silent war
Roberts, I.
  London's pride

Staples, M. J.
  Churchill's people
  Fire over London
  The family at war
  The young ones
Waite, E.
  Cockney courage
  Trouble and strife
Willsher, A.
  All shadows fly away
Worboyes, S.
  Down Stepney way
  Keep on dancing

LONDON: 1960-80

Carr, R.
  Brixton bwoy
Evans, P.
  A song in your heart
  Near and dear
Kindersley, T.
  Goodbye, Johnny Thunders
Levy, A.
  Never far from nowhere
Marsh, J.
  Iris
Moskowitz, C.
  Wyoming trail
Prince, P.
  Waterloo story
Ray, K.
  Stoats and weasels
Worboyes, S.
  Red sequins
  The dinner lady

LONDON: 1980-2000

Bailey, P.
  Kitty and Virgil
Butler, G.
  Coffin's game
Evans, P.
  The carousel keeps turning
Healy, D.
  Sudden times
Howatch, S.
  A question of integrity
Huggins, D.
  Luxury amnesia
Newland, C.
  Society within
Richards, B.
  Throwing the house out of the
    window
Stewart, S.
  Sharking

LONDON: BERMONDSEY

Bowling, H.
  As time goes by

LONDON: CAMDEN TOWN

Charles, P.
  Fountain of sorrow
  Last boat to Camden Town
Owen, J.
  Camden girls

LONDON: EAST END

Bowling, H.
  Down Milldyke way
  One more for Saddler Street
  The Chinese lantern
  The glory and the shame
  The whispering years
  When the pedlar called
Chapman, E.
  Damaged fruit
Cole, H.
  Julia's war
Davey, A. R.
  Winter in Paradise Square
Dunn, N,
  My silver shoes
Grey, P.
  Cutter's Wharf
Hudson, M.
  Tell me no secrets
King, A.
  A handful of sovereigns
  Bow belles
  Frankie's manor
Oldfield, J.
  After hours
  All fall down
O'Neill, G.
  Cissie Flowers
  Dream on
  The lights of London
Roberts, I.
  London's pride
Spencer, S.
  South of the river
Staples, M. J.
  Churchill's people
  The Camberwell raid
  The ghost of Whitechapel
  The young ones
Waite, E.
  Cockney courage
Warner, E.
  A sparrow from the smoke
Williams, D.
  Ellie of Elmleigh Square
  Katie's kitchen

Worboyes, S.
  Down Stepney way
  Keep on dancing
  Red sequins
  The dinner lady

LONDON: HACKNEY
Dennis, F.
  The last blues dance

LONDON: KENSINGTON
Smith, C.
  Kensington Court
Thomas, L.
  Kensington Heights

LONDON: SOUTHWARK
Stewart, S.
  Playing with stars

LONDON: ST. PAUL'S CATHEDRAL
Harbinson, W. A.
  Resurrection

LONDON: STEPNEY
Willsher, A.
  All shadows fly away

LONELINESS
Buchan, J.
  High latitudes
Collins, M.
  Emerald underground
Veciana-Suarez, A.
  The chin kiss king
Williams, C.
  Head injuries

LONELY HEARTS CLUBS
Masters, P.
  A wreath for my sister

LONGEVITY
Irving, C.
  The spring

LOSS ADJUSTERS
Lupoff, R. A.
  The Bessie Blue killer

LOTTERIES
Baldacci, D.
  The winner
Cory, C.
  The guest

LOVE
Alliott, C.
  The real thing
Appignanesi, L.
  The things we do for love
Bailey, P.
  Kitty and Virgil
Barrie, A.
  The butterfly
Bayley, J.
  George's lair
Bell, J.
  Silk town
Bennett, A.
  A strong hand to hold
Benson, P.
  The shape of clouds
Bingham, C.
  Love song
  The nightingale sings
Birch, C.
  Come back, Paddy Riley
Blair, J.
  Portrait of Charlotte
  The other side of the river
Bloom, A.
  Love invents us
Bowling, H.
  The Chinese lantern
Boyt, S.
  The characters of love
Bradford, B. T.
  A secret affair
Brewer, J.
  A crack in forever
Brierley, D.
  The horizontal woman
Brindley, L.
  Autumn comes to Mrs. Hazell
  Indian summer
  The Kerry dance
Bron, E.
  Double take
Clayton, V.
  Dance with me
Cleaver, C.
  The wishing tree
Cookson, C.
  The bonny dawn
Cowie, V.
  The devil you know
Cox, J.
  A time for us
  Somewhere, someday
Cunningham, P.
  Consequences of the heart
Curry, J.
  Counting the ways
  Peacock's Acre

LOVE LETTERS
Schine, K.
  The love letter

LOYALTY
Ashford, J.
  Loyal disloyalty

LUST
Merriman, C.
  State of desire
Spade, J.
  Passion play

MACARTHUR, DOUGLAS, US SOLDIER, 1880-1964
Webb, J.
  The Emperor's General

MACHIAVELLI, NICCOLO, ITALIAN STATESMAN, 1469-1527
Wilson, D.
  The swarm of heaven

MADEIRA
Spencer, S.
  The paradise job

MAFIA
Bonansinga, J. R.
  Bloodhound
Elliott, J.
  Nowhere to hide
Farrow, J.
  City of ice
Giancana, S.
  30 seconds
Lyons, D.
  Dog days
Oldham, N.
  A time for justice
Puzo, M.
  The last Don
Seymour, G.
  Killing ground
Shames, L.
  Virgin heat
Wilson, R.
  Blood is dirt
Woods, S.
  Choke

MAGAZINE INDUSTRY
Coleridge, N.
  Streetsmart
  With friends like these
Edwards, R. D.
  Publish and be murdered

MAGELLAN, FERDINAND, PORTUGUESE NAVIGATOR, 1480-1521
Baccino Ponce de Leon, N.
  Five black ships

MAGICIANS
Bedford, M.
  The Houdini girl
Christopher, N.
  Veronica
Moore, B.
  The magician's wife
O'Connell, C.
  Shell game
Patchett, A.
  The magician's assistant
Smith, D.
  The illusionist

MAGISTRATES
Frewen, F.
  A woman's judgement

MALAYSIA
Lim, C.
  The tear drop story woman

MALE PROSTITUTES
McCabe, P.
  Breakfast on Pluto

MALE RAPE
Strong, T.
  The poison tree

MALI: 1980-2000
Sweetman, D.
  A tribal fever

MALICE
Morrow, B.
  Giovanni's gift

MALTA
Harvey, C.
  The brass dolphin

MAMMOTHS
Baxter, S.
  Mammoth

MANCHESTER
Blincoe, N.
  Manchester slingback
Caveney, P.
  1999

Gash, J.
   Prey dancing
Goring, A.
   No enemy but winter
Hopkins, B.
   Our kid
Lightfoot, F.
   Manchester pride
McDermid, V.
   Blue genes
McDonald, J. F.
   Tribe
Spencer, S.
   Murder at Swann's Lake
Staincliffe, C.
   Dead wrong
   Go not gently
Vann, K. le
   Trailers
Warren, T.
   Full steam ahead

MANHUNTS

Armstrong, V.
   Dead in the water
Baldacci, D.
   Absolute power
Chisnell, M.
   The delivery
Gilstrap, J.
   At all costs
   Nathan's run
Holden, C.
   The last sanctuary
Katzenbach, J.
   State of mind
Lee, T.
   Queen's flight
North, D.
   Violation
Oldham, N.
   A time for justice
Palmer, F.
   Hoodwinked
Scholefield, A.
   Night moves
White, R.
   Siberian light

MANUSCRIPTS

Estleman, L. D.
   The hours of the virgin

MAORIS

Corbalis, J.
   Tapu
Duff, A.
   What becomes of the broken hearted?

Grace, P.
   Baby No-eyes
   Potiki

MARINE ARCHAEOLOGISTS

Roberts, N.
   The reef

MARKS, GRACE, CONVICTED MURDERESS, 1827-?

Atwood, M.
   Alias Grace

MARRIAGE

Asher, J.
   The question
Barrie, A.
   The butterfly
Bergman, M.
   Mirror, mirror
Billington, R.
   Perfect happiness
Bond, F. A.
   Changing step
Bosley, D.
   Let me count the ways
Boylan, C.
   Beloved stranger
Brampton, S.
   Concerning Lily
Brookfield, A.
   A summer affair
Cato, A.
   Still lives
Curry, J.
   Counting the ways
   Peacock's Acre
Curtis, N.
   The last place you look
Fergusson, L.
   The chase
Freely, M.
   The other Rebecca
Goldsmith, O.
   The switch
Goodwin, S.
   Sheer chance
Graham, L.
   The dress circle
Haines, C.
   Touched
Halligan, M.
   Wishbone
Harris, E.
   Singing in the wilderness
Harrison, S.
   Flowers won't fax
Henley, J.
   Family ties

Living lies
Hijuelos, O.
  Empress of the splendid season
Howard, A.
  When morning comes
Huth, A.
  Easy silence
Hylton, S.
  Separate lives
Jacobs, A.
  Our Lizzie
James, E.
  Act of faith
Kay, J.
  Trumpet
Kay, R.
  Out of bounds
Kennedy, W.
  The flaming corsage
Keyes, M.
  Watermelon
Kimball, M.
  Mouth to mouth
Larkin, M.
  For better, for worse
Laszlo, M. de
  The patchwork marriage
Leigh, E.
  The perfect marriage
Lisle, J.
  Journeys from home
Lyons, G.
  Daniella's decision
Mansell, J.
  Mixed doubles
Marsh, W.
  Facing the music
  The quick and the dead
Mason, R.
  The drowning people
Middleton, S.
  Against the dark
  Live and learn
Monroe, D.
  Newfangled
Morgan, S.
  Delphinium blues
Mourby, A.
  The four of us
Noll, I.
  Where shadows walk
Nugent, F.
  Drawing from life
Odone, C.
  A perfect wife
Palmer, E.
  The golden rule
Peck, D.
  The law of enclosures

Purves, L.
  A long walk in wintertime
  More lives than one
Rautbord, S.
  The Chameleon
Renton, A.
  Maiden speech
Rhodes, P.
  The trespassers
Roth, P.
  I married a communist
Sandys, E.
  Enemy territory
Saville, D.
  The hawk dancer
  The honey makers
Sheepshanks, M.
  Facing the music
Sole, R.
  The photographer's wife
Steel, D.
  Granny Dan
Stirling, J.
  The workhouse girl
Street, P.
  The General's wife
Swinfen, A.
  The travellers
Thornley, R.
  Seventeen seventeen Jerome
Trapido, B.
  The travelling horn player
Upcher, C.
  The visitor's book
Whitaker, P.
  Eclipse of the sun
Willett, M.
  The dipper

MARRIAGE GUIDANCE
Wendorf, P.
  The marriage menders

MARY CELESTE (SHIP)
Freemantle, B.
  The Mary Celeste

MARY MAGDALENE, FOLLOWER OF CHRIST
Boast, P.
  Sion

MARY, QUEEN OF SCOTS, 1542-87
Dunbar, I.
  The Queen's bouquet
Tannahill, R.
  Fatal majesty

MASON, CHARLES, BRITISH SURVEYOR, 1728-86
Pynchon, T.
Mason and Dixon

MASSAGE PARLOURS
Darrieussecq, M.
Pig tales

MATHEMATICIANS
Petsinis, T.
The French mathematician
Woolfe, S.
Leaning towards infinity

MATISSE, HENRI, FRENCH PAINTER, 1869-1954
Everett, P.
Matisse's war

MAXWELL, JOHN, LORD HERRIES, WARDEN OF THE WEST MARCH, D. 1594
Tranter, N.
The Marchman

MAYANS
Sands, M.
Serpent and storm

MEDIA
Constantine, S.
Thin air
Elegant, R. S.
The big brown bears
Odone, C.
A perfect wife
Patterson, R. N.
No safe place

MEDICAL RESEARCH
Aird, C.
After effects
Glass, S.
The interpreter
Holms, J.
Thin ice
Johansen, I.
Long after midnight
Mawson, R.
The Lazarus child
McClure, K.
Pandora's helix

MEDICAL THRILLERS
Barnard, C.
The donor

Cook, R.
Chromosome 6
Contagion
Invasion
Toxin
Vector
Cordy, M.
The miracle strain
Crichton, M.
A case of need
Gerritsen, T.
Harvest
Life support
Lancaster, G.
Payback
McClure, K.
Donor
Pandora's helix
Morton, C. W.
Rage sleep
Olgin, H. A.
Remote intrusion
Rayner, C.
Fifth member
Stanway, A.
Vaxxine

MEDICI FAMILY
Proud, L.
A tabernacle for the sun

MEMORIES
English, L.
Children of light
Mackenna, J.
A haunted heart
Nadas, P.
The end of a family story
Steel, D.
Granny Dan

MEMORY
Sebald, W. G.
Vertigo
Wicks, S.
The key
Wiggins, M.
Almost heaven

MEN AND WOMEN
Gordon, J.
My fair man

MENTAL HOSPITALS
Wilson, J.
Omega cluster

MENTAL ILLNESS
Blaine, M.
Whiteouts
Boyle, J.
Hero of the underworld
Jones, M.
Sick at heart
Owens, A.
For the love of Willie
Paling, C.
Deserters
Wilson, P.
Do white whales sing at the edge of
the world?

MENTALLY DISTURBED
Kennedy, S.
Charlotte's friends

MERCENARIES
Carter, N.
King of coins
Knave of swords
Jecks, M.
The Crediton killings

MERCHANT VENTURERS
Dunnett, D.
Caprice and Rondo

MERCY KILLINGS
Jardine, Q.
Gallery whispers
Lescroart, J. T.
The mercy rule

MERLIN, MAGICIAN
Whyte, J.
The sorcerer

MERSEYSIDE
Samson, K.
Awaydays

MESSIANISM
Bateman, C.
Turbulent priests
Kleier, G.
The last day
Lockhart, D.
The paradise complex

METEOROLOGISTS
Francis, D.
Second wind

MEW, CHARLOTTE, ENGLISH POET, 1869-1928
Parris, P. B.
His arms are full of broken things

MEXICAN CIVIL WAR, 1910
Gonzales-Rubin, J.
Loving you was my undoing

MEXICO, ANCIENT
Sands, M.
Serpent and storm

MEXICO: 19TH CENTURY
Fuentes, C.
The crystal frontier
Mastretta, A.
Lovesick

MEXICO: 1930-59
McCarthy, C.
Cities of the plain

MEXICO: 1980-2000
Woods, J. G.
The General's dog

MEXICO: PUERTO VALLARTA
Waller, R. J.
Puerto Vallarta squeeze

MICHAEL, ARCHANGEL
Greeley, A. M.
Contract with an angel

MICROBIOLOGISTS
Puckett, A.
Shadows behind a screen

MIDDLE AGE
Howard, E. J.
Falling
Jackson, S.
A little surprise
Kaye, G.
Late in the day
Lord, G.
Sorry, we're going to have to let you
go
Maitland, S.
Brittle joys
Mead, J.
Charlotte Street
Rowntree, K.
An innocent diversion
Stevens, A.
November tree

MIDDLE CLASSES
Middleton, S.
Against the dark

MIDDLE EAST
Kleier, G.
The last day
Maalouf, A.
Ports of call

MIDDLE EAST: 12TH CENTURY
Ali, T.
The book of Saladin

MIDDLE EAST: 1980-2000
Brown, D.
Shadows of steel
Micou, P.
The leper's bell

MIDLIFE CRISIS
Crewe, C.
The last to know
Huth, A.
Easy silence
Zigman, L.
Dating big bird

MIDWIVES
Bohjalian, C.
Midwives
Crewe, C.
Falling away
Lawrence, M.
The burning bride

MILLENNIUM
Andersen, K.
Turn of the century
Kleier, G.
The last day
Lord, G.
A party to die for

MILLENNIUM BUG
Pineiro, R. J.
01-01-00

MILLINERS
Stubbs, J.
The witching time

MIND BENDING
La Plante, L.
Mind kill

MINERS' STRIKE, 1984
Trotter, J. M.
Never stand alone

MISCARRIAGE
Collen, L.
Getting rid of it

MISCARRIAGES OF JUSTICE
Grant-Adamson, L.
Lipstick and lies
Lindsay, F.
Kissing Judas
McCrumb, S.
The ballad of Frankie Silver
Roberts, B.
Robbery with malice
Rubens, B.
I, Dreyfus
Taylor, A. G.
Unsafe convictions

MISFITS
Huggins, D.
Luxury amnesia

MISSING CHILDREN
Battison, B.
Jeopardy's child
Daish, E.
Emma's journey
Dalton, M.
First impression
Greensted, R.
Lost cause
Grimes, M.
Biting the moon
King, L. R.
With child
Land, J.
Pillars of Solomon
McNeill, E.
Money troubles
Mitchard, J.
The deep end of the ocean
O'Connell, C.
Judas child
Price, R.
Freedomland
Rankin, I.
Dead souls
Taylor, A.
The four last things
Thompson, K.
Thin air

MISSING PERSONS
Baldacci, D.
Total control
Bannister, J.
The primrose convention
Barnard, R.
No place of safety

Bell, P.
Blood ties
Benali, A.
Wedding by the sea
Bolitho, J.
Sequence of shame
Burke, J.
Remember me, Irene
Craig, K.
Short fuse
Dobyns, S.
The church of dead girls
Dunant, S.
Mapping the edge
Falconer, C.
Disappeared
Francis, C.
A dark devotion
Graham, C.
Faithful unto death
Hightower, L.
No good deed
Hillerman, T.
The fallen man
Jenkins, J.
Columbus day
Jennings, L.
Beauty story
Joseph, A.
The quick and the dead
Kadow, J.
Burnout
Kelly, S.
The ghosts of Albi
Laurence, J.
Appetite for death
Lindsay, F.
A kind of dying
Lovesey, P.
The vault
Melville, A.
The longest silence
Page, E.
Hard evidence
Perry, A.
The twisted root
Perry, T.
Shadow woman
Podrug, J.
Frost of heaven
Sedley, K.
The brothers of Glastonbury
Simpson. D.
Dead and gone
Smith, F. A.
Stone dead
Smith, M. C.
Rose

Stewart, S.
Postcards from a stranger
Tremayne, P.
The monk who vanished
Wilson, R.
A darkening stain

MISSIONARIES
Horne, U.
Blow the wind southerly
Jeal, T.
The missionary's wife
Kingsolver, B.
The poisonwood Bible

MISTRESSES
Asher, J.
The question

MITHRAISM
Harris, E.
The sacrifice stone

MIXED MARRIAGES
Bowling, H.
The Chinese lantern
Liu, A. P.
Cloud mountain
Roy, L.
Lady Moses
Soueif, A.
The map of love

MODELS
Brodie, A.
Face to face
Daish, E.
Catrina
Saunders, J.
A different kind of love

MODOTTI, TINA, MEXICAN COMMUNIST LEADER, 1896-1941
Poniatowski, E.
Tinisima

MONASTERIES
Cusack, W.
The edge of vengeance
Sedley, K.
The Saint John's fern

MONEY LAUNDERING
Hammond, G.
Follow that gun
Parker, B.
Criminal justice

MONKS

Kadare, I.
The three-arched bridge
Sedley, K.
The weaver's inheritance

MONSTERS

Wilson, C.
Extinct

MORECAMBE

Williams, C.
Head injuries

MOTHERS AND CHILDREN

Cooper, N.
Creeping ivy
Curtis, N.
The last place you look
Drabble, M.
The witch of Exmoor
Evans, P.
Near and dear
Goldsmith, O.
Marrying Mom
Goudge, E.
Trail of secrets
Kidman, F.
Ricochet baby
Miller, S.
The distinguished guest
Morrissy, M.
Mother of Pearl
Purves, L.
Regatta
Renton, A.
Winter butterfly
Sharam, K.
A hard place
Thorne, N.
Worlds apart
Woodhouse, S.
Other lives
Woolfe, S.
Leaning towards infinity
Worboyes, S.
The dinner lady

MOTHERS AND DAUGHTERS

Badami, A. R.
Tamarind mem
Brett, B.
Mother
Chai, A. J.
The last time I saw mother
Cohen, A.
Dream on
Cook, K,
What girls learn

Corbett, V. and others
Double trouble
Cox, J.
Love me or leave me
Davidson, C. T.
The priest fainted
Delinsky, B.
Shades of Grace
Denker, H.
A place for Kathy Cameron
Dunn, N,
My silver shoes
Ellis, J.
Single mother
Fitch, J.
White oleander
Forster, M.
The memory box
Francis, J.
Somebody's girl
Frederiksson, M.
Hanna's daughters
Gibbons, K.
Sights unseen
Graham, M.
Out of the night
Gunn, K.
The keepsake
Hamilton, R.
The Bells of Scotland Road
Haran, M.
A family affair
Soft touch
Howard, A.
Beyond the shining water
Hucker, H.
The real Claudia Charles
Hutchinson, M.
No place of angels
James, S.
Summer storm
Jenkins, J.
Columbus day
Jenny, Z.
The pollen room
Johnston, J.
Two moons
Jonker, J.
Stay as sweet as you are
Kagan, E.
Blue heaven
Keller, N. O.
Comfort woman
Krantz, J.
The jewels of Tessa Kent
Magrs, P.
Does it show?
Mandeville, J.
Careful mistakes

Maraire, N.
  Zenzele
Mitchard, J.
  The most wanted
Moggach, D.
  Close relations
Murphy, B.
  Janey's war
Murray, A.
  Kate & Olivia
Owens, V. S.
  Generations
Pietrzyk, L.
  Pears on a willow tree
Randall, A.
  Kilkenny bay
Robinson, R.
  This is my daughter
Roe, J.
  Eating grapes downwards
Rogers, J.
  Island
Sallis, S.
  The keys to the garden
Scofield, S.
  Plain seeing
Strout, E.
  Amy and Isabelle
Tate, J.
  No one promised me tomorrow
Veciana-Suarez, A.
  The chin kiss king
Whitmee, J.
  Thursday's child
Wicks, S.
  Little thing
Williams, D.
  Wishes and tears

MOTHERS AND SONS
Atkins, A.
  On our own
Fraser, C. M.
  Kinvara wives
Jones, M.
  Sick at heart
Lipsky, D.
  The art fair
Mulholland, S.
  Woman's work
Mulrooney, G.
  Araby
Nolan, C.
  The banyan tree
Ridgway, K.
  The long falling
Stock, F.
  A foreign country

Wall. J.
  Mother love
Whitnell, B.
  The candlewood tree
Winton, T.
  Blueback

MOTHERS-IN-LAW
Charles, K.
  Strange children
Gregory, P.
  The little house
Laszlo, M. de
  The patchwork marriage

MOTOR RACING
Hammond, G.
  Fine tune
Hooper, K.
  Elusive dawn
Oliver, M.
  The golden road
Stimson, T.
  Pole position

MOUNTAINEERING
Cohen, R.
  Above the horizon
Moffat, G.
  A wreath of dead moths

MOVING HOUSE
White, G.
  Chain reaction

MOZART, WOLFGANG AMADEUS, COMPOSER, 1756-91
Dracup, A.
  Mozart's darling

MULL
Stirling, J.
  The island wife

MULTIPLE MURDERS
Airth, R.
  River of darkness
Johansen, I.
  And then you die. . .
Kellerman, F.
  Serpent's tooth
Sakamoto, K.
  The electrical field

MULTIPLE PERSONALITY
Maxim, J. R.
  Mosaic

MULTIPLE SCLEROSIS
James, E.
  A sense of belonging

MULTI-RACIAL COMMUNITIES
Bandele-Thomas, B.
  The street
Vakil, A.
  Beach boy

MUMMIES
Russell, N.
  The dried-up man

MURDER
Adams, J.
  Cast the first stone
  Fade to grey
Aird, C.
  After effects
Andrews, D.
  Murder with peacocks
Armstrong, D.
  Thought for the day
Badenoch, A.
  Mortal
Bailey, M.
  Haycastle's cricket
Baker, J.
  Walking with ghosts
Bannister, J.
  The hireling's tale
Battison, B.
  Poetic justice
  The witch's familiar
Bedford, M.
  The Houdini girl
Berne, S.
  A crime in the neighbourhood
Bolitho, J.
  An absence of angels
  Buried in Cornwall
  Sequence of shame
  Snapped in Cornwall
  Victims of violence
Bradford, B. T.
  Dangerous to know
Braun, L. J.
  The cat who said cheese
Brett, S.
  Dead room farce
Brindley, L.
  Tantalus
Brookmyre, C.
  Quite ugly one morning
Brown, L.
  Double wedding ring
Burke, J.
  Dear Irene

Burley, W. J.
  Wycliffe and the redhead
Burns, J.
  Snap
Butler, G.
  A double coffin
  Coffin's game
  Coffin's ghost
Carson, P.
  Scalpel
Charles, K.
  Strange children
Clayton, M.
  Dead men's bones
  Death is the inheritance
  The prodigal's return
  The word is death
Cleary, J.
  Dilemma
  Endpeace
Cleeves, A.
  High Island blues
  The crow trap
Cohen, A.
  Poisoned pen
Collier, I.
  Spring tide
Cooper, N.
  Fruiting bodies
Cornwell, P.
  Cause of death
Crombie, D.
  Kissed a sad goodbye
  Leave the grave green
Cutler, J.
  Dying for millions
  Dying on principle
  Dying to write
Daley, R.
  Wall of brass
Dewhurst, E.
  Death of a starnger
  The verdict on winter
Dexter, C.
  Death is now my neighbour
  The remorseful day
Doherty, P. C.
  A tournament of murders
  The devil's hunt
  The field of blood
Duffy, M.
  Music in the blood
Eccles, M.
  A species of revenge
  Cast a cold eye
  The Superintendent's daughter
Edwards, R. D.
  Murder in a cathedral

Pawson, S.
  The Judas sheep
Pears, I.
  Death and restoration
Penn, J.
  Bridal shroud
  Sterner stuff
Perry, A.
  Bedford Square
  Brunswick Gardens
  Pentecost Alley
  Traitor's Gate
Puckett, A.
  Chilling out
Rayner, C.
  Fourth attempt
Reah, D.
  Only darkness
Rendell, R.
  Harm done
Rhea, N.
  Death of a princess
Rhodes, E.
  The merry month of May
Robb, J. D.
  Glory in death
Robinson, P.
  Wednesday's child
Roome, A.
  Bad Monday
Ross, A.
  Double vision
Ross, J.
  Murder! murder! burning bright
Rowe, R.
  The Germanicus mosaic
Royce, K.
  Shadows
Sandford, J.
  Secret prey
Scholefield, A.
  Night moves
Scottoline, L.
  Rough justice
Sedley, K.
  The wicked winter
Sherwood, J.
  Shady borders
Siddons, A. R.
  Fault lines
Simons, P.
  Red leaves
Simpson. D.
  Dead and gone
Smith, F. A.
  Candles for the dead
Smith, F. E.
  Fatal flaw

Spring, M.
  Nights in white satin
Stallwood, V.
  Oxford shift
Staynes, J. & Storey, M.
  Quarry
Stockley, G.
  Blind judgment
Strong, T.
  The death pit
Taylor, A. G.
  The mortal sickness
Templeton, A.
  Night and silence
  The trumpet shall sound
Thomas, S.
  Dead clever
Thompson, G.
  The homecoming
Thomson, J.
  Burden of innocence
Todd, C.
  Search the dark
Todd, M.
  Jail bait
  Man eater
Tope, R.
  A dirty death
Tremayne, P.
  The spider's web
Trevor, J.
  The same corruption there
Tripp, M.
  The suitcase killings
Trow, M. J.
  Lestrade and the devil's own
Turnbull, P.
  Embracing skeletons
  Fear of drowning
Weldon, T.
  The surgeon's daughter
Whitehead, B.
  Secrets of the dead
Williams, D.
  Dead in the market
Wilson, D.
  Cumberland's cradle
Wilson. D.
  The Borgia chalice

MUSEUMS
Moncur, A.
  A good looking man
Norman, H.
  The museum guard
Vidal, G.
  The Smithsonian Institution

MUSIC FESTIVALS
Templeton, A.
The trumpet shall sound

MUSIC HALLS
Worboyes, S.
Keep on dancing

MUSICIANS
Hansen, E. F.
Psalm at journey's end
Hayes, K.
Cloud music
Hudson, M.
The music in my head
Joss, M.
Funeral music
Leavitt, D.
The page turner
Lingard, A.
The fiddler's leg
Maurensig, P.
Canone inverso
McVeigh, A.
Ghost music
Nicholson, G.
Flesh guitar
Pewsey, E.
Unholy harmonies
Proulx, A.
Accordion crimes
Rice, A.
Violin
Rushdie, S.
The ground beneath her feet
Seaward, B.
The avalanche
Seth, V.
An equal music
Sheepshanks, M.
Facing the music
Sverak, Z.
Kolya
Templeton, A.
The trumpet shall sound
Tremain, R.
Music and silence

MYSTERY STORIES
Andrews, D.
Murder with peacocks
Apostolou, A.
A murder in Thebes
Armstrong, V.
Dead in the water
Babson, M.
Miss Petunia's last case
Bailey, M.
Haycastle's cricket

Bannister, J.
The primrose convention
Barr, N.
Endangered species
Barron, S.
Jane and the genius of the place
Jane and the man of the cloth
Jane and the unpleasantness at
Scargrave Manor
Jane and the wandering eye
Black, V.
Vow of adoration
Vow of compassion
Vow of poverty
Bolitho, J.
Buried in Cornwall
Braun, L. J.
The cat who knew Shakespeare
The cat who played post office
The cat who said cheese
The cat who sang for the birds
The cat who saw stars
The cat who tailed a thief
Brett, S.
Mrs. Pargeter's plot
Brindley, L.
Tantalus
Brought
Brought to book; edited by P. Sumner
Buckley, F.
The doublet affair
The Robsart mystery
Burke, J.
Liar
Chadwick, W.
Framed
Christie, A.
While the light lasts (short stories)
Clare, A.
Fortune like the moon
Clark, M. J.
Do you want to know a secret?
Clynes, M.
The relic murders
Cook, J.
Blood on the Borders
Death of a lady's maid
Kill the witch
Cutler, J.
Dying on principle
Dying to write
Davis, L.
One virgin too many
Two for the lions
Death
Death in Dixie; edited by B. S.
Mosiman
Dewhurst, E.
The verdict on winter

Arms of Nemesis
Catilina's riddle
Schechter, H
Nevermore
Sedley, K.
The Saint John's fern
The weaver's inheritance
Straley, J.
The curious eat themselves
Sussman, S.
Audition for murder
Terry, C.
My beautiful mistress
Todd, M.
Man eater
Wolf whistle
Tremayne, P.
Act of mercy
The monk who vanished
The spider's web
The subtle serpent
Valley of the shadow
Truman, M.
Murder at the F. B. I.
Vine, B.
The brimstone wedding
Walters, M.
The echo
Williams, J. M.
Scherzo
Wilson, D.
The swarm of heaven
Wishart, D.
Germanicus
The Lydian baker

MYTHOLOGY, CELTIC
Mosse, K.
Crucifix Lane

MYTHOLOGY, GREEK
Davidson, C. T.
The priest fainted

NANNIES
Francis, J.
Another man's child
Haslam, J.
Rosy Smith
Mulholland, S.
Woman's work

NAPOLEON I, EMPEROR OF FRANCE, 1796-1821
Gavin, C.
One candle burning

NAPOLEONIC WARS, 1792-1815
Howard, R.
Bonaparte's conquerors
Bonaparte's invaders
Bonaparte's sons
Mallinson, A.
A close run thing

NATIONAL PARKS
Barnes, S.
Rogue lion safaris

NATIONALISM
King, J.
England away

NATIVE AMERICANS
Bryers, P.
The prayer of the bone
Gear, K. O.
People of the masks
Hogan, L.
Solar storms
Knight, A.
Angel eyes
LaFavor, C.
Along the Journey river
Martin, L. J.
Sounding drum
McMurty, L. & Ossana, D.
Zeke and Ned
Taylor, J.
Lakota winds
Treuer, D.
Little
The Hiawatha

NATIVE AMERICANS: BLACKFOOT
Munn, V.
Blackfeet season

NATIVE AMERICANS: CHEROKEE
Conley, R. J.
The Peace Chief

NATIVE AMERICANS: COMANCHE
McMurtry, L.
Comanche moon

NATIVE AMERICANS: LAKOTA-SIOUX
Chiaventone, F. J.
A road we do not know
London, D.
Sun dancer

NETHERLANDS: 20TH CENTURY
Moring, M.
In Babylon
Mulisch, H.
The discovery of heaven

NETHERLANDS: AMSTERDAM
Moggach, D.
Tulip fever

NETHERLANDS: FRISIA
Llewellyn, S.
The shadow in the sands

NEW AGE TRAVELLERS
Hines, J.
Autumn of strangers

NEW ZEALAND: 19TH CENTURY
Corbalis, J.
Tapu

NEW ZEALAND: 1930-59
Cox, M. I.
Holding back the dark

NEW ZEALAND: 1960-80
Aitken, G.
Fifty ways of saying fabulous
Reidy, S.
The visitation

NEW ZEALAND: 1980-2000
Duff, A.
What becomes of the broken hearted?
Gee, M.
Loving ways
Grace, P.
Potiki
Kidman, F.
Ricochet baby
Summers, E.
Caleb's kingdom
Thomas, P.
Guerrilla season

NEWCASTLE UPON TYNE
Waites, M.
Little triggers
Mary's prayer

NEWSPAPER INDUSTRY
Archer, J.
The fourth estate

NICARAGUA: 1980-2000
Goldman, F.
The ordinary seaman

NIGERIA: 1960-80
Okri, B.
Dangerous love
Infinite riches

NIXON, RICHARD MILHOUS, US PRESIDENT, 1913-94
Maxwell, M.
That other lifetime

NOMADIC TRIBES
Lee, M.
The lost tribe

NORFOLK
Barker, R.
Hens dancing
Cooper, B.
The Blacknock woman
The travelling dead
Ferrari, L.
The girl from Norfolk with the flying table
Francis, C.
A dark devotion
Purves, L.
A long walk in wintertime
Saxton, J.
Still waters
Sutton, H.
Bank Holiday Monday

NORTH AFRICA
Nicole, C.
Guns in the desert

NORTH POLE
Barrett, A.
The voyage of the Narwhal

NORTH SEA FERRIES
Callison, B.
Ferry down

NORTHERN IRELAND
Clarke, S.
Underworld
Conway, S.
Damaged
Dunlop, A.
Kissing the frog
McEldowney, E.
Murder at Piper's Gut
O'Connell, S.
Angel bird

NORTHERN IRELAND: DERRY
Anthony, P.
    The fragile peace
Deane, S.
    Reading in the dark
Madden, D.
    One by one in the darkness
Urch, M.
    Violent shadows

NORTHUMBERLAND
Cleeves, A.
    The baby-snatcher
    The crow trap
Collier, I.
    Innocent blood
    Requiem
    Spring tide
Cookson, C.
    The bonny dawn
    The branded man
    The solace of sin
Gill, E.
    Snow angels
Lewis, R.
    Angel of death
    Suddenly as a shadow
    The ghost dancers
    The shape-shifter
Marysmith, J.
    Waterwings
Trotter, J. M.
    Chasing the dream

NORWAY: 1900-29
Prideaux, S.
    Magnetic north

NORWAY: 1930-59
Haff, B. H.
    Shame

NOSTALGIA
Latham, E.
    Silences of the heart

NOTTINGHAM
Gibb, N.
    Blood red sky
Harvey, J.
    Easy meat
    Last rites
    Still water

NOUVEAU RICHE
Thorne, N.
    Old money

NOVELS IN VERSE
Murray, L.
    Fredy neptune

NOVELS WITHIN A NOVEL
Paddock, T.
    Beware the dwarfs

NUCLEAR PLANTS
Graham, A.
    The shaft

NUCLEAR WEAPONS
Kanon, J.
    Los Alamos
Martini, S.
    Critical mass
Millar, P.
    Stealing thunder
Stevenson, R. L.
    Bright star

NUNS
Black, V.
    Vow of adoration
    Vow of compassion
    Vow of poverty
Bragg, M.
    Credo
Day, M.
    Lambs of God
Joseph, A.
    A dark and sinful death
    The quick and the dead
Leon, D.
    The death of faith
Lobb, F.
    The vow
Newman, J.
    Life class
Tremayne, P.
    The monk who vanished
    The subtle serpent

NURSES
Cohen, A.
    Angel of retribution
Craig, M.
    When the lights come on again
Green, C.
    Deadly partners
Horne, U.
    A time to heal

NURSING HOMES
Mitchell, K.
    A rage of innocents

OBESITY

Green, J.
Jemima J.
Leigh, E.
Moving in

OBSESSION

Adams, J.
Final frame
Baker, S.
The loving game
Benison, T.
A rational man
Burdett, J.
A personal history of Thirst
Capriolo, P.
The woman watching
Charles, K.
Unruly passions
Devon, G.
Wedding night
Drake, A.
Master of destiny
Dufort, N.
Defrosting Edmund
Duncan, G.
Hope
Elgin, E.
One summer at Deer's Leap
Emerson, S.
Heat
Erskine, B.
On the edge of darkness
Evans, P.
Freezing
Fairbairns, Z.
Other names
Fernyhough. C.
The auctioneer
Ferris, P.
Infidelity
Forster, M.
Shadow baby
French, N.
Killing me softly
Fritchley, A.
Chicken feed
Hall, M.
The art of breaking glass
Hendricks, V.
Iguana love
Hunter, E.
Privileged conversation
Jardine, Q.
Skinner's mission
Kellerman, F.
Prayers for the dead
Krausser, H.
The great Bagarozy

Listfield, E.
The last good night
Martin, D.
Cul-de-sac
McEwan, I.
Enduring love
McGrath, P.
Asylum
Munoz Molina, A.
Winter in Lisbon
Noll, I.
Hell hath no fury
O'Flanagan, S.
Tomcat in love
Paige, F.
The confetti bed
Perriam, W.
Coupling
Ronan, F.
Lovely
Rosen, J.
Eve's apple
Rufin, J. C.
The Abyssinian
Seaward, B.
The avalanche
Shute, J.
Sex crimes
Slavin, J.
Writing on the water
Smith, C.
Double exposure
Smith, M. A.
New America
Staynes, J. & Storey, M.
Quarry
Taylor, D.
Pig in the middle
Tiffin, P.
Watching Vanessa
Wilkins, C.
The horizontal instrument
Wilson, T.
Cruel to be kind
Zigman, L.
Animal husbandry

OBSTETRICIANS

Cuthbert, M.
The silent cradle

OCCULT

Irwin, R.
Satan wants me
Reed, J.
Dorian

OFFICE LIFE
Barnacle, H.
Day one
Mackesy, S.
The temp
McCabe, J.
Stickleback

OIL RIGS
Brookmyre, C.
One fine day in the middle of the
night

OLD AGE
Glaister, L.
Sheer blue bliss
King, F.
Ash on an old man's sleeve
Middleton, S.
Necessary ends
Minot, S.
Evening
Sobin, G.
A play of light
Sterling, B.
Holy fire
Storey, D.
A serious man
Waugh, H.
The chaplet of pearls

OLD PEOPLE'S HOMES
Aird, C.
Stiff news
Rubens, B.
The waiting game

OLYMPIC GAMES
Bock, D.
Olympia
Cleary, J.
Five ring circus

OPAL MINING
Hospital, J. T.
Oyster
Shaw, P.
The opal seekers

OPERA
Edmonds, L.
Aria

OPERA COMPANIES
Gano, J.
Arias of blood

ORCHESTRAS
Cooper, J.
Appassionata
McVeigh, A.
Ghost music

ORGANISED CRIME
Battison, B.
Flying pigs
Truths not told
Connelly, M.
Trunk music
Duffy, M.
Music in the blood
Hudson, M.
Tell me no secrets
Knox, B.
The counterfeit killers
Lindsey, D. L.
Requiem for a glass heart
Ludlum, R.
The Matarese countdown
Lustbader, E.
Dark homecoming
Masters, A.
The good and faithful servant
Price, R. T.
Grievous
Nickers
Rankin, I.
The hanging garden

ORNITHOLOGISTS
Luard, N.
Silverback

ORPHANAGES
Strayhorn, S. J.
Black night

ORPHANS
Andrews, V.
Orphans
Bradshaw, R.
Alone beneath the heavens
Davidson, D.
The Three Kings
Eaton, P.
Silver Joey
Francis, J.
For the sake of the children
Jeffrey, E.
Far above rubies
McCoy, K.
Cobblestone heroes
Pemberton, V.
Nellie's war
Ross, M.
Tomorrow's tide

OSTRICH FARMING
Landsman, A.
The devil's chimney

OUTLAWS
Fackler, E.
Breaking even

OXFORD
Cato, A.
Still lives
Dexter, C.
Death is now my neighbour
The remorseful day
Doherty, P. C.
The devil's hunt
Marston, A. E.
The stallions of Woodstock
Melville, A.
Role play
Morson, I.
Falconer and the face of God
Falconer and the great beast
Ovenden, K.
The greatest sorrow
Pears, I.
An instance of the fingerpost
Sinclair, J.
Dangerous games
Stallwood, V.
Oxford blue
Oxford fall
Oxford knot
Oxford shift
Strong, T.
The poison tree

PACIFIC ISLANDS
Lancaster, G.
The Saturday girl
Yoshimoto, B.
Amrita

PAEDOPHILES
Battison, B.
Jeopardy's child
Campbell, S.
Touched
Homes, A. M.
The end of Alice
McDermid, V.
A place of execution
Purves, L.
More lives than one
Rankin, I.
Dead souls

PAGANISM
Marysmith, J.
Waterwings

PAGEANTS
Burke, J.
Bareback
Maynard, N.
Pageant

PAINTINGS
Bayley, J.
The red hat
Chadwick, W.
Framed
Hook, P.
The soldier in the wheatfield
Kilmer, N.
Dirty linen
Lipsky, D.
The art fair
Malcolm, J.
Into the vortex
Olshan, J.
Vanitas
Skeggs, D.
The phoenix of Prague
Stephens, K.
Felstead

PAISLEY
Hood, E.
Another day
Neill, I.
Sweet will be the flower

PAKISTAN: 1980-2000
Shamsie, K.
In the city by the sea

PAKISTAN: KARACHI
Sadiq, Z.
38 Bahadurabad

PANAMA CANAL
Zencey, E.
Panama

PAPER MAKING
Davies, J. W.
To the ends of the earth

PARAMEDICS
Connelly, J.
Bringing out the dead

PARANORMAL
Ambrose, D.
Superstition

Geller, U.
Ella

PARAPSYCHOLOGY
Geller, U.
Dead cold
Lawrence, M. C.
Aquarius descending
Murder in Scorpio
The cold heart of Capricorn
Rogan, B.
Suspicion

PARENT TEACHER ASSOCIATIONS
Zubro, M.
Are you nuts?

PARENTS AND CHILDREN
Astley, J.
Every good girl
Seven for a secret
Fenton, K.
Balancing on air
Gordimer, N.
The house gun
Ingman, H.
Waiting at the gate
Kapur, M.
Difficult daughters
Kelly, S.
A complicated woman
Lisle, J.
A perfect match
McPhee, M.
Bright angel time
Price, R.
The promise of rest
Purves, L.
A long walk in wintertime
Ryan, J.
Dismantling Mr. Doyle
Singer, N.
My mother's daughter
Thomas, R.
Moon island
Townsend, S.
Ghost children
Wickham, M.
Swimming pool Sunday

PARODIES
Milligan, S.
Black Beauty

PARTIES
Lord, G.
A party to die for

Parker, U-M.
Secrets of the night

PATHOLOGISTS
Rayner, C.
Fifth member

PEARL FISHING
Morrissey, D.
Tears of the moon

PEEPING TOMS
Taylor, A.
The lover of the grave

PENAL COLONIES
Courtenay, B.
The potato factory
Davies, J. W.
To the ends of the earth
Garner, A.
Strandloper

PENFRIENDS
Blake, C.
Foreign correspondents

PENNINES
Howard, A.
The shadowed hills

PENSIONS
Ormerod, R.
The vital minute

PEPYS, ELIZABETH, WIFE OF SAMUEL
George, S.
The journal of Mrs. Pepys

PERCEPTION
Bernief, J.
Eclipse

PERFUME INDUSTRY
Kessler, D.
The other victim

PERON, EVA, ARGENTINIAN LEADER, 1919-52
Martinez, T. E.
Santa Evita

PERON, JUAN DOMINGO, ARGENTINIAN STATESMAN, 1895-1974
Martinez, T. E.
The Peron novel

PERSECUTION
Clayton, M.
  The word is death
Kennealy, J.
  The forger

PERSIA, ANCIENT
Hudson, J. F.
  Hadassah

PERSONAL DEVELOPMENT COURSES
Bannister, J.
  The Lazarus Hotel

PERU
Guttridge, P.
  Two to tango
Vargas Llosa, M.
  Death in the Andes

PHARMACISTS
Noll, I.
  The pharmacist

PHILATELY
Maitland, B.
  The Chalon heads

PHILIPPINES
Chai, A. J.
  The last time I saw mother
Garland, A.
  The Tessaract
Hawksley, H.
  Absolute measures
Mo, T.
  Renegade or halo?

PHILOSOPHERS
Blevins, W.
  The rock child
Brownrigg, S.
  The metaphysical touch

PHILOSOPHY
Gaarder, J.
  The solitaire mystery
Mulisch, H.
  The discovery of heaven

PHOTOGRAPHERS
Bainbridge, B.
  Master Georgie
Baker, A. L.
  New York Graphic
Bannister, J.
  Critical angle

Bigsby, C.
  Still lives
Clark, R.
  Mr. White's confession
Hammond, G.
  Flamescape
Houston, P.
  Waltzing the cat
Melville, A.
  The eyes of the world
Morrell, D.
  Double image
Palmer, W.
  The pardon of Saint Anne
Rawle, G.
  Diary of an amateur photographer
Sole, R.
  The photographer's wife
Swinfen, A.
  A running tide

PHYSICISTS
Millar, P.
  Stealing thunder

PIANO ACCORDIONS
Proulx, A.
  Accordion crimes

PICARESQUE NOVELS
Bidisha
  Seahorses
Billington, R.
  Magic and fate
De Grazia, D.
  American skin
Donleavy, J. P.
  Wrong information is being given out at Princeton
Drummond, B.
  Bad wisdom
Egolf, T.
  Lord of the barnyard
Farrington, T.
  The Californian book of the dead
Gilfillan, R.
  The snake-oil Dickens man
Girardi, R.
  The pirate's daughter
Grunberg, A.
  Blue Mondays
Hawkins, T.
  The anarchist
Hustvedt, S.
  The enchantment of Lily Dahl
Kluge, P. F.
  Biggest Elvis
Maw, J.
  Nothing but trouble

McInerney, J.
  Model behaviour
Murakami, H.
  The wind-up bird chronicle
North, F.
  Chloe
O'Connell, J.
  The skin palace
Ridley, J.
  Love is a racket
Robbins, H.
  The predators
Sillitoe, A.
  The broken chariot
Thomas, L.
  Chloe's song
Vargas Llosa, M.
  The notebooks of Don Rigoberto
Whyte, C.
  The gay decameron
Wiggins, T.
  Zeitgeist

PIGS
Darrieussecq, M.
  Pig tales

PILGRIMAGES
Blackburn, J.
  The leper's companion
Doherty, P. C.
  A tournament of murders
Robb, C.
  A gift of sanctuary
Tremayne, P.
  Act of mercy

PIONEERS
Holland, C.
  An ordinary woman

PIRACY
Griffin, N.
  The requiem shark
MacLeod, A.
  The changeling
Palliser, M.
  Matthew's prize
Smith, W.
  Birds of prey
Summers, R.
  A safe haven

PLAGUES
Ouellette, P.
  The third pandemic

PLYMOUTH
Thompson, E. V.
  Somewhere a bird is singing

POETS
Crombie, D.
  Dreaming of the bones
Cunningham, M.
  The hours
Smith, M.
  Reprisal

POISON PEN LETTERS
Cohen, A.
  Poisoned pen
Grey, P.
  Good Hope Station
Ingman, H.
  Waiting at the gate

POISONING
Gregory, S.
  A deadly brew
Jecks, M.
  Belladonna at Belstone
Johnston, P.
  Water of death

POKER (GAME)
Gorman, E.
  The poker club

POLAND: 19TH CENTURY
Nattel, L.
  The river midnight

POLAND: 20TH CENTURY
Brierley, D.
  The horizontal woman

POLAND: 1980-2000
Powers, C. T.
  In the memory of the forest

POLICE INFORMERS
Jones, J.
  After Melissa
  Baby talk

POLICE WORK
Abel, K.
  The blue wall
Adams, J.
  Fade to grey
Amis, M.
  Night train
Bannister, J.
  Broken lines
  No birds sing

The counterfeit killers
Krich, R. M.
  Blood money
Lawton, J.
  Old flames
Mahoney, D.
  Black and white
Masters, A.
  The good and faithful servant
McBain, E.
  The big bad city
McGown, J.
  Verdict unsafe
Newman, R.
  Manners
O'Connell, C.
  Killing critics
Olden, M.
  The ghost
Oldham, N.
  Nightmare city
  One dead witness
  The last big job
Palmer, F.
  Black gold
  Dark forest
  Final score
  Hoodwinked
  Red gutter
  Witching hour
Parker, R. B.
  Night passage
  Trouble in Paradise
Parker, T. J.
  Where serpents lie
Paul, B.
  Full frontal murder
Paul, W.
  Sleeping partner
Pawson, S.
  Deadly friends
  Last reminder
  Some by fire
Pearson, R.
  Beyond recognition
Pennac, D.
  The fairy gunmother
Rankin, I.
  Black and blue
  Dead souls
  The hanging garden
Rhea, N.
  Confession
Robb, J. D.
  Ceremony in death
  Glory in death
  Naked in death
  Rapture in death
  Vengeance in death

Rowlands, B.
  An inconsiderate death
Saer, J. J.
  The investigation
Sandford, J.
  Sudden prey
Santiago, S.
  Streets of fire
Scholefield, A.
  Night moves
Taylor, A. G.
  In guilty night
Turnbull, P.
  Fear of drowning
  The man with no face
Walters, M.
  The breaker
Watson, I. K.
  Cops and other robbers
Westermann, J.
  The Honor Farm
Whitehead, B.
  Death at the Dutch House
Williams, T.
  Big Italy

POLITICAL LOBBYISTS
Baker, J.
  Walking with ghosts
Thynne, J.
  The shell house

POLITICAL OPPRESSION
Brierley, D.
  The horizontal woman

POLITICAL PRISONERS
Booth, M.
  The industry of souls

POLITICAL THRILLERS
Adams, J.
  Hard target
Allbeury, T.
  Shadow of a doubt
Archer, J.
  The eleventh commandment
Armstrong, C.
  Heat
Backhouse, F.
  By other means
  Within the walls
Baldacci, D.
  Saving faith
Barnard, R.
  Touched by the dead
Bedell, G.
  Party tricks

Uris, L.
  A god in ruins
Westermann, J.
  Ladies of the night
Whiting, C.
  Death trap
Willett, S.
  The betrayal
Williams, B.
  Stealth bomber
Yallop, D.
  Unholy alliance
York, A.
  Tallent for democracy

POLITICIANS
Butler, G.
  A double coffin
Cameron, J.
  Brown bread in Wengen
Cohen, M. B.
  Brass monkeys
Constantine, K. C.
  Family values
Currie, E.
  A woman's place
Dobbs, M.
  Goodfellowe MP
  The Buddha of Brewer Street
Ellison, R.
  Juneteenth
Flynn, V.
  Term limits
Francis, D.
  10lb penalty
George, E.
  In the presence of the enemy
Greenwood, E. & Grubb, J.
  Body politic
Hannam, V.
  Change of key
  Division belle
Harrod-Eagles, C.
  Blood sinister
Hatfield, K.
  Angels alone
Jowitt, S.
  In the red
Keays, S.
  The black book
Lefcourt, P.
  The woody
Lott, T.
  White City blue
Mahoney, D.
  Black and white
McEwan, I.
  Amsterdam

Moncur, A.
  The harlot's prerogative
Mortimer, J.
  The sound of trumpets
Myerson, J.
  Your father
Ozick, C.
  The Puttermesser papers
Pascoe, D.
  Fox on the run
Patterson, J.
  Jack and Jill
Patterson, R. N.
  No safe place
Pearce, M.
  Death of an effendi
Perry, A.
  Ashworth Hall
Rayner, C.
  Fifth member
Renton, A.
  Maiden speech
Royce, K.
  Shadows
Sheldon, S.
  The best laid plans
Toner, M.
  Seeing the light
Waites, M.
  Little triggers

PONTYPRIDD
Collier, C.
  Broken rainbows
  Past remembering

POP MUSICIANS
Ferrari, L.
  The girl from Norfolk with the flying
    table
Jackson, S.
  Caught up in the rapture
Kluge, P. F.
  Biggest Elvis
Strongman, P.
  Cocaine

POPES
West, M.
  Eminence

PORNOGRAPHERS
O'Connell, J.
  The skin palace

PORNOGRAPHY
Johnson, B.
  Bad moon rising

Larsen, M.
  Uncertainty
Trow, M. J.
  Maxwell's movie
Vinci, S.
  A game we play

PORTLAND, W. J. CAVENDISH-SCOTT-BENTINCK, 5TH DUKE OF
Jackson, M.
  The underground man

PORTSMOUTH
Harry, L.
  Keep smiling through
  Love and laughter
  Moonlight and lovesongs

PORTUGAL: 15TH CENTURY
Zimler, R.
  The last Kabbalist of Lisbon

PORTUGAL: 17TH CENTURY
Vaz, K.
  Mariana

PORTUGAL: 19TH CENTURY
Hodge, J. A.
  Caterina

PORTUGAL: 1960-80
Dearing, S.
  The bull is not killed

PORTUGAL: DOURO
Aspler, T.
  Death on the Douro

PORTUGAL: LISBON
Wilson, R.
  A small death in Lisbon

POST TRAUMATIC STRESS DISORDER
Buchanan, E.
  Margin of error
Lennon, J. R.
  The light of falling stars

POSTAL SERVICE
Medwed, M.
  Mail

POTATO GROWING
Heiney, P.
  Golden apples

POVERTY
Andrews, L.
  Liverpool songbird
  Take these broken wings
Andrews, L. M.
  The ties that bind
Broomfield, J.
  A song in the street
Carr, I.
  Lovers meeting
Chapman, E.
  Damaged fruit
Doyle, R.
  A star called Henry
Flynn, K.
  No silver spoon
Fuentes, C.
  The crystal frontier
Hamilton, R.
  Paradise Lane
  The Bells of Scotland Road
Howard, A.
  Angel meadow
Hutchinson, M.
  Abel's daughter
Jeffrey, E.
  Far above rubies
Jonker, J.
  Sadie was a lady
King, A.
  A handful of sovereigns
Lightfoot, F.
  Manchester pride
Lord, E.
  The turning tides
MacDonald, E.
  Steelworkers Row
Mo, T.
  Renegade or halo?
Murray, A.
  Orphan of Angel Street
Newland, C.
  Society within
Niekerk, M.
  Triomf
O'Neill, G.
  The lights of London
Page, L.
  Any old iron
  At the toss of a sixpence
  Just by chance
Patchett, A.
  Taff
Tate, J.
  Riches of the heart
Thompson, E. V.
  Lewin's Mead
Williams, D.
  Ellie of Elmleigh Square

Katie's kitchen

POWER
Hamer, M.
Predator
Robbins, H.
The stallion

PREACHERS
Robertson, W.
The jagged window

PREGNANCY
Barnes, Z.
Bumps
Cowan, A,
Common ground
Fforde, K.
Life skills
Fuller, J.
A skin diary
Goodwin, S.
Sheer chance
Haran, M.
All that she wants
Jackson, S.
A little surprise
Jacob, A.
Fermentation
Parker, I.
These foolish things

PREHISTORIC ANIMALS
Alten, S.
Meg

PREHISTORIC MAN
Darnton, J.
Neanderthal
Kerr, P.
Esau

PREMONITIONS
Michaels, F.
Split second

PRESIDENTIAL ELECTIONS
Didion, J.
The last thing he wanted
Doyle, R.
Executive action

PRESIDENTS
Herman, R.
Edge of honour

PRESSURE GROUPS
Pearce, M.
The fig tree murder

Phillips, M.
The dancing face

PRIESTS
Adam, P.
Unholy trinity
Cornwell, J.
Fear and favour
Gorman, E.
Harlot's moon
Greeley, A. M.
Happy are the oppressed
Happy are those who mourn
Harris, J.
Chocolat
Kienzle, W. X.
Call no man father
Requiem for Moses
The man who loved God

PRISON CAMPS
Murphy, Y.
The sea of trees

PRISON LIFE
Burke, J.
Half of paradise
Cole, M.
Two women
Gregory, D.
The cornflake house
Joseph, A.
The dying light
MacSweeney, D.
Lovers
St. Aubin de Teran, L.
The palace
Waters, S.
Affinity

PRISONERS OF WAR
Glaister, L.
Easy peasy
Thompson, E. V.
Cast no shadows
White, M. C.
A brother's blood

PRIVATE EYE STORIES
Andrews, P.
Own goals
Arnote, R.
Fast lane
Baker, J.
Death minus zero
King of the streets
Barnes, L.
Cold case

Find my way home
Quick before they catch us
Tripp, M.
Deadly ordeal
Trocheck, K. H.
Heart trouble
Strange brew
Walsh, M.
As time goes by
Wesley, V. W.
No hiding place
Where evil sleeps
Wessel, J.
Pretty ballerina
This far, no further
Wings, M.
She came to the Castro
Winslow, D.
Isle of joy
Womack, S.
Chain of fools
Wright, E.
Death of a Sunday writer

PROPERTY DEVELOPERS
Colborn, N.
The congregation
Gash, J.
Different women dancing
Trevor, J.
Time to die

PROSTITUTES
Belle, J.
Going down
Duncan, G.
Hope
George, E.
In pursuit of the proper sinner
Gregson, J. M.
Girl gone missing
Hall, P.
Perils of the night
Kasischke, L.
Suspicious river
Myerson, J.
Me and the fat man
Oates, J. C.
Man crazy
O'Neill, G.
The lights of London
Roth, J.
The string of pearls
Waters, S.
Tipping the velvet

PROTEST GROUPS
Clayton, M.
The prodigal's return

Haymon, S. T.
Death of a hero
Hey, S.
Sudden unprovided death
Kingston, B.
Laura's way
Rendell, R.
Road rage
Thomas, P.
Guerrilla season

PROVINCIAL TOWNS
Baker, L.
The flamingo rising
Cook, T. H.
Breakheart Hill
Cory, C.
The guest
Dallas, S.
The Persian Pickle Club
Dobyns, S.
The church of dead girls
Eidson, T.
All God's children
Grazebrook, S.
Page two
Hayman, C.
Missing
Hoffman, A.
Here on earth
Local girls
Peck, D.
Now it's time to say goodbye
Pewsey, E.
Unholy harmonies
Poolman, J.
Interesting facts about the State of
Arizona
Rogan, B.
Rowing in Eden
Santiago, E.
America's dream
Spencer, L.
Then came heaven
Stubbs, J.
The witching time
Thompson, G.
A shop in the High Street
Sophie Street
Watson, L.
White crosses
Wilson, P.
Noah, Noah

PSYCHIATRIC HOSPITALS
Mina, D.
Garnethill

PSYCHIATRISTS

Bannister, J.
    The primrose switchback
Black, E.
    The broken hearts club
Carr, C.
    The angel of darkness
Davidson, T.
    Scar culture
Krausser, H.
    The great Bagarozy
McGrath, P.
    Asylum
Title, E.
    Chain reaction

PSYCHICS

Bonansinga, J. R.
    Bloodhound
Geller, U.
    Ella
Glass, J.
    Eyes

PSYCHOLOGICAL PROFILING

Asher, H.
    The predators
McDermid, V.
    The wire in the blood

PSYCHOLOGICAL THRILLERS

Ablow, K. R.
    Denial
Appignanesi, L.
    The dead of winter
Auerbach, J.
    Catch your breath
Baer, W. C.
    Kiss me, Judas
Baker, K.
    Reckoning
Baker, S.
    Falling in deep
Bannister, J.
    The Lazarus Hotel
Beckett, S.
    Where there's smoke
Belsky, R.
    Loverboy
Blauner, P.
    The intruder
Brenchley, C.
    Dispossession
Brett, B.
    Dreaming of water
Brindle, J.
    The hiding game
    The seeker

Buchanan, D.
    Different rules
Campbell, B.
    Don't talk to strangers
Caputo, P.
    Equation for evil
Cave, E.
    The lair
Charles, K.
    Unruly passions
Clark, M. H.
    Pretend you don't see her
Clark, M. J.
    Do you promise not to tell?
Cohen, S. M.
    Becker's ring
Connelly, M.
    The poet
Cook. T. H.
    Instruments of night
Craig, K.
    Closer
Curtis, J.
    The confessor
Davis, R.
    The right to silence
Deaver, J.
    The Coffin Dancer
Delaney, F.
    The amethysts
Dobyns, S.
    The church of dead girls
Doughty, L.
    Dance with me
Dronfield, J.
    Resurrecting Salvador
Due, T.
    My soul to keep
Dunant, S.
    Transgressions
Fielding, J.
    Missing pieces
Ford, L.
    Double exposure
Fox, , Z. A.
    Cradle and all
    When the wind blows
French, J.
    The killer within
French, N.
    The safe house
Fyfield, F.
    Blind date
    Staring at the light
    Without consent
Galleymore, F.
    Safe
Glaister, L.
    Sheer blue bliss

140

I spy
Woods, S.
  Inperfect strangers
Yglesias, R.
  Dr. Neruda's cure for evil
Yorke, M.
  A question of belief
  The price of guilt

PSYCHOLOGISTS
Kennett, S.
  Gray matter
Kline, P.
  Living in dread

PSYCHOPATHS
Airth, R.
  River of darkness
Bedford, M.
  Acts of revision
Ferguson, F.
  With intent to kill
Hall, P.
  The Italian girl
Huberman, C.
  Eminent domain
Johansen, I.
  The killing game
Olden, M.
  The ghost
Sandford, J.
  Mind prey
Starling, B.
  Messiah
Templeton, A.
  Night and silence
Walker, R. W.
  Darkest instinct
Walters, M.
  The breaker

PSYCHOTHERAPY
Hoskyns, T.
  The talking cure
Kershaw, V.
  Juicy Lucy
MacSweeney, D.
  Lovers

PUBLIC EXECUTIONERS
Binding, T.
  A perfect execution

PUBLISHERS
McDermid, V.
  Booked for murder

PUBLISHING
Baylis, M.
  Stranger than Fulham
Goldsmith, O.
  Bestseller
Pennac, D.
  Write to kill

PUERTO RICO
Ferre, R.
  Eccentric neighbourhoods
Spark, D.
  Coconuts for the saint

PUPPY FARMING
Burgh, A.
  Breeders

PYRRHUS, SON OF ACHILLES
Merlis, M.
  Pyrrhus

QUILTING
Brown, L.
  Double wedding ring
Rice, L.
  Cloud nine

RABBIS
Kemelman, H.
  That day the Rabbi left town

RABBITS
Adams, R.
  Tales from Watership Down

RACE RELATIONS
Danticat, E.
  The farming of bones
Devoto, P. C.
  My last days as Roy Rogers
George, E.
  Deception on his mind
Katzenbach, J.
  Hart's war
Phillips, C.
  The nature of blood
Rhodes, J. P.
  Magic city

RACISM
Caputo, P.
  Equation for evil
Ellison, R.
  Juneteenth
French, A.
  I can't wait on God
Hall, P.
  Dead on arrival

Leitch, M.
  The smoke king
Matthiessen, P.
  Lost man's river
Peck, D.
  Now it's time to say goodbye
Wideman, J. C.
  The cattle killing

RADIO BROADCASTING
Fenton, K.
  Balancing on air
Kurland, M.
  The girl in the high-heeled shoes
Paling, C.
  The silent sentry

RADIO JOURNALISTS
Kessler, D.
  Tarnished heroes
Niles, C.
  Crossing live

RADIO SERIES, NOVELS BASED ON
Toye, J.
  The Archers; family ties
  The Archers; looking for love

RAILWAY ENGINEERING
Jackson, J.
  The iron road
Jacobs, J.
  Jessie
Wiggin, H.
  Trouble on the wind

RAIN-MAKERS
Moloney, S.
  A dry spell

RAMESES II, EGYPTIAN PHARAOH, 1304-1237BC
Jacq, C.
  The battle of Kadesh
  The son of the light
  The temple of a million years

RAPE
Ashford, J.
  Loyal disloyalty
Davis, R.
  The right to silence
Fyfield, F.
  Without consent
Harvey, J.
  Easy meat

McGown, J.
  Verdict unsafe
Pawson, S.
  Deadly friends
Tripp, M.
  Deadly ordeal
Walters, M.
  The breaker

RAPISTS
Ross, A.
  Shot in the dark
Van Pelt, N.
  Stomp

RASPUTIN, GRIGORI, RUSSIAN ELDER, 1871-1916
Armitage, A.
  A winter serpent

READING
Schlink, B.
  The reader

RECEPTIONISTS
Forrester, A. G.
  Ringing for you

RECLUSES
Wall, A.
  The lightning cage

RECOVERED MEMORY SYNDROME
Nevin, J.
  Past recall

REDDITCH, WORCESTERSHIRE
Fraser, S.
  The imperialists

REDUNDANCY
Heffernan, W.
  The dinosaur club
Lord, G.
  Sorry, we're going to have to let you go
Westlake, D. E.
  The axe

REFUGEES
Swinfen, A.
  The travellers

REGISTRY OFFICES
Saramago, J.
  All the names

REGRESSION
Deveraux, J.
 Legend
Greeley, A. M.
 Irish lace
Grimsley, J.
 My drowning
Long, J.
 Ferney
Tanner, J.
 The shores of midnight

REHABILITATION CLINICS
Keyes, M.
 Rachel's holiday

REINCARNATION
Pullinger, K.
 Weird sister

RELATIONSHIPS
Barfoot, J.
 Some things about flying
Hauptmann, G.
 In search of an impotent man
Kureishi, H.
 Intimacy

RELICS
Siebert, S.
 Cleopatra's needle

RELIGIONS
Clement, C.
 Theo's odyssey

RELIGIOUS COMMUNITIES
Dunn, S.
 The light of the body

RELIGIOUS CULTS
Campion, A.
 Holy smoke
Due, T.
 My soul to keep
Mann, J.
 Hanging fire
Walker, M. W.
 Under the beetle's cellar

RELIGIOUS FANATICS
Harrod-Eagles, C.
 Blood lines
Myerson, J.
 The touch
Smith, M. A.
 New America

RELIGIOUS FUNDAMENTALISM
Collins, L.
 Tomorrow belongs to us

RELIGIOUS RELICS
Behrens, R.
 The lost scrolls of King Solomon
King, L. R.
 A letter of Mary
Macdonald, M.
 Ghost walk
Wood, B.
 The prophetess

RELIGIOUS SECTS
Macaulay, T.
 Brutal truth

REMORSE
Wilson, T.
 Cruel to be kind

REPENTANCE
Mosley, W.
 Always outnumbered, always
 outgunned

RESEARCHERS
Preston, C.
 Jackie by Josie

RESTAURANTS
Letts, B.
 The Honk and Holler opening soon
Neel, J.
 To die for

RESURRECTION
Klavan, A.
 Hunting down Amanda

RETRIBUTION
Cohen, A.
 Angel of retribution

REUNIONS
Carroll, J.
 The marriage of sticks
Cartwright, J.
 Leading the cheers
Crane, T.
 Siena summer
Dewar, I.
 It could happen to you
Drury, A.
 Public men
Ellis, K.
 The Armada boy

Ewing, B.
  The actresses
Falconer, C.
  Disappeared
Hucker, H.
  Trials of friendship
Hunter, A.
  Over here
Larkin, M.
  Full circle
McCrum, R.
  Suspicion
McNaught, J.
  Night whispers
Richards, E.
  Every day
Sallis, S.
  Come rain or shine
Smith, C.
  Family reunion

REVENANTS
Blacker, T.
  Revenance

REVENGE
Anthony, E.
  The legacy
Badenoch, A.
  Driver
Bedford, M.
  Acts of revision
Bolitho, J.
  Finger of fate
Brown, D.
  The tin man
Browne, G. C.
  Ghosts in sunlight
Burke, J.
  Death by marzipan
Burley, W. J.
  Wycliffe and the redhead
Butler, G.
  Coffin's ghost
Charles, P.
  Fountain of sorrow
Conran, S.
  The revenge of Mimi Quinn
Cook, S.
  Rotten apple
Corley, E.
  Requiem mass
Dershowitz, A. M.
  Just revenge
Eccles, M.
  Cast a cold eye
  The Superintendent's daughter
Fiennes, R.
  The sett

Fotheringham, P. M.
  Seasnake
Fox, , Z. A.
  When the wind blows
Fullerton, A.
  Wave cry
Gill, B.
  The death of an Irish sea wolf
Gorman, E.
  Runner in the dark
Granger, A.
  A word after dying
Gray, C.
  Crossbow
Gulvin, J.
  Close quarters
Hamilton, R.
  The corner house
Holt, H.
  Dead and buried
  The only good lawyer
James, P. D.
  A certain justice
Jardine, Q.
  Murmuring the judges
  Skinner's ghosts
Jecks, M.
  Moorland hanging
Kerr, P.
  A five year plan
Kessler, D.
  Reckless justice
La Plante, L.
  Mind kill
Lambkin, D.
  The hanging tree
Leather, S.
  The tunnel rats
Lord, G.
  A party to die for
Lyons, D.
  Dog days
Magnan, P.
  The murdered house
Martin, D.
  Cul-de-sac
Masters, A.
  I want him dead
Masters, P.
  And none shall sleep
Melville, J.
  Revengeful death
Miller, J. R.
  The last family
Morgan, S.
  Delphinium blues
O'Connell, C.
  Flight of the stone angel

Oldham, N.
　One dead witness
Palmer, F.
　Final score
Patterson, J.
　Cat and mouse
Pemberton, L.
　Dancing with shadows
Penn, J.
　Bridal shroud
Pottinger, S.
　A slow burning
Power, M. S.
　Dealing with Kranze
Pullinger, K.
　Weird sister
Robinson, P.
　HMS Unseen
Rogers, J.
　Island
Rowlands, B.
　Smiling at death
Sandford, J.
　Sudden prey
Scanlan, P.
　Mirror, mirror
Scholefield, A.
　Night moves
Shames, L.
　Virgin heat
Simpson. D.
　Dead and gone
Stainforth, D.
　Intimate enemy
Swindells, M.
　Sunstroke
Trevor, J.
　The same corruption there
Wilson, J.
　Flatmate
Woodrell, D.
　Tomato red

REVOLUTIONARIES
Roig, J. M.
　The landscape collector

REVOLUTIONS
Cordell, A.
　Send her victorious

RHODES, CECIL, SOUTH AFRICAN STATESMAN, 1853-1902
Harries, A.
　Manly pursuits

RITUAL MURDER
Harstad, D.
　Eleven days

ROBBERY
Branton, M.
　The house of whacks
Bunker, E.
　Dog eat dog
Gash, J.
　The rich and the profane
Greeley, A. M.
　The bishop and the three kings
Hammond, G.
　A running jump
Hebden, J.
　Pel and the precious parcel
　Pel the patriarch
Hodge, J. A.
　Unsafe hands
Joss, M.
　Funeral music
Lansdale, J. R.
　Freezer burn
Leonard, E.
　Out of sight
Lovesey, P.
　Bloodhounds
Ormerod, R.
　Final toll
Pawson, S.
　Some by fire
Phillips, M.
　The dancing face
Rowlands, B.
　An inconsiderate death
Spencer, S.
　The paradise job
Summers, J.
　Crime and ravishment
Whitehead, B.
　Death at the Dutch House

ROBSART, AMY, WIFE OF ROBERT DUDLEY, EARL OF LEICESTER, D. 1560
Buckley, F.
　The Robsart mystery

ROCK MUSICIANS
Caveney, P.
　Bad to the bone
Cutler, J.
　Dying for millions
Earnshaw, T.
　Helium
Edmonds, L.
　Losing you
Guttridge, P.
　Two to tango
Kennedy, P.
　The Exes

Leonard, E.
  Be cool
McDermid, V.
  Blue genes
Perrotta, T.
  The wishbones
Rathbone, J.
  Trajectories
Roome, A.
  Bad Monday
Sampson, K.
  Powder
Staynes, J. & Storey, M.
  Quarry

ROLE REVERSAL
Mourby, A.
  We think the world of him
Whittaker, O.
  The house husband

ROMANIA: 1980-2000
Bailey, P.
  Kitty and Virgil
Manea, N.
  The black envelope
Muller, H.
  The land of green plums

ROMANS IN BRITAIN
Kearsley, S.
  The shadowy horses
Wishart, D.
  The horse coin

ROME, ANCIENT
Davis, L.
  A dying light in Corduba
  One virgin too many
  The course of honour
  Three hands in the fountain
  Two for the lions
Jackman, S.
  Death wish
Leckie, R.
  Scipio
Massie, A.
  Antony
  Nero's heirs
McCullough, C.
  Caesar
  Caesar's women
Saylor, S.
  A murder on the Appian Way
  Arms of Nemesis
  Catilina's riddle
  Rubicon
Stewart, J.
  The centurion

Todd, M.
  Jail bait
  Man eater
  Virgin territory
  Wolf whistle
Wishart, D.
  Germanicus
  Nero
  Sejanus
  The Lydian baker

ROMNEY MARSH
Lake, D.
  Death on the Romney Marsh

ROWING
Dunn, C.
  Dead in the water

ROYAL FAMILY
Preston, P.
  Bess
Vickers, E.
  The way of gentleness

ROYALTY
Benison, C. C.
  Death at Buckingham Palace
Norman, D.
  Shores of darkness
Roth, J.
  The string of pearls

RUNAWAYS
Crewe, C.
  The last to know
Greenwood, T.
  Breathing water

RUNNING
Foster, D.
  In the new country

RURAL AREAS, PRESERVATION OF
North, S.
  The lie of the land

RURAL LIFE
Anderson-Dargatz, G.
  The cure for death by lightning
Barker, R.
  Hens dancing
Bingham, C.
  The kissing garden
Brewis, H.
  Night shift
Dawson, J.
  Trick of the light

Elis, I. F.
   Shadow of the sickle
Gebler, C.
   How to murder a man
Grace, P.
   Potiki
Grimsley, J.
   Winter birds
Hayes, K.
   Cloud music
Horwood, W.
   The Willows at Christmas
Kavanagh, P.
   Gaff topsails
Lively, P.
   Heat wave
MacDonald, E.
   Catch the moment
Marshall, S.
   A late lark singing
O'Riordan, K.
   The boy in the moon
Russell, N.
   The dried-up man
Sebald, W. G.
   The rings of Saturn
Stranger, J.
   The guardians of Staghill
Taylor, A.
   The woman of the house
Woodman, R.
   Captain of the Caryatid

RUSSIA: 19TH CENTURY
Armitage, A.
   A winter serpent
Heaven, C.
   The love child
Pearce, M.
   Dmitri and the milk-drinkers
   Dmitri and the one-legged lady

RUSSIA: 20TH CENTURY
Kharitanov, M.
   Lines of fate
Makine, A.
   Le testament Francais
Nicole, C.
   Death of a tyrant

RUSSIA: 1900-29
Carlisle, H.
   The idealists
Ironside, E.
   The accomplice
Nicole, C.
   The red gods
Solzhenitsyn, A.
   November 1916

RUSSIA: 1930-59
Kharitanov, M.
   Under house arrest
Rybakov, A.
   Dust and ashes

RUSSIA: 1960-80
Booth, M.
   The industry of souls

RUSSIA: 1980-2000
Harris, R.
   Archangel
Jones, M.
   Caviar
Robertson, W.
   The self-made woman
Savarin, J. J.
   Horsemen in the shadows

RUSSIA: 2000-
Forsyth, F.
   Icon

RUSSIA: MOSCOW
Ratushinskaya, I.
   Fictions and lies
Wroe, G.
   Slaphead

RUSSIA: ST PETERSBURG
Creswell, S.
   Sam Golod
Richards, J.
   The gods of fortune

RUSSIAN MAFIA
Jones, M.
   Caviar

RUSSIAN REVOLUTION, 1917-21
Spencer, S.
   The silent land

RUSSIANS ABROAD: FRANCE
Makine, A.
   The crime of Olga Arbyeline

S. A. S.
Clarke, S.
   Operation Millennium
   Opium road
Howard, J.
   Blood money
   Direct action
Kerrigan, J.
   Revenge!
   Surprise attack

Ryan, C.
  Stand by, stand by
  Tenth man down
  Zero option
Whiting, C.
  The Balkan chase

S. B. S.
Blake, I.
  The Burma offensive
Harding, D.
  Operation Stormwind
  The Finland mission

SABOTAGE
Robertson, G.
  The Sunday man

SAFARI PARKS
Ross, J.
  Murder! murder! burning bright

SAHARA DESERT
Wilson, G.
  The Carthaginian hoard

SAILING
Purves, L.
  Regatta

SAINTS
Roberts, M.
  Impossible saints

**SALADIN, SULTAN OF EGYPT
AND SYRIA, 1138-93**
Ali, T.
  The book of Saladin

SALESMEN
Greensted, R.
  Raw nerve
Kennedy, D.
  The job

SALFORD
Connor, A.
  Midnight's smiling

SALVAGE
Stevenson, R. L.
  Torchlight

SALVATION ARMY
Thompson, E. V.
  Somewhere a bird is singing

SAMOA
Figiel, S.
  Where we once belonged

SATANISM
Taylor, A.
  The four last things

SATELLITES, COMMUNICATION
Smethurst, W.
  Pasiphae

SATIRES
Baddiel, D.
  Whatever love means
Barnes, J.
  England, England
Berens, J.
  The highwayman
Blinn, J.
  The aardvark is ready for war
Brussig, T.
  Heroes like us
Dooling, R.
  Brainstorm
Doughty, L.
  Honey-dew
Duffy, S.
  Singling out the couples
Dunn, S.
  The light of the body
Eberstadt, F.
  When the sons of heaven meet the
    daughters of the Earth
Feeny, C.
  Musical chairs
Fowler, B.
  Scepticism Inc.
Goldsmith, O.
  The switch
Janowitz, T.
  A certain age
Millet, L.
  Omnivore
Norwich, W,
  Learning to drive
Oakley, A.
  Overheads
Smith, R.
  I must confess
Sosnowski, D.
  Rapture
Sutcliffe, W.
  Are you experienced?
Tesich, S.
  Karoo

Williams, S.
  Metal fatigue
Wood, N. L.
  Faraday's orphans
Zahn, T.
  Vision of the future

SCIENTIFIC RESEARCH
Davies, J.
  The fourth dimension
Goddard, R.
  Out of the sun
Mezrich, B.
  Threshold
Robinson, J.
  The monk's disciples

SCIENTISTS
Appignanesi, L.
  The things we do for love
Hewson, D.
  Solstice
McGrail, A.
  Mrs. Einstein
Scott, H.
  Skeptic

SCIPIO AFRICANUS, ROMAN GENERAL, 236-182BC
Leckie, R.
  Scipio

SCOTLAND: 10TH CENTURY
Tranter, N.
  High kings and Vikings

SCOTLAND: 11TH CENTURY
Drake, S.
  Come the morning

SCOTLAND: 13TH CENTURY
Tranter, N.
  Envoy extraordinary
  Sword of state

SCOTLAND: 15TH CENTURY
Tranter, N.
  A flame for the fire
  The lion's whelp

SCOTLAND: 16TH CENTURY
Davis, M. T.
  Burning ambition
Dunbar, I.
  The Queen's bouquet
Tannahill, R.
  Fatal majesty
Tranter, N.
  A flame for the fire

A rage of regents
  The Marchman

SCOTLAND: 17TH CENTURY
Gleeson, J.
  The moneymaker
Tranter, N.
  Poetic justice
Whyte, C.
  The warlock of Strathearn

SCOTLAND: 19TH CENTURY
Blair, E.
  An apple from Eden
Fraser, C. M.
  Noble seed
Knight, A.
  Murder by appointment
  The Coffin Lane murders
MacDonald, E.
  Catch the moment
  Kirkowen's daughter
Short, A.
  The herring summer
Stirling, J
  The island wife
  The wind from the hills
Withall, M.
  The gorse in bloom

SCOTLAND: 20TH CENTURY
O'Flanagan, S.
  Our fathers

SCOTLAND: 1900-29
Blair, E.
  Flower of Scotland
Craig, M.
  The river flows on
Davidson, D.
  Blood sinister
  The Three Kings
Davis, M. T.
  The Clydesiders
Douglas, A.
  Catherine's land
Hood, E.
  Another day
Muir, K.
  Suffragette city
Neill, I.
  Sweet will be the flower
Paige, F.
  The lonely shore
Ramsay, E.
  Harvest of courage
  Walnut shell days
Stirling, J.
  The piper's tune

Withall, M.
  Where the wild thyme grows

SCOTLAND: 1930-59
Blair, E.
  Goodnight, sweet prince
Craig, M.
  The river flows on
Davidson, D.
  The girl with the creel
Douglas, A.
  As the years go by
  Catherine's land
Henderson, M.
  The holy city
Kay, N.
  Gift of love
  Lost dreams
MacDonald, E.
  Steelworkers Row
Massie, A.
  Shadows of empire
McNeill, E.
  Money troubles
Owens, A.
  For the love of Willie
Ramsay, E.
  The quality of mercy
Stirling, J.
  Prized possessions
Withall, M.
  Fields of heather

SCOTLAND: 1960-80
Dillon, D.
  Itchycooblue
Fraser, C. M.
  A Rhanna mystery

SCOTLAND: 1980-2000
Fraser, C. M.
  Wild is the day
Hood, E.
  Time and again
Knox, B.
  The counterfeit killers
Raife, A.
  Belonging
  Grianan
Scottoline, L.
  Rough justice
Warner, A.
  The sopranos

SCOTLAND: BORDERS
Burke, J.
  Bareback
Hammond, G.
  A shocking affair

Follow that gun
  Sink or swim
Kearsley, S.
  The shadowy horses
Tranter, N.
  The Marchman

SCOTLAND: FIFE
Hammond, G.
  Dogsbody
Huth, A.
  The wives of the fishermen
Smart, H.
  The wild garden
Veevers, M.
  Bloodlines

SCOTLAND: HEBRIDES
Denham, B.
  Black rod
Lingard, A.
  Figure in a landscape
McLaren, J.
  7th sense
Withall, M.
  The gorse in bloom

SCOTLAND: HIGHLANDS
Duffy, M.
  Music in the blood
Holms, J.
  Foreign body
Knox, B.
  Blood proof
Moffat, G.
  A wreath of dead moths
Raife, A.
  Sun on snow
  The larach
Strong, T.
  The death pit
Withall, M.
  Fields of heather
  Where the wild thyme grows

SCOTLAND: ISLANDS
Swinfen, A.
  A running tide

SCREEN WRITERS
Wheeler, P.
  Losing the plot

SEA STORIES
Carey, L.
  The mermaids singing

SEA STORIES: AIRCRAFT CARRIERS
Greeley, A. M.
  Blackie at sea

SEA STORIES: CRUISERS
Titchmarsh, A.
  The last lighthouse keeper

SEA STORIES: FREIGHTERS
Llewellyn, S.
  The iron hotel
Medland, M.
  Point of honour

SEA STORIES: LINERS
Beaven, D.
  Acts of mutiny
Hansen, E. F.
  Psalm at journey's end
Lord, G.
  A party to die for
Winterson, J.
  Gut symmetries
Woodman, R.
  Act of terror

SEA STORIES: MERCHANT SHIPS
Woodman, R.
  The cruise of the "Commissioner"

SEA STORIES: SAILING SHIPS
Freemantle, B.
  The Mary Celeste
Garrison, P.
  Fire and ice
Griffin, N.
  The requiem shark
Kinsolving, W.
  Mister Christian
Palliser, M.
  Matthew's prize
Parkinson, D.
  The fox and the faith
Smith, W.
  Birds of prey
Woodman, R.
  Under sail

SEA STORIES: SUBMARINES
Cobb, J.
  Stormdragon
DiMercurio, M.
  Barracuda final bearing
  Piranha: firing point
Fullerton, A.
  Final dive

Robinson, P.
  HMS Unseen
  Kilo class
  Nimitz class
Smedley, R. B.
  Hidden strengths

SEA STORIES: YACHTS
Llewellyn, S.
  The shadow in the sands
Pizzey, E.
  The wicked world of women

SEARCH FOR IDENTITY
Allen, C. V.
  Somebody's baby
Brandreth, G.
  Who is Nick Saint?
Dorfman, A.
  The nanny and the iceberg
Duffy, M.
  Restitution
Frederiksson, M.
  Simon and the oaks
Glanfield, J.
  The cuckoo wood
Hegi, U.
  Salt dancers
King, R.
  Alba
Kundera, M.
  Identity
Lawrenson, D.
  The moonbathers
Levy, A.
  Fruit of the lemon
Lyons, G.
  Daniella's decision
Marciano, F.
  Rules of the wild
Matthews, C.
  More to life than this
Morrow, B.
  Giovanni's gift
Oldfield, P.
  A woman alone
Paton Walsh, J.
  The serpentine cave
Rayner, A.
  An accidental daughter
Roy, L.
  Lady Moses
Saramago, J.
  All the names
Siddons, A. R.
  Up island
Singer, N.
  My mother's daughter

Stuart, A.
Barefoot angel

SEASIDE ROCK
Thornton, M.
A stick of Blackpool rock

SEASIDE TOWNS
Brayfield, C.
Sunset
Connolly, J.
Summer things
Craze, G.
By the shore
Flynn, R.
A fine body of men
A public body
Busy body
The body beautiful
Harrison, S.
That was then
Maskell, V.
Shopkeepers
Rees, E.
Undertow
Thompson, G.
A corner of a small town
Thorne, M.
Tourist

SECOND MARRIAGES
Alexander, K.
Love and duty
Blake, C.
Second wives
Henley, J.
Stepping aside
Mackie, G.
Second marriage
Monk, C.
Different lives

SECRET SOCIETIES
Read, P. P.
Knights of the Cross
Wall, A.
Bless the thief

SECRETS
Bayley, J.
George's lair
Delaney, F.
Pearl
Hunter, S.
Black light
Irving, C.
The spring
Kalberer, R.
Lethal

Purcell, D.
Sky
Ramus, D.
The gravity of shadows
Royle, N.
The matter of the heart
Scholefield, A.
The drowning mark
Simons, P.
Red leaves
Sinclair, E.
The path through the woods
Watson, S.
The perfect treasure
White, G.
The beggar bride

SECURITY EXPERTS
Dailey, J.
Illusions

SECURITY SERVICES
Paretsky, S.
Hard time
Rucka, G.
Smoker
Urban, M. L.
The illegal

SEDUCTION
Harvey, S.
Misbehaving

SELF-MUTILATION
Levenkron, S.
The luckiest girl in the world

SENSES
Hodgson, B.
The sensualist

SEPOY REBELLION, 1856
Sinclair, K.
From a far country

SERIAL KILLINGS
Adams, J.
Final frame
Alexie, S.
Indian killer
Aspler, T.
The beast of Barbaresco
Battison, B.
Mirror image
Belsky, R.
Loverboy
Playing dead
Bolitho, J.
Finger of fate

Bonner, H.
   A fancy to kill for
Butler, G.
   A grave Coffin
Cannell, S. J.
   Final victim
Carr, C.
   The angel of darkness
Case, J.
   The genesis code
Child, L.
   Killing floor
Connelly, M.
   The poet
Connolly, J.
   Every dead thing
Conrad, P.
   Limousine
Cornwell, P.
   Unnatural exposure
Curtis, J.
   The confessor
Davis, K.
   Possessions
Davis, R.
   The right to silence
Deaver, J.
   The bone collector
Glass, J.
   Eyes
Grippando, J.
   The informant
Hall, J. W.
   Buzz cut
Hall, O. M.
   Ambrose Bierce and the Queen of
      Spades
Hutson, S.
   Purity
Janes, J. R.
   Sandman
Kadow, J.
   Shooting stars
Katzenbach, J.
   State of mind
Kennett, S.
   Gray matter
King, L. R.
   With child
Krich, R. M.
   Speak no evil
Lean, F.
   The reluctant investigator
Lovesey, P.
   Death duties
McDermid, V.
   The wire in the blood
Melo, P.
   The killer

Melville, J.
   Stone dead
   The woman who was not there
Nabb, M.
   The monster of Florence
O'Nan, S.
   The speed queen
Passman, D.
   The visionary
Patterson, J.
   Pop goes the weasel
Pennac, D.
   The fairy gunmother
Pepper, M.
   Man on a murder cycle
Rayner, C.
   Fifth member
Rees, E.
   The book of dead authors
   Undertow
Reichert, M. Z.
   Deja dead
Roberts, N.
   Montana sky
Robinson, L. R.
   Intensive care
Ross, A.
   Shot in the dark
Rowlands, B.
   Smiling at death
Saer, J. J.
   The investigation
Sandford, J.
   Sudden prey
Sheldon, S.
   Tell me your dreams
Smith, C.
   Family reunion
   Kensington Court
Smith, M. T.
   An American killing
Starling, B.
   Messiah
Strayhorn, S. J.
   Black night
Sullivan, M. T.
   Ghost dance
Title, E.
   Bleeding hearts
Walker, R. W.
   Darkest instinct
Waterhouse, J.
   Shadow walk
Wingfield, R. D.
   Winter Frost

SERIAL RAPISTS
Adams, J.
   Fade to grey

SERINGAPATAM, SIEGE OF, 1799
Cornwell, B.
Sharpe's tiger

SERVANTS
Davidson, D.
The Three Kings
Davis, M. T.
The Clydesiders
Dickinson, M.
Chaff upon the wind
Dymoke, J.
The making of Molly March
Hutchinson, M.
No place of angels
Jeffrey, E.
Hannah Fox
McDonald, R.
Mr. Darwin's shooter
Minton, M.
Fortune's daughter
Montague, J.
Child of the mist
Ross, M.
Like a diamond

SEX
Baker, S.
A certain seduction
The loving game
Davis, B.
The midnight partner
Duncan, G.
Hope
Galleymore, F.
Safe
Gambotto, A.
The pure weight of the heart
Gordon, M.
Spending
Hendricks, V.
Miami purity
Hole, J.
The ultimate aphrodisiac
Jacobson, H.
No more Mister Nice Guy
Kempadoo, O.
Buxton spice
Landsman, A.
The devil's chimney
Lette, K.
Altar ego
Margolis, S.
Neurotica
McKinney, M.
In the dark
Mondesir, S.
Acquired tastes

North, F.
Sally
Oudot, S.
Virtual love
Prantera, A.
Zoe Trope
Roth, H.
From bondage
Segrave, E.
Ten men
Shute, J.
Sex crimes
Simons, P.
The benefits of passion
Stimson, T.
Pole position
Vinci, S.
A game we play
Walker, F.
Snap happy

SEX CRIMES
Flynn, R.
A fine body of men

SHAKESPEARE, WILLIAM, ENGLISH PLAYWRIGHT, 1564-1616
Baldwin, M.
Dark lady
Nye, R.
The late Mr. Shakespeare

SHEEP FARMING
Kuban, K.
Marchlands
McKinley, T.
Matilda's last waltz
Shaw, P.
A cross of stars

SHEFFIELD
Bedford, M.
Exit, orange and red
Jeffrey, E.
Hannah Fox

SHETLAND ISLES
Short, A.
The herring summer

SHIPBUILDING
Andrews, L. M.
From this day forth
Stirling, J.
The piper's tune

SINGLE WOMEN
Ellis, J.
Second time around
Roberts, Y.
The trouble with single women

SINO-JAPANESE WAR
Chang, M.
A choice of evils

SISTERS
Andrews, L. M.
Angels of mercy
Ansa, T. M.
Ugly ways
Birch, C.
Little sister
Bradshaw, R.
Reach for tomorrow
Brookner, A.
Falling slowly
Close, A.
Forspoken
Connor, A.
Green Baize road
Crane, T.
Siena summer
Dunmore, H.
Talking to the dead
Fine, A.
Telling Liddy
Forbes, L.
Bombay ice
Garcia, C.
The Aguero sisters
Goring, A.
No enemy but winter
Hamilton, R.
Miss Honoria West
Hanauer, C.
My sister's bones
My sister's bones
Harte, L.
Losing it
Heyman, K.
Keep your hands on the wheel
Hoffman, A.
Practical magic
Horne, U.
When morning comes
Howard, A.
Angel meadow
Inyama, I.
Sistas on a vibe
Jonker, J.
Try a little tenderness
Kelly, S.
A sense of duty

Lancaster, G.
The precious gift
Larkin, M.
Full circle
Levy, A.
Never far from nowhere
Lipman, E.
The ladies man
Madden, D.
One by one in the darkness
Margolis, S.
Sisteria
Martella, M.
Maddy goes to Hollywood
Maynard, N.
Between the waters
Moggach, D.
Close relations
Murphy, E.
Comfort me with apples
Paige, F.
Kindred spirits
Paretsky, S.
Ghost country
Pemberton, V.
My sister Sarah
Perez, L. M.
Geographies of home
Prone, T.
Racing the moon
Roberts, N.
Montana sky
Roby, K. L.
Here and now
Saunders, K.
Lily-Josephine
Sharam, K.
Dangerous relatioins
Shorten, E.
Katie Colman crosses the water
Stirling, J.
The island wife
The wind from the hills
Tan, A.
The hundred secret senses
Taylor, L.
Going against the grain
Tennant, E.
Elinor and Marianne
Upcher, C.
Grace and Favour
Walker, A.
By the light of my father's smile
Woodford, P.
Jane's story
Worboyes, S.
Red sequins

SPACE TRAVEL
Booth, M.
  Adrift in the oceans of mercy
McCarthy, W.
  Blood
Russell, M. D.
  The sparrow

SPAIN: 7TH CENTURY
Tremayne, P.
  Act of mercy

SPAIN: 11TH CENTURY
Michaels, F.
  Tender warrior

SPAIN: 19TH CENTURY
Perez Galdos, B.
  Dona Perfecta
  The disinherited
Perez-Reverte, A.
  The fencing master

SPAIN: 1930-59
Heller, K.
  Snow on the moon
Woods, J. G.
  A murder of no consequence

SPAIN: 1980-2000
Ballard, J. G.
  Cocaine nights
Roig, J. M.
  The landscape collector

SPAIN: BARCELONA
Martell, D.
  Lying, crying, dying
  The republic of night

SPAIN: CATALUNYA
Jardine, Q.
  A coffin for two

SPAIN: IBIZA
Butts, C.
  Is Harry on the boat?

SPAIN: MADRID
Perez Galdos, B.
  The disinherited

SPAIN: MALLORCA
Jeffries, R.
  A maze of murders
  An artistic way to go
  An enigmatic disappearance
  The ambiguity of murder

SPANISH CIVIL WAR, 1936-39
Burton, B.
  Not just a soldier's war
Carr, I.
  Chrissie's children
Clarasc, M.
  Wandering Angus

SPECULATORS
Plain, B.
  Fortune's hand

SPEECH DISORDERS
Shields, D.
  Dead languages

SPIN DOCTORS
Harding, D.
  Bad influence

SPIRITUAL AWAKENING
Brady, J.
  Heaven in high gear
Ekman, K.
  The forest of hours

SPIRITUALISM
Chopra, G.
  Child of the dawn
Jacques, J.
  Someone to watch over me
Rogow, R.
  The problem of the spiteful
    spititualist
Shepherd, S.
  Twilight curtain
Stewart, G.
  Kenny Rogers sings the blues
Waters, S.
  Affinity

SPONSORSHIP
Gordon, M.
  Spending

SPORT
Hamer, M.
  Predator
Taylor, T.
  Kicking around

SPORTS CLUBS
Keegan, A.
  Razorbill

SPURN HEAD
Bedford, W.
  The freedom tree

SPY STORIES

Allbeury, T.
  Aid and comfort
  The long run
  The reckoning
Anthony, E.
  Albatross
Archer, G.
  Fire hawk
Benson, R.
  High time to kill
  The facts of death
  Tomorrow never dies
  Zero minus ten
Brierley, D.
  The cloak-and-dagger girl
Brown, G.
  The contractor
Davison, P.
  The crooked man
Deighton, L.
  Charity
Egleton, C.
  Blood money
  Dead reckoning
  Warning shot
Finney, P.
  Unicorn's blood
Flannery, S.
  Achilles heel
Fraser, S.
  The target
Freedman, M.
  Mamzer
Freemantle, B.
  Charlie's chance
  The iron cage
Furst, A.
  The world at night
Gardner, J.
  COLD
Gilbert, M.
  Into battle
Hall, A.
  Quiller Balalaika
Hawksley, H.
  Ceremony of innocence
Hetzer, M.
  The forbidden zone
Jackson, J. H.
  Cold cut
Kanon, J.
  Los Alamos
  The prodigal spy
Kent, G.
  Night trap
Lawton, J.
  Old flames

Le Carre, J.
  The tailor of Panama
Littell, R.
  Walking back the cat
Lyall, G.
  All honourable men
  Flight from honour
Maxim, J. R.
  Haven
McKay, R.
  The leper colony
McNab, A.
  Crisis four
Pattinson, J.
  Avenger of blood
Pownall, D.
  The catalogue of men
Royce, K.
  Ghostman
Sallis, J.
  Death will have your eyes
Shelby, P.
  Gatekeeper
Tan, M.
  A. k. a. Jane
  Run, Jane, run

SQUATTERS

Lemaitre, C.
  April rising
Michael, L.
  All the dark air
Plate, P.
  Police and thieves

SRI LANKA: 1900-29

Selvaduri, S.
  Cinnamon gardens

SRI LANKA: 1930-59

Gunesekera, R.
  The sandglass
Roberts, K.
  The flower boy

SRI LANKA: 1980-2000

Adamson, P.
  Facing out to sea

ST. IVES, CORNWALL

Hayes, K.
  Still life on sand
Paton Walsh, J.
  The serpentine cave

STAFFORDSHIRE

Masters, P.
  A wreath for my sister
  Catch the fallen sparrow

Scaring crows
Paige, F.
So long at the fair

STALIN, JOSEPH, RUSSIAN LEADER, 1879-1953
Nicole, C.
Death of a tyrant

STALKERS
Howatch, S.
The high flyer
Staynes, J. & Storey, M.
Quarry
Sullivan, M. T.
The purification ceremony
Tiffin, P.
Watching Vanessa
Wallace, M.
Current danger

STATELY HOMES
Bentley, U.
The sloping experience
Fforde, K.
Stately pursuits
Gano, J.
Inspector Proby's weekend
Jennings, L.
Beauty story
Marsh, J.
Fiennders keepers
Pewsey, E.
Unaccustomed spirits
Sherwood, J.
Shady borders
Thorne, N.
In this quiet earth
Worboys, A.
House of destiny

STEEL ERECTORS
McCann, C.
This side of brightness

STEEL INDUSTRY
Bedford, M.
Exit, orange and red

STEPFATHERS AND STEPSONS
Beckett, S.
Owning Jacob

STEPMOTHERS
Alexander, K.
Love and duty
McGowan, F.
A better life

Richards, E.
Rescue
Robinson, R.
This is my daughter
Trollope, J.
Other people's children

STEPMOTHERS AND STEPDAUGHTERS
Thornton, M.
Forgive our foolish ways

STEPSISTERS
Marsh, W.
Sisters under the skin

STOCK EXCHANGE
Robinson, J.
A true and perfect knight

STOCKBROKERS
Buchan, E.
Against her nature
Stainforth, D.
Intimate enemy

STONEHENGE
Cornwell, B.
Stonehenge

STORY TELLING
Chissick, R.
Catching shellfish between the tides

STREAM OF CONSCIOUSNESS NOVELS
McManus, A.
I was a mate of Ronnie Laing
North, S.
By desire
Parks, T.
Europa
Waterhouse, K.
Good grief

STRESS
White, G.
Chain reaction

STRIPPERS
Heyman, K.
Keep your hands on the wheel

STUDENT RIOTS
Ying, H.
Summer of betrayal

Strayhorn, S. J.
  Black night
Wycliffe, J.
  The lost

SUPERNATURAL: HAUNTED HOUSES
Thorne, N.
  Repossession

SUPERNATURAL: POSSESSION
Smethurst, W.
  Pasiphae
Thorpe, A.
  Pieces of light

SUPERNATURAL: VAMPIRES
Grimson, T.
  Stainless
Holland, T.
  Supping with panthers
Kalogridis, J.
  Lord of the vampires
Monahan, B. J.
  The blood of the covenant
Newman, K.
  The bloody Red Baron; Anno Dracula 1918
Rice, A.
  Pandora
  The vampire Armand
  Vittorio, the vampire
Savage, T.
  Valentine
Shepard, J.
  Nosferatu in love
Slawberg, H.
  Count Dracula
Spruill, S. G.
  Daughter of darkness
  Lords of light

SUPERNATURAL: VOODOO
Montero, M.
  You, darkness
Somtow, S. P.
  Darker angels

SUPERNATURAL: WITCHCRAFT
Doherty, P. C.
  The rose demon
  The soul slayer
Potter, C.
  The witch
  The witch's son
Pullinger, K.
  Weird sister
Whyte, C.
  The warlock of Strathearn

SURFING
Nunn, K.
  Tapping the source
  The dogs of winter

SURREALIST NOVELS
Goytisolo, J.
  The Marx family saga

SURROGATE MOTHERS
Ellis, K.
  The merchant's house

SURVIVAL
Bober, R.
  What news of the war?
Chorlton, W.
  Latitude zero
Marshall, J. V.
  White-out
Sullivan, M. T.
  The purification ceremony
West, P.
  Terrestrials

SUSPENSE STORIES
Buchanan, E.
  Act of betrayal
Clark, M. H.
  Moonlight becomes you
  We'll meet again
  You belong to me
Devon, G.
  Wedding night
Erickson, L.
  Night whispers
Erskine, B.
  House of echoes
  On the edge of darkness
Ferrigno, R.
  Dead silent
Galleymore, F.
  Widow maker
Garrison, P.
  Fire and ice
Harris, E.
  The twilight child
Hewson, D.
  Epiphany
Hey, S.
  Scare story
Lee, T.
  Queen's flight
Lutz, J.
  The ex
Maclean, C.
  The silence
Parker, U-M.
  Secrets of the night

Patterson, J.
  Hide and seek
Sinclair, J.
  Dangerous games
Sullivan, M. T.
  The purification ceremony
Todd, C.
  Staying cool
Yorke, M.
  Act of violence

SUSSEX
Carr, A.
  Dark harvest
Hartnett, D. W.
  Brother to dragons
Shaw, S.
  Act of darkness

SWANSEA
Edwards, D.
  Dreaming of tomorrow
  Follow every rainbow
Gower, I.
  Dream catcher
  The wild seed
Thompson, T.
  The homecoming

SWEDEN: 1930-59
Frederiksson, M.
  Simon and the oaks

SWEDEN: 20TH CENTURY
Frederiksson, M.
  Hanna's daughters

TABLE TENNIS
Jacobson, H.
  The mighty Walzer

TAJIKISTAN
Darnton, J.
  Neanderthal

TALISMANS
Phillips, M.
  The dancing face

TALL PEOPLE
Canals, C.
  Berta la Larga

TANGIERS
Lynton, P.
  Farewell to Barbary

TATTOOS
Hill, T.
  Skin

TEA PARTIES
Mulholland, S.
  Lingerie tea

TEACHERS
Bailey, J.
  Promising
Blauner, P.
  Man of the hour
Doughty, A.
  A few late roses
Evans, F.
  The family next door
Hamilton, J.
  The short history of a prince
Kay, R.
  Out of bounds
Melville, A.
  Role play
North, F.
  Polly
Purves, L.
  More lives than one
Robertson, W.
  Cruelty games
Taylor, L.
  Reading between the lines
Thornton, M.
  The sound of the laughter
Trow, M. J.
  Maxwell's movie
  Maxwell's war
Whitaker, P.
  Eclipse of the sun

TELEPATHY
McLaren, J.
  7th sense
Wilson, F. P.
  Mirage

TELEVISION ADDICTS
Baylis, M.
  Stranger than Fulham

TELEVISION BROADCASTING
Rhodes, P.
  With hearts and hymns and voices
Robertson, D.
  Daybreak

TELEVISION COMMERCIALS
Jennings, L.
  Beauty story

TELEVISION DIRECTORS
Ross, A.
  Double vision

TELEVISION INDUSTRY
DeAndrea, W. L.
  Killed in the fog

TELEVISION JOURNALISTS
Clark, M. J.
  Do you want to know a secret?
Gibb, N.
  Blood red sky
Hayter, S.
  The last manly man
Racina, T.
  Hidden agenda
Sandford, J.
  The night crew

TELEVISION PRESENTERS
Corbett, V. and others
  Double trouble
Flagg, F.
  Welcome to the world, baby girl!
Titchmarsh, A.
  Mr. MacGregor

TELEVISION PRODUCERS
Howell, L.
  The director's cut
North, S.
  Seeing is deceiving

TELEVISION SERIES, NOVELS BASED ON
Cave, P.
  No bananas
Cherryh, C. J.
  Lois and Clark
Gaiman, N.
  Neverwhere
Harrington, W.
  The Hoffa connection (Columbo)
La Plante, L.
  The Governor 2
  Trial and retribution
Martin, D.
  Forever yours (Heartbeat)
McGregor, T.
  Kavanagh QC 2
  Wokenwell
Mortimore, J.
  The mad woman in the attic (Cracker)
Silver, R.
  Madson

TEMPS
Mackesy, S.
  The temp

TENEMENTS
Douglas, A.
  Catherine's land

TENNIS
Brandner, G.
  The players
Davison, E.
  The game
Mawe, E.
  Grown men
Woods, S.
  Choke

TENNYSON, ALFRED, 1ST BARON, POET, 1809-92
Truss, L.
  Tennyson's gift

TERRORISTS
Brookmyre, C.
  One fine day in the middle of the night
Burnell, M.
  The rhythm section
Butler, G.
  Coffin's game
Clancy, T.
  Rainbow six
Deaver, J.
  The devil's teardrop
Easterman, D.
  The final judgement
Gulvin, J.
  Nom de guerre
  Storm crow
Harry, E. L.
  Protect and defend
Hellenga, R.
  The fall of a sparrow
Jackson, J. H.
  Dead headers
Jardine, Q.
  Gallery whispers
  Skinner's ordeal
Johansen, I.
  And then you die. . .
Land, J.
  Dead simple
Leather, S.
  The bombmaker
Lutz, J.
  Final seconds

Martell, D.
   Lying, crying, dying
   The republic of night
Morgenroth, K.
   Kill me first
O'Rourke, F. M.
   The poison tree
Porter, H.
   Remembrance Day
Prantera, A.
   Letter to Lorenzo
Reeves-Stevens, J.
   Icefire
Robinson, P.
   Nimitz class
Silva, D.
   The marching season
Smith, M. A.
   Jeremiah; terrorist prophet
Weber, K.
   The music lesson
Woodman, R.
   Act of terror

THAMES, RIVER
Maynard, N.
   Pageant

THEATRES
Cook, J.
   Murder at the Rose
Henderson, L.
   Freeze my Margarita
Lee, C.
   The killing of Cinderella
Lessing, D.
   Love, again
Lusby, J.
   Flashback
Maitland, B.
   All my enemies
McCafferty, J.
   Finales and overtures
Sher, A.
   The feast
Sherrin, N.
   Scratch an actor
Terry, C.
   My beautiful mistress

THEME PARKS
Guttridge, P.
   The once and future con

THEOLOGICAL COLLEGES
Greenwood, D. M.
   Heavenly vices
Simons, P.
   The benefits of passion

THERMOPYLAE, BATTLE OF, 400BC
Pressfield, S.
   Gates of fire

THIRD WORLD WAR
Clancy, T.
   SSN
Harry, E. L.
   Protect and defend

THRILLERS
Ablow, K. R.
   Projection
Adam, P.
   Unholy trinity
Alletzhauser, A.
   Quake
Anderson, K. J. & Beason, D.
   Ignition
Andrews, C.
   Deep as the marrow
Andrews, L.
   The sinister side
Anscombe, R.
   Shank
Anthony, E.
   The legacy
Armstrong, V.
   The wrong road
Arnott, J.
   The long firm
Ashford, J.
   Loyal disloyalty
Aspler, T.
   The beast of Barbaresco
Babson, M.
   The multiple cat
Badenoch, A.
   Driver
   Mortal
Baker, J.
   Walking with ghosts
Baker, K.
   Engram
   Inheritance
Baldacci, D.
   Absolute power
Bannister, J.
   Critical angle
   The primrose switchback
Barnard, R.
   The habit of widowhood (stories)
Barnes, S.
   Rogue lion safaris
Barrett, M.
   Intimate lies

Fiennes, R.
  The sett
Follett, J.
  Sabre
Follett, K.
  The third twin
Fotheringham, P. M.
  Seasnake
Fowler, C.
  Disturbia
Francis, C.
  A dark devotion
  Keep me close
Francis, D.
  Second wind
  To the hilt
Francome, J.
  False start
  Tip off
Frayn, M.
  Headlong
French, N.
  Killing me softly
  The memory game
Fritchley, A.
  Chicken out
Gaarder, J.
  The solitaire mystery
Gadney, R.
  The Achilles heel
Garber, J. R.
  In a perfect state
  Vertical run
Gash, J.
  A rag, a bone and a hank of hair
  The possessions of a lady
Gately, I.
  The assessor
Geller, U.
  Dead cold
Gellis, R.
  A mortal bane
Gerritsen, T.
  Bloodstream
Giancana, S.
  30 seconds
Gillespie, E.
  Five dead men
Gilstrap, J.
  Nathan's run
Glass, S.
  The interpreter
Goddard, R.
  Out of the sun
  Set in stone
Gom, L.
  Freeze frame
Gorman, E.
  Runner in the dark

The poker club
Graham, A.
  The shaft
Grant-Adamson, L.
  Undertow
Gray, C.
  Crossbow
Graziunas, D.
  Thinning the predators
Greeley, A. M.
  Irish mist
Grimes, M.
  Biting the moon
  Hotel Paradise
Grippando, J.
  Found money
Grisham, J.
  The testament
Guttridge, P.
  The once and future con
Hall, G.
  Mortal remains
Hall, J. W.
  Body language
  Buzz cut
Hamer, M.
  Dead on line
Hammond, G.
  Dogsbody
  Flamescape
  Sink or swim
Harcourt, P.
  Shadows of the past
Harding, D.
  Bad influence
Harrington, E.
  Daddy darling
Harris, E.
  The sacrifice stone
Hawes, J.
  Rancid aluminium
Hawksley, H.
  Absolute measures
Hayman, C.
  Greed, crime, sudden death
Hellenga, R.
  The fall of a sparrow
Henderson, L.
  The strawberry tattoo
Hendricks, V.
  Iguana love
Higgins, G. V.
  A change of gravity
Higson, C.
  Getting rid of Mr. Kitchen
Hill, J. S.
  Ghirlandaio's daughter
Hill, T.
  Underground

TOUR DE FRANCE
North, F.
Cat

TOURISTS
Jeffries, R.
A maze of murders

TOYS
McBain, E.
Gladly the cross-eyed bear

TRACKER DOGS
Lord, G.
The sharp end

TRADESCANT, JOHN, THE ELDER, ENGLISH GARDENER, 1570-C1638
Gregory, P.
Earthly joys
Virgin earth

TRANSPLANT SURGERY
Lustbader, E.
Dark homecoming
Woodford, P.
Jane's story

TRANSPORT SYSTEMS
Billheimer, J.
The contrary blues

TRANSVESTITES
Buxton, J.
Pity
Graham, L.
The dress circle
Mootoo, S.
Cereus blooms at night

TRAUMA CLINICS
Mawson, R.
The Lazarus child

TRAUMAS
Black, E.
The broken hearts club

TRAVEL
Dewar, I.
It could happen to you

TRAVELLERS
McDonald, J. F.
Tribe
Palmer, F.
Witching hour

TRAVELLING THEATRE COMPANIES
Grazebrook, S.
Foreign parts

TREASURE
Fritchley, A.
Chicken out
Keating, H. R. F.
The soft detective
Roberts, N.
The reef
Stevenson, R. L.
Torchlight

TREES
Bail, M.
Eucalyptus

TRIADS
Falconer, C.
Triad
Luk, H.
China bride
West, C.
Death of a red mandarin

TRIALS
Ashford, J.
A web of circumstances
Cleary, J.
Dilemma
Fast, H.
Redemption
Godden, R.
Cromartie v. the god Shiva
Griffin, G.
An operational necessity
McGown, J.
Verdict unsafe
Patterson, J.
Hide and seek
Sheldon, S.
Tell me your dreams
Turow, S.
The laws of our fathers
Van Wormer, L.
Jury duty

TROJAN WAR
McCullough, C.
The song of Troy

TURKEY: 17TH CENTURY
Chamberlin, A.
The reign of favoured women

TURKEY: 1900-29
Yasar Kemal
  Salman the solitary

TURKEY: 1980-2000
Melville, A.
  The longest silence
Pamuk, O.
  The new life

TURKEY: ISTANBUL
Nadel, B.
  Belshazzar's daughter

TUTANKHAMUN, PHARAOH, D. 1340BC
Holland, T.
  The sleeper in the sands

TWINS
Baker, A.
  A Mersey duet
Follett, K.
  The third twin
Ford, L.
  Double exposure
Kearney, R.
  Walking at sea level
Lamb, W.
  I know this much is true
Lightfoot, F.
  Larkrigg Fell
Murphy, B.
  A restless peace
Nicholson, J.
  The tribes of Palos Verdes
Roy, A.
  The god of small things
Steel, D.
  Mirror image
Wilson, F. P.
  Mirage
Worboys, A.
  You can't sing without me

TYCOONS
Hayman, C.
  Greed, crime, sudden death

TYNESIDE
Cookson, C.
  Riley
  The bondage of love
  The desert crop
  The upstart
Jacques, J.
  Wrong way up the slide

UGANDA
Foden, G.
  The last king of Scotland

UKRAINE: 20TH CENTURY
Ratushinskaya, I.
  The Odessans

UNCLES AND NEPHEWS
Shamsie, K.
  In the city by the sea

UNCLES AND NIECES
Melville, A.
  The eyes of the world
Mukerjee, R.
  Toad in my garden
Stout, M.
  One thousand chestnut trees

UNDERTAKERS
Spence, A.
  Way to go

UNITED STATES: 18TH CENTURY
Coyle, H.
  Savage wilderness
Gabaldon, D.
  Drums of autumn
Lawrence, M.
  Blood red roses
  Hearts and bones
Lightfoot, F.
  Rhapsody Creek
Pynchon, T.
  Mason and Dixon
Stone, I.
  The President's lady
Wideman, J. C.
  The cattle killing

UNITED STATES: 19TH CENTURY
Allende, I.
  Daughter of fortune
Banks, R.
  Cloudsplitter
Blake, M.
  Marching to Valhalla
Burke, J.
  Two for Texas
Carr, C.
  The angel of darkness
Chiaventone, F. J.
  A road we do not know
Deveraux, J.
  Legend
Eidson, T.
  Hannah's gift

Fackler, E.
  Breaking even
Fleming, T.
  The wages of fame
Garwood, J.
  For the roses
Hall, O. M.
  Ambrose Bierce and the Queen of
  Spades
Harrod-Eagles, C.
  The outcast
Holland, C.
  An ordinary woman
Jones, R. F.
  Deadville
Lawrence, M.
  The burning bride
McMurtry, L.
  Comanche moon
McMurty, L. & Ossana, D.
  Zeke and Ned
Ross, D. F.
  Arizona!
  Celebration!
  New Mexico!
  Oklahoma!
Schechter, H
  Nevermore
Skimin, R.
  The river and the horsemen
Turner, N.
  These is my words
Vanderhaeghe, G.
  The Englishman's boy
Williamson, P. G.
  Heart of the West

UNITED STATES: 20TH CENTURY
Ardizzone, T.
  In the garden of Papa Santuzzu
Auchincloss, L.
  The education of Oscar Fairfax
DeLillo, D.
  Underworld
Dorris, M.
  Cloud chamber
Jong, E.
  Of blessed memory
Pietrzyk, L.
  Pears on a willow tree
Roth, P.
  American pastoral
Updike, J.
  In the beauty of the lilies

UNITED STATES: 1900-29
Belfer, L.
  City of light

Haines, C.
  Touched
Jakes, J.
  America dreams
Kennedy, W.
  The flaming corsage
Liu, A. P.
  Cloud mountain
MacDonald, A.
  Fall on your knees
Maxwell, W.
  The folded leaf
McMurtry, L. & Ossana, D.
  Pretty Boy Floyd
Parker, J.
  The stars shine bright
Rhodes, J. P.
  Magic city
Seymour, A.
  The sins of the mother
Spencer, L.
  That Camden summer
Vanderhaeghe, G.
  The Englishman's boy

UNITED STATES: 1930-59
Cunningham, M.
  The hours
Dallas, S.
  The Persian Pickle Club
Estleman, L. D.
  Jitterbug
French, A.
  I can't wait on God
Hodge, J. A.
  Susan in America
Lee, M.
  Through the storm
McCracken, E.
  The giant's house
McKinney-Whetstone, D.
  Tumbling
Shearer, C.
  The wonder book of the air
Singer, I. B.
  Shadows on the Hudson
Steel, D.
  Silent honour
Tilghman, C.
  Mason's retreat

UNITED STATES: 1960-80
Baker, L.
  The flamingo rising
Briscoe, C.
  Big girls don't cry
Menaker, D.
  The treatment

Rivers, C.
Camelot
Shearer, C.
The wonder book of the air

UNITED STATES: 1980-2000
Daish, E.
Emma's journey
Desai, A.
Fasting, feasting
Didion, J.
The last thing he wanted
Isaacs, S.
Red white and blue

UNITED STATES: ARIZONA
Hammick, G.
The Arizona game
Mapson, J.
Loving Chloe
Poolman, J.
Interesting facts about the State of
Arizona

UNITED STATES: ARKANSAS
Hunter, S.
Black light

UNITED STATES: ATLANTA
Willard, F.
Down on Ponce

UNITED STATES: ATLANTA
Smith, F. M.
Flight of the blackbird

UNITED STATES: BALTIMORE
Schechter, H
Nevermore

UNITED STATES: BOSTON
Preston, C.
Jackie by Josie

UNITED STATES: BUFFALO
Belfer, L.
City of light

UNITED STATES: CALIFORNIA
Huneven, M.
Round rock
Lawrence, M. C.
The cold heart of Capricorn
Nicholson, J.
The tribes of Palos Verdes
Rawley, D.
Slow dance on the fault line
Saunders, J.
Journey's end

Siddons, A. R.
Fault lines

UNITED STATES: CHARLOTTE
Cornwell, P.
Hornet's nest

UNITED STATES: CHICAGO
Branton, M.
The house of whacks
Gaitano, N.
Spent force
Reaves, S.
Bury it deep

UNITED STATES: COLORADO
Dailey, J.
Illusions
Deveraux, J.
Legend
Irving, C.
The spring

UNITED STATES: CONNECTICUT
DelVeccio, J. M.
Darkness falls

UNITED STATES: DAKOTA
London, D.
Sun dancer
O'Brien, D.
Brendan Prairie

UNITED STATES: DETROIT
Estleman, L. D.
Jitterbug
Stress
The hours of the virgin
Kienzle, W. X.
Call no man father

UNITED STATES: FLORIDA
Baker, L.
The flamingo rising
Hailey, A.
Detective
Hall, J. W.
Body language
Hiaasen, C.
Lucky you
Stormy weather
Matthiessen, P.
Lost man's river
McNaught, J.
Night whispers
Norman, G.
Blue streak
Parker, B.
Blood relations

Shames, L.
  Mangrove squeeze
  Tropical depression
  Welcome to Paradise
Shorten, E.
  Katie Colman crosses the water
Woods, S.
  Choke

UNITED STATES: GEORGIA
Ansa, T. M.
  The hand I fan with
  Ugly ways
Ellis, J.
  Far to go

UNITED STATES: HIGH PLAINS
Wheeler, R. S.
  The buffalo commons

UNITED STATES: HOLLYWOOD
Bram, C.
  Father of Frankenstein
Collins, J.
  LA connections
  Vendetta; Lucky's revenge
Ellis, J.
  A woman for all seasons
Forbes, B.
  The memory of all that
Grant, R. E.
  By design
Hunt, M.
  Like Venus fading
Kaminsky, S. M.
  Dancing in the dark
La Plante, L.
  Cold heart
Leigh, J.
  House of destiny
Leonard, E.
  Be cool
Maracotta, L.
  The dead celeb
  Turn around, you're dead
Martella, M.
  Maddy goes to Hollywood
Norman, B.
  Death on Sunset
Richardson, J. H.
  The viper's club
Ridley, J.
  Love is a racket
Vanderhaeghe, G.
  The Englishman's boy

UNITED STATES: IOWA
Gorman, E.
  The silver scream

Harstad, D.
  Eleven days

UNITED STATES: KANSAS
Eidson, T.
  All God's children
Peck, D.
  Now it's time to say goodbye

UNITED STATES: LAS VEGAS
Kellerman, F.
  Moon music
Michaels, F.
  Vegas rich
  Vegas sunrise
Potter, J.
  Greedy mouth

UNITED STATES: LONG ISLAND
De Mille, N.
  Plum Island
Maclean, C.
  The silence

UNITED STATES: LOS ANGELES
Connelly, M.
  Trunk music
Craig, K.
  Some safe place
Ferrigno, R.
  Dead man's dance
Jackson, S.
  Caught up in the rapture
Krich, R. M.
  Blood money
Naylor, C.
  Catching Alice
Thornley, R.
  Seventeen seventeen Jerome

UNITED STATES: LOUISIANA
Burke, J.
  Half of paradise
Hill, E.
  Satisfied with nothin'
Neil, B.
  A history of silence
O'Connell, C.
  Flight of the stone angel
Wells, R.
  Divine secrets of the ya-ya sisterhood

UNITED STATES: MAINE
Bryers, P.
  The prayer of the bone
White, M. C.
  A brother's blood

UNITED STATES: MARYLAND
Tilghman, C.
Mason's retreat

UNITED STATES: MASSACHUSETTS
Hodge, J. A.
Susan in America
Parker, R. B.
Trouble in Paradise
Siddons, A. R.
Up island
Updike, J.
Toward the end of time

UNITED STATES: MIAMI
Buchanan, E.
Act of betrayal
Suitable for framing
Veciana-Suarez, A.
The chin kiss king

UNITED STATES: MICHIGAN
Cartwright, J.
Leading the cheers
Hamilton, S.
A cold day in Paradise

UNITED STATES: MINNESOTA
Treuer, D.
Little

UNITED STATES: MISSOURI
Esstman, B.
Mare's milk

UNITED STATES: MONTANA
Moffat, G.
Private sins
Roberts, N.
Montana sky
Watson, L.
Justice
White crosses
Williamson, P. G.
Heart of the West

UNITED STATES: NEBRASKA
McNeal, T.
Goodnight, Nebraska

UNITED STATES: NEVADA
Dailey, J.
Notorious
Ridley, J.
Stray dogs

UNITED STATES: NEW ENGLAND
Coomer, J.
Beachcombing for a shipwrecked god
Francis, S. A.
Angels in the architecture
Hoffman, A.
Here on earth
North, F.
Polly
Watkins, P.
The story of my disappearance

UNITED STATES: NEW HAMPSHIRE
Shreve, A.
The weight of water

UNITED STATES: NEW MEXICO
McCarthy, C.
Cities of the plain
McGarrity, M.
Mexican hat
Tularosa
Wheeler, R. S.
Flint's truth

UNITED STATES: NEW ORLEANS
Cameron, S.
French quarter

UNITED STATES: NEW YORK CITY
Abel, K.
The blue wall
Baker, A. L.
New York Graphic
Baker, K.
Dreamland
Carr, C.
The angel of darkness
Collins, M.
Emerald underground
Connelly, J.
Bringing out the dead
Daley, R.
Wall of brass
Eberstadt, F.
When the sons of heaven meet the daughters of the Earth
Ellis, B. E.
Glamorama
Granelli, R.
Out of nowhere
Harrison, C.
Manhattan nocturne
Henderson, L.
The strawberry tattoo

Kurland, M.
  The girl in the high-heeled shoes
Lustbader, E.
  Pale Saint
Mahoney, D.
  Black and white
McCann, C.
  This side of brightness
McDermott, A.
  Charming Billy
Muir, K.
  Suffragette city
O'Connell, C.
  Killing critics
Ozick, C.
  The Puttermesser papers
Roth, H.
  From bondage
Santiago, S.
  Streets of fire
Selby, H.
  The willow tree
Tillman, L.
  No lease on life
Winn, M.
  Redtails in love

UNITED STATES: NEW YORK STATE
Ferriss, L.
  Against gravity

UNITED STATES: NORTH CAROLINA
Grimsley, J.
  Winter birds
McCrumb, S.
  The ballad of Frankie Silver

UNITED STATES: NORTH DAKOTA
Moloney, S.
  A dry spell

UNITED STATES: OKLAHOMA
McMurtry, L.
  The late child
Morrison, T.
  Paradise
Rhodes, J. P.
  Magic city

UNITED STATES: PALM BEACH
Sanders, L.
  Guilty pleasures

UNITED STATES: PENNSYLVANIA
Constantine, K. C.
  Family values

UNITED STATES: PHILADELPHIA
Campbell, B. M.
  Singing in the comeback choir
Griffin, W. E. B.
  Special operations
  The victim
Lashner, W.
  Veritas
McKinney-Whetstone, D.
  Tumbling
Wideman, J. C.
  The cattle killing

UNITED STATES: PITTSBURGH
French, A.
  I can't wait on God

UNITED STATES: SAN FRANCISCO
Farrington, T.
  The Californian book of the dead
Hall, O. M.
  Ambrose Bierce and the Queen of Spades
King, L. R.
  To play the fool

UNITED STATES: SEATTLE
Alexie, S.
  Indian killer
Pearson, R.
  Beyond recognition

UNITED STATES: SOUTH CAROLINA
Siddons, A. R.
  Low country

UNITED STATES: SOUTH WESTERN STATES
Hillerman, T.
  The first eagle

UNITED STATES: SOUTHERN STATES
Grimsley, J.
  Dream boy
Jackson, B. K.
  The view from here
Price, R.
  Roxanna Slade

UNITED STATES: ST. LOUIS
Kennett, S.
Gray matter

UNITED STATES: TENNESSEE
Patchett, A.
Taff

UNITED STATES: TEXAS
Burke, J.
Two for Texas
Cleeves, A.
High Island blues
Eidson, T.
Hannah's gift
McMurtry, L.
Comanche moon
Duane's depressed

UNITED STATES: VIRGINIA
Hoffman, W.
Tidewater blood

UNITED STATES: WASHINGTON D. C.
Baldacci, D.
Absolute power
Berne, S.
A crime in the neighbourhood
Emerson, S.
Heat
Roosevelt, E.
Murder in the map room

UNITED STATES: WASHINGTON STATE
Dawson, J.
Trick of the light
Moffat, G.
Running dogs
Sloan, S. R.
An isolated incident

UNITED STATES: WESTERN STATES
Fackler, E.
Breaking even
Jones, R. F.
Deadville
Ross, D. F.
Oklahoma!

UNITED STATES: WYOMING
Kuban, K.
Marchlands

UNIVERSITIES
Bowen, G.
A killing spring
Cato, A.
Still lives
McInerny, R.
Lack of the Irish
Oakley, A.
Overheads
Selby, M.
Gargoyles and port
Thomas, S.
Dead clever

UPPER CLASSES
Auchincloss, L.
The education of Oscar Fairfax
Harrod-Eagles, C.
Dangerous love
Thorne, N.
Old money

VALLON, ANNETTE, 1ST WIFE OF WILLIAM WORDSWORTH
Baldwin, M.
The first Mrs. Wordsworth

VATICAN
Adam, P.
Unholy trinity
Cartmell, S.
Papal whispers
West, M.
Eminence

VENEZUELA
Koning, C.
Undiscovered country
Torres, A. T.
Dona Ines versus oblivion

VENTRILOQUISTS
Melville, P.
The ventriloquist's tale

VESPASIAN, EMPEROR OF ROME, AD9-79
Davis, L.
The course of honour

VETERINARY SURGEONS
Dewhurst, E.
Alias the enemy
McCormac, R.
Playing dead
Patterson, J.
When the wind blows

Scott, M.
  Night mares

VIETNAM WAR, 1963-
Davies, L.
  Wilderness of mirrors
DelVeccio, J. M.
  The 13th valley
Hunter, S.
  Time to hunt
Huong, D. T.
  Novel without a name
Leather, S.
  The tunnel rats
Quinnell, A. J.
  Message from hell

VIETNAM: 1980-2000
Butler, R. O.
  The dark green sea

VIGILANTES
Walker, M. W.
  All the dead lie down

VILLAGE LIFE
Andrews, L.
  The sinister side
Babson, M.
  Miss Petunia's last case
Blacker, T.
  Revenance
Bonner, H.
  A passion so deadly
Boucheron, R.
  Farewell
  Friends and neighbours
  The butterfly field
Burgh, A.
  Breeders
Carr, A.
  The last summer
Colborn, N.
  The congregation
Cook, G.
  Roscarrock
Corlett, W.
  Two gentlemen sharing
Courtney, E.
  Love me never
Cusk, R.
  The country life
De Bernieres, L.
  The war of Don Emmanuel's nether
    parts
Fawcett, P.
  Village wives
Fforde, K.
  Stately pursuits

Fielding, K.
  A secret place
  Ravensdale spring
Fraser, C. M.
  Kinvara wives
Frewen, F.
  The sunlight in the garden
  The tortoise shell
Gee, S.
  The hours of the night
Granger, T.
  A word after dying
Grant-Adamson, L.
  The girl in the case
  The girl in the case
Gulvin, J.
  Close quarters
Heiney, P.
  Domino's effect
Hines, J.
  Autumn of strangers
Hodge, J. A.
  Unsafe hands
Ingman, H.
  Waiting at the gate
James, E.
  A breath of fresh air
  Time for a change
Karon, J.
  A Light in the Window
  These high, green hills
Kingston, B.
  Laura's way
Lively, P.
  Spiderweb
Long, J.
  Ferney
Mackay, S.
  The orchard on fire
Marlow, A.
  Mermaid's ground
  No love lost
Marsh, J.
  Fiennders keepers
Marshall, S.
  Strip the willow
Marysmith, J.
  Waterwings
Mayhew, M.
  Old soldiers never die
Newberry, S.
  The painted sky
Odone, C.
  The shrine
Ogilvy, I.
  Loose chippings
  The Polkerton giant
Prideaux, S.
  Rude mechanicals

Pullinger, K.
Weird sister
Purser, A.
Mixed doubles
New every morning
Orphan lamb
Thy neighbour's wife
Ransmayr, C.
The dog king
Read, Miss
A peaceful retirement
Rhea, N.
Constable about the parish
Constable at the dam
Constable at the gate
Constable in the farmyard
Constable over the stile
Constable under the gooseberry bush
Rhodes, E.
Midsummer meeting
Rhodes, P.
With hearts and hymns and voices
Rose, L.
Heaven's door
Kingdom come
Scanlan, P.
Promises, promises
Scholefield, A.
The drowning mark
Selby, M.
A wing and a prayer
All that glisters
Sharma, Y.
The buffalo thief
Shaw, R.
Scandal in the village
The village show
Village gossip
Village matters
Village secrets
Simpson, D.
Once too often
Tayler, P.
Moving on
Templeton, A.
Past praying for
Thorne, N.
In this quiet earth
Past love
Repossession
Thorpe, A.
Pieces of light
Trevor, J.
Time to die
Upcher, C.
The visitor's book
Wendorf, P.
The toll house

Wiggin, H.
Trouble on the wind
Wilbourne, D.
A vicar's diary

VIOLENCE
Caveney, P.
1999
Cook, T. H.
Breakheart Hill
Gerritsen, T.
Bloodstream
Gordimer, N.
The house gun
Gray, C.
Crossbow
Lee, T.
Queen's flight
McEldowney, E.
The sad case of Harpo Higgins
Melo, P.
The killer
Peck, D.
Now it's time to say goodbye
Sharam, K.
Rough exposure
Weldon, T.
The surgeon's daughter
Yorke, M.
Act of violence
Zahavi, H.
Donna and the fatman

VIOLINS
Maurensig, P.
Canone inverso

VIRTUAL REALITY
Oudot, S.
Virtual love
Priest, C.
The extremes
Ridpath, M.
Trading reality
Williams, T.
River of blue fire

VIRUSES
Case, J.
The first horseman
Hillerman, T.
The first eagle
Kerr, P.
The second angel
Scott, M.
Night mares
Stewart, C.
The kill box

Wallace, C.
The Pied Piper's poison

VISIONS
Reidy, S.
The visitation

VOLCANOES
Du Brul, J. B.
Vulcan's forge
Kissick, G.
Winter in Volcano

WAITRESSES
Waite, E.
Nippy

WALES: 14TH CENTURY
Robb, C.
A gift of sanctuary

WALES: 19TH CENTURY
Fuller, J.
A skin diary
Gower, I.
Firebird
Sweet Rosie

WALES: 20TH CENTURY
Evans, M.
Inheritors

WALES: 1900-29
Edwards, D.
Follow every rainbow
Gower, I.
Dream catcher
The wild seed
McKenzie, H.
The way things were

WALES: 1930-59
Collier, C.
Broken rainbows
Past remembering
Edwards, D.
Dreaming of tomorrow
Elis, I. F.
Return to Lleifior
Shadow of the sickle
McKenzie, H.
The way things were
Saunders, J.
Journey's end
Secombe, F.
Pastures new
Templeton, A.
Night and silence

Thompson, G.
A corner of a small town
A shop in the High Street
The Weston women

WALES: 1960-80
Edwards, D.
Better love next time
Thompson, G.
Sophie Street

WALES: 1980-2000
Fraser, A.
Dangerous deception
Merriman, C.
State of desire
Taylor, A. G.
In guilty night
Thompson, G.
Maisie's way
Unlocking the past
Wilson, J.
Omega cluster

**WALLIS, ALFRED, ENGLISH
PAINTER, 1855-1942**
Everett, P.
The voyages of Alfred Wallis

WAR
Anderson, S.
Triage
Arnison, J.
Expendable lives
Turtledove, H.
How few remain

WAR CRIMES
Dias, D.
Rule of law
Harcourt, P.
Shadows of the past
Ransmayr, C.
The dog king
Rodin, R. L.
Articles of faith

WAR CRIMINALS
Schlink, B.
The reader
Wilson, J.
Turmfalke: case 3788

WAR WIDOWS
Bryant, J.
Waiting for the tide

WAREHOUSES
Prince, P.
  Waterloo story

WARWICK
Marston, E.
  The foxes of Warwick

WATER
Drewe, R.
  The drowner

WEALTH
Ashworth, S.
  Money talks
Berry, E.
  The scourging of poor little Maggie
Birmingham, S.
  The wrong kind of money
Chiu, M. L.
  Gone forever
Fraser, C. M.
  An inheritance
Geary, T.
  Shouting at the ship men
Grippando, J.
  Found money
Haley, J.
  Written in water
Hawksley, H.
  Absolute measures
Lashner, W.
  Veritas
Lim, C.
  The bondmaid
Lyons, G.
  The other cheek
McKinney, M.
  In the dark
Perrick, P.
  Evermore
Rautbord, S.
  The Chameleon
Robbins, H.
  The stallion
Siddons, A. R.
  Low country

WEAPONS
Kent-Payne, V.
  Longdon

WEATHER
Canals, C.
  Berta la Larga
Fane, J.
  Money matters

WEDDINGS
Andrews, D.
  Murder with peacocks
Benali, A.
  Wedding by the sea
Brookner, A.
  Visitors
Jonker, J.
  Down our street
Walker, F.
  Well groomed

WELSH BORDERS
Gee, S.
  The hours of the night

WEREWOLVES
Dickason, C.
  Quicksilver

WEST COUNTRY
Bonner, H.
  A passion so deadly
Jecks, M.
  Squire Throwleigh's heir
  The leper's return

WEST INDIES
Benitez Rojo, A.
  A view from the mangrove
Francis, D.
  Second wind
Whitnell, B.
  Deep waters

WEST INDIES: 17TH CENTURY
Tomson, J. M.
  Eden

WEST INDIES: 1980-2000
Mootoo, S.
  Cereus blooms at night

WEST INDIES: ANGUILLA
Lovelace, E.
  Salt
McLaurin, D.
  Tropical darkness

WEST INDIES: DOMINICAN REPUBLIC
Danticat, E.
  The farming of bones

WEST INDIES: HAITI
Montero, M.
  You, darkness

WEST INDIES: JAMAICA
Kennaway, G.
  One people
Levy, A.
  Fruit of the lemon
Wesley, V. W.
  Where evil sleeps

WEST INDIES: MARTINIQUE
Chamoiseau, P.
  Texaco

WEST INDIES: ST. LUCIA
Pemberton, L.
  Sleeping with ghosts

WEST INDIES: TRINIDAD
Brand, D.
  At the full and change of the moon
Carrington, R.
  A thirst for rain

WHISKY DISTILLING
Knox, B.
  Blood proof

WHITBY
Blair, J.
  The other side of the river
Reed, C. W.
  To reason why

WHITE SLAVE TRADE
Orton, J.
  Between us girls
Thompson, E. V.
  Somewhere a bird is singing

WIDOWS
Anderson, B.
  Proud garments
Clayton, V.
  Past mischief
Crowell, J.
  Necessary madness
Evans, P.
  A smile for all seasons
Francis, J.
  Kitty and her boys
James, E.
  A breath of fresh air
Johnson, P.
  Under construction
Meynard, Y.
  A certain smile
Newberry, S.
  A charm of finches
Nolan, C.
  The banyan tree

Parsons, J.
  The courtship gift
Raife, A.
  Drumveyn
Randall, A.
  Kilkenny bay
Sharam, K.
  A hard place
Shreve, A.
  The pilot's wife
Sutherland, T.
  An accidental life
Waterhouse, K.
  Good grief
Wideman, J. C.
  Two cities

WILD LIFE, PRESERVATION OF
Evans, N.
  The loop
Morrissey, D.
  When the singing stops

WILLIAM THE CONQUEROR, KING, 1027-87
Rathbone, J.
  The last English king

WINDSOR
Melville, J.
  Stone dead
  The woman who was not there

WINE TRADE
Aspler, T.
  Death on the Douro
  The beast of Barbaresco
Darcy, E.
  The secrets within
Dibdin, M.
  A long finish
Friedman, R.
  Vintage
Knox, E.
  The vintner's luck

WISHES
Delinsky, B.
  Three wishes

WITCHES
Strong, T.
  The death pit
Stubbs, J.
  The witching time

WITNESSES
Hoag, T.
  Ashes to ashes

Kellerman, J.
  Billy Straight

WOLLSTONECRAFT, MARY, FEMINIST AND WRITER, 1759-97
Roberts, M.
  Fair exchange

WOLVES
Evans, N.
  The loop
Horwood, W.
  Seekers at the Wulfrock

WOMEN
Beard, J. A.
  The boys of my youth
Brownrigg, S.
  Ten women who shook the world
Carey, L.
  The mermaids singing
Dunlop, A.
  Kissing the frog
Faith, P.
  Hello, Mr. Magpie
Harris, S.
  Wasting time
Landsman, A.
  The devil's chimney
Langley, L.
  False pretences
Oudot, S.
  All that I am
Parkin, S.
  Take me home
Ross, L.
  All the blood is red
Syal, M.
  Life isn't all ha ha hee hee

WOMEN CLERGY
Cannam, H.
  First parish

WOMEN EXECUTIVES
Bryan, L.
  Gorgeous
Buchan, J.
  High latitudes
Corbett, V.
  Unfinished business
Cowie, V.
  Designing woman
Holt, F.
  Some you win
Kelly, T.
  The cut
Palmer, E.
  Flowering Judas

Swindells, M.
  Winners and losers

WOMEN MYSTICS
Davies, S.
  Impassioned clay

WOMEN'S CLUBS
Dallas, S.
  The Persian Pickle Club

WOMEN'S LAND ARMY
Cox, M. I.
  Holding back the dark
Jacques, J.
  Someone to watch over me
Roberts, I.
  Walker Street

WOMEN'S RIGHTS
Faulk, A. G.
  Holding out
Ferriss, L.
  The misconceiver
Naish, N.
  A time to learn
Ng, M.
  Eating Chinese food naked
Paige, F.
  The lonely shore
Weldon, F.
  Big women

WOOLF, VIRGINIA, ENGLISH NOVELIST, 1882-1941
Cunningham, M.
  The hours

WORDSWORTH, WILLIAM, ENGLISH POET, 1770-1850
Baldwin, M.
  The first Mrs. Wordsworth

WORKAHOLICS
O'Flanagan, S.
  Suddenly single

WORKING CLASSES
Blair, E.
  An apple from Eden
Blanchard, S.
  The paraffin child
King, J.
  The football factory

WORKING MOTHERS
Barnes, Z.
  Bumps

Delinsky, B.
A woman's place
Shorten, E.
A new woman

WORLD WAR 1
Andrews, L. M.
Angels of mercy
Bryant, J.
Waiting for the tide
Chambers, J.
Vale Valhalla
Hartnett, D. W.
Brother to dragons
Howard, A.
When morning comes
Monk, C.
On the wings of the storm
Murphy, T.
Christ in khaki
Ramsay, E.
Harvest of courage
Reed, C. W.
To reason why
Williams, B.
Death before dishonour

WORLD WAR 1: ENGLAND
Carr, A.
Dark harvest
Hutchinson, M.
Bitter seed

WORLD WAR 1: FRANCE
Gilbert, M.
Over and out

WORLD WAR 1: INTELLIGENCE SERVICES
Hudson, H.
Winter roses

WORLD WAR 1: ROYAL NAVY
Carr, A.
The last summer
Drummond, E.
Act of valour
Grieve, P.
Upon a wheel of fire
Hill, R.
The wood beyond
McCutchan, P.
Tom Chatto, RNR
Turtledove, H.
The Great War; American front

WORLD WAR 2
Haig, K.
Apple blossom time

Lord, E.
For all the bright promises
Marshall, J. V.
White-out
Staples, M. J.
The family at war

WORLD WAR 2: AIR TRANSPORT AUXILIARY
Gould, C.
Spitfire girls

WORLD WAR 2: ATOMIC WEAPONS
Cregan, C.
Ground zero

WORLD WAR 2: BRITISH ARMY: COMMANDOS
Savage, A.
Commando

WORLD WAR 2: BRITISH ARMY: SAS
Clarke, S.
The desert raiders

WORLD WAR 2: BURMA
Blake, I.
The Burma offensive

WORLD WAR 2: CHANNEL ISLANDS
Bachmann, D.
A sound like thunder
Binding, T.
Island madness

WORLD WAR 2: ENGLAND
Bennett, A.
A strong hand to hold
Carey, H.
On a wing and a prayer
Some sunny day
Cox, M. I.
Holding back the dark
Fraser, S.
Specs war
Grey, P.
Good Hope Station
Harry, L.
Moonlight and lovesongs
James, B.
The last enemy
Kingston, B.
Avalanche of daisies
Lee, M.
Put out the fires

Matthew, C.
  A nightingale sang in Fernhurst Road
Murphy, B.
  Janey's war
Murray, A.
  Birmingham blitz
Oldfield, J.
  All fall down
Palmer, E.
  The dark side of the sun
Pemberton, V.
  Nellie's war
  The silent war
Saxton, J.
  You are my sunshine
Staples, M. J.
  Churchill's people
  Fire over London
Stephens, K.
  Dark before dawn
Stewart, S.
  Playing with stars
Thomas, L.
  Other times
Thorne, N.
  A time of hope

WORLD WAR 2: EVACUEES

Chapman, J.
  The soldier's girl
Hedgecoe, J.
  Breakfast with Dolly
Saunders, J.
  Journey's end
Staples, M. J.
  Bright day, dark night
Thornton, M.
  Wish upon a star

WORLD WAR 2: FAR EAST

Coppel, A.
  The burning mountain
Glaister, L.
  Easy peasy
Hart, E.
  Star of the rising sun
Keller, N. O.
  Comfort woman
Murphy, Y.
  The sea of trees
Savage, A.
  The sword and the jungle
Smith, F. E.
  Saffron's trials
Webb, J.
  The Emperor's General

WORLD WAR 2: FRANCE

Everett, P.
  Matisse's war
Faulks, S.
  Charlotte Gray
Fullerton, A.
  Return to the field
Janes, J. R.
  Gypsy
  Madrigal
  Sandman
Palmer, W.
  The pardon of Saint Anne

WORLD WAR 2: GERMAN ARMY

Kessler, L.
  Death from Arctic skies
  Death's eagles
  March of death
  Operation Fury
  The Wotan mission

WORLD WAR 2: GERMAN NAVY

Harding, D.
  Sink the Scharnhorst

WORLD WAR 2: GERMANY

Hook, P.
  The soldier in the wheatfield
Savage, A.
  The sword and the prison

WORLD WAR 2: GREECE

Llewellyn, S.
  Thunderbolt from Navarone

WORLD WAR 2: INTELLIGENCE SERVICES

Bailey, H.
  After the cabaret
Carey, H.
  On a wing and a prayer
Cregan, C.
  Valkyrie
Fullerton, A.
  In at the kill
Furst, A.
  Red gold
Griffin, W. E. B.
  Blood and honor
Kessler, L.
  The Bormann mission
Laker, P.
  The fragile hour
Leslie, P.
  Action in the Arctic
  Baltic commando
  Blitz harvest

Savage, A.
  The Afrika Korps
  The traitor within
Silva, D.
  The unlikely spy
Thayer, J. L.
  Five past midnight

WORLD WAR 2: INTERNEES
Steel, D.
  Silent honour

WORLD WAR 2: ITALY
Ginzburg, N.
  All our yesterdays
Kessler, L.
  The Churchill papers

WORLD WAR 2: JERSEY
Blair, E. N.
  Half hidden

WORLD WAR 2: MALTA
Harvey, C.
  The brass dolphin
Rinaldi, N.
  The jukebox queen of Malta

WORLD WAR 2: NETHERLANDS
Clegg, A.
  Where birds don't sing
  Windmills

WORLD WAR 2: NORTH AFRICA
Jackson, R.
  Desert combat
Savage, A.
  Stop Rommel!
  The Afrika Korps
Sykes, E.
  Smelling of roses

WORLD WAR 2: NORWAY
Haff, B. H.
  Shame
Laker, R.
  The fragile hour

WORLD WAR 2: PACIFIC
Tillman, B.
  Hellcats

WORLD WAR 2: POLAND
Crane, T.
  The raven hovers

WORLD WAR 2: PRISONERS OF WAR
Hart, E.
  Star of the rising sun
Katzenbach, J.
  Hart's war
Langley, B.
  Fellrunner
Savage, A.
  The sword and the prison
Stanley, G.
  Nagasaki six

WORLD WAR 2: REFUGEES
Heller, K.
  Snow on the moon
Michaels, A.
  Fugitive pieces
Wallace, C.
  The Pied Piper's poison

WORLD WAR 2: RESISTANCE MOVEMENT
Chapman, J.
  This time last year
Clarasc, M.
  Wandering Angus
Crackanthorpe, D.
  Stolen marches
Faulks, S.
  Charlotte Gray
Fullerton, A.
  Return to the field
Leslie, P.
  Flames over Provence

WORLD WAR 2: ROYAL AIR FORCE
Beaty, D.
  The ghosts of the eighth attack
Blair, J.
  The restless spirit
Drummond, E.
  The savage sky
Jackson, R.
  Desert combat
  Flames over France
  Flames over Norway
  Fortress England
  The intruders
  The rising sun
McGraw, M.
  After Dunkirk
Savarin, J. J.
  Norwegian fire
  Typhoon strike
Stanford, N.
  The magpie secret

WORLD WAR 2: ROYAL AIR FORCE: BOMBER COMMAND
Mayhew, M.
The crew

WORLD WAR 2: ROYAL MARINES
Reeman, D.
Dust on the sea

WORLD WAR 2: ROYAL NAVY
Elgin, E.
Where bluebells chime
Fullerton, A.
Band of brothers
Harding, D.
Sink the Ark Royal
Sink the Graf Spee
Sink the Prince of Wales
Sink the Tirpitz
Reeman, D.
A dawn like thunder
Battlecruiser

WORLD WAR 2: RUSSIA
Nicole, C.
The scarlet generation
Robbins, D.
War of the rats

WORLD WAR 2: SCANDINAVIA
Petterson, P.
To Siberia

WORLD WAR 2: SCOTLAND
Craig, M.
When the lights come on again

WORLD WAR 2: UNITED STATES ARMY AIR FORCE
Thorn, J.
Mustang summer

WORLD WAR 2: UNITED STATES MARINES
Griffin, W. E. B.
Behind the lines
In danger's path
Steel, D.
Silent honour

WORLD WAR 2: WALES
Collier, C.
Broken rainbows

WORLD WAR 2: WAR CRIMINALS
Griffin, G.
An operational necessity

WORLD WAR 2: WEST INDIES
Tinniswood, P.
Dolly's war

WORLD WAR 2: WESTERN FRONT
Kessler, L.
Patton's wall

WRESTLING
Cody, L.
Musclebound
Hammond, G.
A running jump
Jardine, Q.
Wearing purple

WRONGFUL ACCUSATION
Korelitz, J. H.
The Sabbathday river

YOBS
Crow, H.
Lee Trebilcock in the twentieth
century

YORK
Marston, A. E.
The lions of the north
Smith, A.
Big soft lads
Turnbull, P.
Embracing skeletons
Whitehead, B.
Death at the Dutch House
Secrets of the dead
Yeomans, A.
Where are you, Henry?

YORKSHIRE
Barnard, R.
The corpse at the Haworth Tandoori
Barraclough, J.
First finds
First loves
No time like the present
Bedford, W.
The freedom tree
Blair, J.
The restless spirit
The seaweed gatherers
Brindley, L.
Lizzie
Elgin, E.
Windflower wedding
Haley, J.
When beggars die